CONTEMPORARY AMERICAN FICTION

HIGHER EDUCATION

Lisa Pliscou was born and raised in Southern California and in Mexico. She graduated from Harvard University with a degree in English, and has worked primarily in publishing with a brief stint in investment banking. This is her first novel.

Higher

EDUCATION

LISA PLISCOU

PENGUIN
BOOKS

PENGUIN BOOKS
Published by the Penguin Group
Viking Penguin Inc., 40 West 23rd Street,
New York, New York 10010, U.S.A.
Penguin Books Ltd, 27 Wrights Lane,
London W8 5TZ, England
Penguin Books Australia Ltd, Ringwood,
Victoria, Australia
Penguin Books Canada Ltd, 2801 John Street,
Markham, Ontario, Canada L3R 1B4
Penguin Books (N.Z.) Ltd, 182–190 Wairau Road,
Auckland 10, New Zealand

Penguin Books Ltd, Registered Offices:
Harmondsworth, Middlesex, England

First published in 1989 in simultaneous hardcover
and paperback editions by Viking Penguin Inc.
Published simultaneously in Canada

1 2 3 4 5 6 7 8 9 10

LIBRARY OF CONGRESS CATALOGING IN PUBLICATION DATA
Pliscou, Lisa.
Higher education / Lisa Pliscou.
p.   cm.
ISBN 0 14 01.1344 4
I. Title.
[PS3566.L54H5   1989b]
813'.54—dc19
88-23221

Printed in the United States of America by
R. R. Donnelley & Sons Company, Harrisonburg, Virginia
Set in Meridien
Designed by Fritz Metsch

For Jeanette
with thanks to Irene, Nan, Jay,
and Charlie

Higher

EDUCATION

*D*ear god.

I see my roommate from freshman year approaching through the Wigglesworth archway off Mass Ave. Her breasts seem larger than ever, and as she walks toward me her chest sways formidably. Left, right. Left, right.

Flooded by dread, I consider diverting left and up the steps toward Lamont, or veering a trickier right toward the language labs and slipping into the lounge where I can hide behind an Italian edition of *Vogue* for a few minutes. In the meantime I make my eyes go as blank as possible, trying to look preoccupied, if not totally oblivious. Contemplating Proust, perhaps. Lost to the world. Possibly stoned.

But it is too late. Jeanne has seen me, and I have no choice but to continue moving in a straight line, clutching my notebook and paperback Roget's a little more tightly to my own meager bosom.

"*Buon giorno,* Miranda!" Her voice as ever is vibrant and lively. "*Comment ça va, chérie?*"

"Hey, Jeanne." Even with my habitual slouch I'm still a good half-foot taller than she is. "How's everything?"

"Oh, I can't complain." She beams up at me through a fuzzy mass of dark erratic curls.

"Great." I nod. "So what's new?"

"Well," she says brightly, and I brace myself. "Carl and I are running the model U.N. this year, and I'm still taking jazz dance classes up at South House twice a week. Plus I'm having my thesis typed for me, which means I have to keep running every five minutes to the typist's to proofread. And of course I'm getting ready for my internship in Washington next year—"

There's something I want to do tonight, but I can't seem to recall what it is. Arching an eyebrow, I cast about in my mind for a sense of impending pleasure, discomfort, or boredom. Tracking down reserve readings for Soc Sci 33? Carrying my dirty socks down five flights of stairs to the laundry room? Hanging out in Tommy's Lunch improving my Defender score?

"—and Carl keeps begging me to spend the summer with him in Greece—"

A synapse twitches and now I remember: I'm supposed to call Dean tonight, to confirm a date hastily arranged this afternoon while his girlfriend dallied behind in the lunch line.

"—and I was going to have dinner at Adams House, but then I remembered that it's Oxfam night so there's no interhouse."

"Oxfam night?" I test myself to see if I know Dean's number by heart. *4-9-8—*

"You know, skipping a meal for world hunger. Harvard Students for Oxfam, remember?" Jeanne eyes me sternly. "The proceeds go to needy third-world children."

"Oh, yeah. Right." Suddenly I realize that I'm ravenous. The two blocks to the dining hall seem to stretch ahead like miles.

"You signed up, didn't you?"

"Well, actually—" My stomach rumbles, and I slide my notebook and Roget's down over my abdomen. "A whole bunch of us are having a picnic out by the Charles."

"At six o'clock at night?"

"Kind of romantic, don't you think?" I give her a crooked half-smile. "Want to come?"

"That's okay. I stopped over at the Lowell House tea for a quick bite."

"You're a fan of the cucumber sandwiches, aren't you?"

"What a memory you have." She laughs. "Homemade baklava, *chérie*. And the pâté—well, you know me and pâté."

Fat cow. "Sounds kind of boring."

"Boring?" Her breasts are still jiggling merrily. "Even the cucumber sandwiches?"

"Especially the cucumber sandwiches."

"You funny old Val Gal. Still into yogurt and granola, eh?"

4-9-8-3-7— "What?"

"Of course you are. You're still the same old beanpole."

"Fer sure," I say amiably, wondering if she's still squeezing her pimples and leaving neat little apostrophes of pus on the bathroom mirror.

"I know there's so much to catch up on, kiddo, but there's a Democratic Club meeting over in Emerson, and I'm afraid I've got to run."

Try waddle. "Well, it was nice seeing you again."

"Why don't we get together for lunch sometime?"

"Sure. And thanks for reminding me about Oxfam."

"*Pas de problème*, sweetie." Flashing a sunny smile, Jeanne motors off, readjusting her enormous green backpack over her shoulder.

"Yeah, *ciao,*" I call, making a grotesque Lucky Jim face at her briskly retreating back.

Walking down Plympton Street I come to the *Crimson* building, its balcony draped with a big white bedsheet spray-painted in spidery neon-orange letters: STOP APARTHEID NOW. Beneath the banner, on the steps leading into the building, six juniors from Leverett House are grasping each other's shoulders and doing precision Rockette kicks to the accompaniment of a ghetto blaster playing "Life Is a Cabaret" at full volume.

Then I pass on. This being mid-April, it's Fools Week at the Lampoon, during which newly inducted members are made to perform a number of eccentric public acts, many of which entail partial nudity and strange hats. Or, in this case, a cancan on the Crimson steps. God only knows what they do in the privacy of their own domain. I've never much liked their magazine, although I must admit I've chuckled at their literary parodies from time to time.

As usual the door to Adams House is locked. Through the grimy barred window I look at Kurt the superintendent in his office, tipped back in his chair with his feet up on the desk, reading a magazine. His steel-gray hair, parted straight down the middle of his scalp, shines dully in the brutal fluorescent light. Squinting, I see he's staring down at an old issue of *Newsweek*. I'd bet a sum equivalent to the proceeds from Oxfam night that there's a copy of *Playboy* tucked inside.

Too lazy to dig out my keys from my bag, I ring the bell and show my teeth in a huge grin. Kurt looks up from Miss April and scrutinizes me through the ironwork. Am I a terrorist bent on blowing up the Adams House library, perhaps, or a foolhardy resident of Quincy House attempting interhouse on Oxfam night? He narrows his eyes, which makes them look even smaller and flintier, and with snail-like deliberation he moves his hand the ten inches it takes to press the buzzer to let me in.

My smile widens, if such a thing is possible, and lightly I pull open the door. This of course is Kurt's retaliation for the fact that every winter, regardless of which section of Adams House I happen to be living in, I nag him ceaselessly about the inadequate heating in my room, running downstairs to pound on his office door as many as six times in one day, a record set my junior year that I believe is still unsurpassed. When Kurt is sufficiently exasperated by my shrill-voiced complaints, he calls up Buildings and Grounds to send over someone from Maintenance. When the B & G man finally arrives, he kicks the radiator a few times, scattering gray slush all over the floor, and curses the superintendent for making him leave his office on such a bitterly cold day. Nodding and waving my arms, I commiserate with him, viciously egging him on, and then he stumps downstairs to harass Kurt, who in turn refuses to give me the standard double apportionment of toilet paper, limiting my dispensation to a single roll per request. Usually I end up stealing four or five rolls at a time from the ladies' room in Mem Hall, thereby avoiding another vitriolic exchange with Kurt, who probably thinks I've stopped going to the bathroom entirely.

Humming, I stop at the C-entry mailboxes and dial the C-45 combination. There's a letter for Jessica from her parents in a fat embossed Yale University envelope, bills from the Coop, an invitation to the Spee Club's annual pajama party, a "Return in 5 Days To" envelope from my mother, and a pink form letter from the Women's Clearinghouse inviting me to a forum on Date Rape, Refreshments Provided.

Dear Mira,

   We got the news about Phi Beta Kappa. Your father says it's all paternal genes, ha ha. We went deep sea fishing in Ensenada last weekend with the Taggarts. The weather was fantastic. Have you heard from Columbia yet about graduate school?

I look up from the letter, tilting my head. Very faintly, I think I hear a baby crying.

For a moment I picture my parents out on the open sea, fishing rods in one hand and long-necked Coronas in the other, laughing at one of Eddie Taggart's incessant scatological jokes. "Mr. and Mrs. Sea and Ski," I mutter, crumpling my mother's note into a little ball and tossing it into the nearest receptacle, which happens to be the exposed case of the Gold Room's grand piano.

"Two points," a voice drawls. I turn to see Jackson stretched out on the burgundy leather sofa by the fireplace, a cigarette in one pale slender hand. "Your aim's superb as always, Randa." He smiles at me through a blue veil of smoke. "But don't you think you could find a more appropriate place for your garbage?"

"My garbage?" I feel my lips curving in a sneer, yet somehow my voice is softer than I intended it to be. "I needed a trash can."

"Darling, you're an English major." He takes a drag on his cigarette and lazily exhales. "Don't you know the difference between a piano and a wastebasket?"

"Is this a trick question?" I stare back at him, envying for perhaps the thousandth time the length and impossible curl of his eyelashes.

It's well past midnight and the *Advocate* party is packed. For the past half-hour Molly and I have been doing go-go routines on the fireplace mantel, high above the crowd. Even though the ledge is barely a foot wide, we've managed to pull off some pretty impressive Supremes imitations, although at one point I had to grab Molly by her polka-dotted miniskirt to keep her from tumbling headlong into the dancers below. Across the room on the massive oak table Billy and Gerard are ripping up back issues of the *Advocate*, sprinkling the pieces on people's heads and howling with laughter.

More and more people keep jamming into the room, which by sheer dint of body heat and kinetic energy gets warmer and warmer. Although the open windows admit the chilly November air, only those at the very fringe of the crowd can feel the steamy coolness, tingling on overheated skin.

Over at the makeshift bar they've run out of mixers and are pouring gin and vodka straight up in clear plastic cups. Jackson, who as *Advocate* Dionysus this year is the official party-thrower, seems unconcerned; the party is another glorious success. Eyes glittering and outlined with brilliant blue kohl, he weaves his way through the crush, stopping here a moment to kiss someone in greeting, there to dance briefly with someone else before moving on, supremely at his ease. He and I haven't spoken, save for a quick kiss exchanged upon my arrival, although at one point as I stood by the fireplace talking with Anthony, our heads close together so we could be heard above the music, Jackson suddenly appeared and swung me up onto the mantel, where Molly had been doing the Pony solo to the last couple of songs.

Now we go from the Ramones right into "Jumpin' Jack Flash" and then to "Twist and Shout," the music reaching a mad crescendo as everyone jumps into the four-part harmonies, singing, sweating, swaying, sinking to the floor in an ecstatic paroxysm. The song ends and now Elvis Costello is singing "My Aim Is True." Swiftly the room quiets, becomes somehow reverent under Elvis' moody spell, and Jackson is standing before me. He holds out his arms, and I descend from the mantelpiece into his embrace, and we're dancing together, my cheek pressed tight against his familiar knobby shoulder.

Later, much later, Jackson closes the front door of the *Advocate* behind the last guest, turns the lock, and leads me upstairs, where he clears one of the sofas of empty beer bottles and forgotten jackets. It's nearly dawn *and it's breathtakingly quiet in the room. As Jackson pulls off his shirt, I sit waiting for him on the sofa, reputedly the very same sofa on which Norman Mailer used to take his daily afternoon naps. "What's so funny?" Jackson whispers, sitting down next to me. "Nothing," I whisper back. "Nothing at all." Leaning forward, I very gently bite him on the salty skin at the base of his throat, still smiling as all thoughts of Norman Mailer swiftly vanish.*

"Have I ever asked you a trick question? Miranda?"

I blink. Jackson has just executed a flawless smoke ring, which he carelessly brushes aside.

"Pay attention, darling. There's going to be a quiz afterwards."

I shudder ever so slightly, wondering if I'm imagining the sudden draft I feel snaking down my spine. "Loan me a cig?" I say, giving him my best glammie smile, a precisely calculated expression displaying equal parts of derision, spurious affability, and indifference. It is an art that I have cultivated in recent years, and which of late I have brought to something close to perfection.

Jackson frowns at me. "Since when do you smoke, Randa?"

"Everyone needs a hobby." I shrug. "What brings you to this den of sin, anyway? Waiting for Godot or something?"

"Meeting somebody."

"There's no interhouse tonight, you know."

"Oh?" He blows another smoke ring. "Why not?"

"Oxblood, Cowland, Starve a Steer for Christ. I forget." I raise my right foot a few inches off the floor and flex the ankle, one two, one two. My shinsplints seem to be bothering me more than usual tonight. "You know. Another one of those massive bleeding-heart gestures that gets a lot of publicity and makes everybody feel guilty for a few hours. But all it really means is that there's no interhouse." One two, one two. "Hope it doesn't interfere with your plans."

"Not really. We'll go out, I guess." He yawns. "What's wrong with your leg?"

I turn away. "Well, I'll see you around."

"Randa?"

"Yeah?"

"D'you think I need a haircut?"

I look over my shoulder. His hair, a tawny brown, curls with artless grace over his collar. *Dear god*, I think unguardedly, *he's Byron, he's Baudelaire*.

"Randa?"

"You look fine." I take my hand from my throat. "How's the French lit coming along these days?"

"Same as usual."

"Good." When I am at the door, he speaks again.

"Hey."

"What."

"Want that cig?"

"No thanks. I was only joking."

After descending the three steps into the dining hall, I pass the enormous portrait of John Quincy Adams, who somehow looks more solemn and dyspeptic than ever, and head for the checker's desk, nimbly avoiding a collision with the house chemistry tutor and one of his students. Sourly I notice that they both wear trousers that are slightly too short, which leads me to ask myself yet again why it is that chemistry majors always look like chemistry majors.

Virginia the checker waves me on into the kitchen, making a little red mark next to my name on her list. "I got you, hon." She is for the most part genial and easygoing but I have seen her on occasion break into a terrifying sprint after unauthorized diners attempting to slip out the back door carrying trays of food. Virginia never buys the sick-roommate story. "If they's so sick," she'll retort, "how come they need two servin's chicken cacciatore?"

My cynical interest in tonight's culinary aberrations notwithstanding, I pass the hot entrées and proceed directly to the chilled metal dairy tins and help myself to a bowl of yogurt. Grinning, Serge tosses me an apple and a whole-wheat roll. Next I jostle my way to the head of the line at the coffee machine. Then, following the obligatory moue of disgust, it's out of the kitchen and into the dining hall. Not unlike Scylla and Charybdis, now that I think of it, impatiently waiting for a pair of overweight sophomores to finish squeezing through the doorway in tandem.

Standing by the salad bar with my tray, I peer about in search of friendly fauna. It's the usual six o'clock scene: a blur of faces and arms and legs and teeth, the cacophony of trays and dishes and silverware clattering, shoes clicking and tapping on the polished wood floor, voices raised in banter and salutation and laughter. The house master's baby is crying again. He's propped up in his high chair at the pre-law table, where Master Ackerman holds court, flanked by two long rows of sycophants who snatch bites of food between nods. His wife sits at the foot of the table, her chin receding desperately as she attempts to shush James P. Ackerman, Jr., who waves his tiny fists about and wails with a fortitude that might come in handy during the Yale game when football season rolls around again.

I wouldn't want to be sitting at that table either, bulging as it is with articulate, neatly dressed overachievers engaging in thoughtful and well-informed conversations about important issues of the day. Dear god.

Their first word was probably "LSAT." It's not that I object so much to their sedately checkered flannel shirts, or even to their inexplicable interest in world affairs. It's the *effort* they display that unnerves me. The trick, I've found, is to breeze into exams, serenely whip your way through a bluebook or two, and leave forty-five minutes early; to ostentatiously skip language lab yet be able to recite your French verbs perfectly the next day; when called upon in English lit to explicate a passage from "Il Penseroso," confess that you haven't read it in years but would be happy to hazard an interpretation, and then launch into a short but brilliant exposition upon Milton's unmatched utilization of imagery and meter.

Smiling maliciously, I loosen the cap on the vinegar cruet. I keep it to myself that I spend a lot of time hunched over my books in the Widener reading room, sequestered among the portly bearded scholars and the haggard Eastern European émigrés who sit reading obscure Czechoslovakian periodicals and chain-smoking till closing time. Or that I'm often in the Widener stacks, borrowing some anonymous graduate student's carrel for a couple of hours to do some writing or reading. If anybody ever asks me, I claim to have been playing video games. Either that or out doing volunteer work for the Radcliffe Foundation.

"Yo, Miranda." It's Carlos loping past, empty plate in hand.

"Thank god." I straighten up. "Where are you sitting?"

"On the right side of the tracks." He gives me a wolfish smile, teeth very white against his skin. "For once."

Although it's perhaps not evident to the untrained eye, the Adams House dining hall embodies an intricate and ever-changing social matrix in which different areas and even specific tables manifest varying degrees of prestige and chic. These days all tables north of the salad bar are déclassé, while those in the extreme southeast corner are the most sought-after seats in the house, veritably bristling with a ridiculous number of chairs. These tables are in such demand that it's risky to vacate your seat for something so trivial as seconds; you may return to find your chair occupied by someone else, your tray mysteriously vanished, your overcoat quite possibly gone.

"Who's at your table?" I ask Carlos. "Anyone remotely humanoid?"

"Sure, I'm sitting with Flopsy, Mopsy, Biopsy, Donner and Blixen. Not to mention the Bobbsey Twins and the Happy Hollisters." He laughs. "Oh yeah. And Bryan and Mark."

"Bryan?" My stomach gives a little twist. "How did he get in? There's no interhouse tonight."

"I snuck him in while Virginia was tackling a couple of guys from Quincy House." Carlos twirls his plate on an index finger. "Why don't you join us? The more the merrier, I always say." He sails off into the kitchen, still twirling his plate, blithely oblivious to the fact that Bryan and I haven't been on speaking terms since the night I slept with his friend Tim, to whom he himself is attracted.

"Why did you do it? That's all I want to know."

Bryan and I look at each other, the silence between us hanging heavier by the second. We're in a practice room at North House; he sits on the piano bench and I'm leaning against the soundproofed wall, hard-pressed to guess which of us is the more stony-faced.

"Well?" he says.

"Three strawberry daiquiris." I shrug. "You know how it is."

"That's not much of an answer."

"It wasn't much of an evening."

"I just want to know why you did it."

"I keep trying to tell you." I draw a long breath, absently noting that my lungs feel tight. What am I supposed to do, blurt out that Jessica was interested in Tim, that he was coming over all the time, we all sort

of hung out together, and somehow he ends up telling me it's me he wants? Tell him that Tim reminds me irresistibly of a Malibu Ken doll? "All I did was lie absolutely still on his bed trying not to puke. Before that I giggled a lot. That's all that happened."

Bryan is tapping out a random tune on the piano. "It just seems so goddam unnecessary, that's all. You knew how I felt about Tim."

"Bryan, Tim was the one who asked me out."

"Did you have to say yes?"

"I always think I'm going to have so much fun with strawberry daiquiris. They just *sound* like fun, don't they? But it never seems to work out that way."

"You could have had Perrier, you know." He's pushing down on the same key over and over again. "And not gotten drunk."

"He was paying."

"Maybe you'd like to talk honestly about this?"

"Can't we just blame it on demon rum and get it over with?"

"It's not that easy, Miranda."

Quelled into silence by his formal use of my name, I'm busy trying to draw a deep breath when Bryan speaks again.

"Maybe you have something else to say?"

"How about playing the theme from Love Story," I suggest. He shoots me a look of such black incredulousness that I raise a hand in self-defense. "Never mind. I was only joking."

"Jesus," he whispers. "Show some goddam emotion, will you?"

"Do I have to?" I lean my head back and watch him as he bends over the keyboard. When I realize that he's crying, I go over to him and put my hand on his shoulder. Now he looks up at me, his face distorted and wet.

"You're completely cool." His voice shakes. "Like a goddam ice queen. Don't you even care?"

"I'm sorry," I say, rasping a little from the tightness in my chest. "I'm really sorry."

"You sure as hell don't show it." He swipes a hand across his cheek. "Just get the hell out of here, okay? Do me a favor and get out of here. Go make some snow angels or something."

After a moment I take my hand off his shoulder; strangely, my palm feels hot, as if it's touched coals. Leaving the practice room, I jog upstairs and go outside to catch the next shuttle bus back down to Harvard Square.

Huddled in my coat, I look out the window at the white snowy streets, wondering why it is I don't seem to feel like crying.

Jessica, after threatening to move off campus and tell the housing office that I'd been keeping snakes in our room, then lapsed into a silent treatment which had me thumbing through Dante's *Inferno* in an effort to see where she derived her methodology. Finally, after two days of her icy glances and stubbornly pursed lips, I cornered her in the bathroom, planted my body as a barricade against the door, and swore to her that I spent the entire night retching into Tim's baseball helmet, which, as far as I was concerned, was only the merest distortion of the truth. Relenting, she snickered at my woeful face, and then we shook hands in a manly sort of way and I took her out to Steve's for ice cream.

But with Bryan it seems that it's more than a simple case of pique. Our freshman-year friendship began in a shared fondness for tiny dark cafés, crashing Fogg Museum art openings, the Talking Heads, and picking the raisins out of the granola tin, and was nourished over the semesters by long telephone conversations at all hours and by our study sessions holed up in his room at North House, him tinkering with a score for composition class, me at my notebook muttering over my Roget's. All this easy camaraderie has somehow been displaced by a tense void between us, looming wider every day; and it's all the more trying since Tim keeps phoning me, and I haven't got much to say to him, except perhaps to inquire if he's ever heard the old expression about loose lips sinking ships.

And so I stand here by the salad bar with my yogurt getting warm, Carlos offering no refuge, and out of the corner of my eye I can see Beatrice and Alicia in their matching leather trousers rustling my way. Grimly I consider handing over my tray to the dishwasher and bagging dinner entirely. *Homemade baklava, chérie.* I try to recall what I had for lunch today. Did I have lunch today?

Then I spot Michael and Walt at a small round table not fifteen feet from the salad bar. Quashing a sigh of relief, I drift toward them as if my destination had been ordained before birth, taking care to avoid all unnecessary and potentially fatal eye contact en route.

After setting down my tray, I pluck a chair from a nearby table and slide into the seat. "Thank god."

"Howdy, you long tall drink of water," Michael says, half-rising and tipping an imaginary ten-gallon to me. He's from Texas and can get away with things like wearing pointy Tony Lamas and opening doors for women. Not many people would guess that he's attended East Coast prep schools since he was ten. "How are you, gal?"

"Oh, I can't complain."

"Miranda," Walt says, shaking his head at my tray, "don't you know what nutrition spelled backwards is?"

"Noitirtun."

"R-e-l-i-e-f." Michael winks at me.

"M-o-n-e-y." Walt is waving his fork for emphasis. Little brown blobs of gravy dot the tabletop.

"Oh, Walt. You're beautiful when you're angry." Smiling, I wipe a little globule of gravy off my arm. After untold hours of computation, Walt has determined exactly how much food he must consume at each sitting in order to get full value for his board plan, which, as for most Harvard students, boils down to three all-you-can-eat meals a day. He does fairly well with lunch and dinner, but breakfast proves to be another kettle of fish, as it were. How much oatmeal, after all, can one person eat? Walt compensates for his physiological limitations by smuggling out several single-serving boxes of cereal a day, thus, he insists, getting his money's worth from his meal plan. This satisfaction is never plainer than when he is showing off an entire wall of his room lined with row upon row of carefully stacked Rice Krispies, Cocoa Puffs, Sugar Smacks, Bran Buds, and Special K boxes.

"I'm not angry, Miranda. But I'll be honest with you, I *am* somewhat concerned."

"Is it because I have food between my teeth?" I smirk radiantly at him, in deference to his avowed intention of becoming a dentist. "Something huge and disgusting?"

"Just a small tree in the very front, darlin'." Michael taps my chin. "It's kinda cute, though."

"I'm not joking, Miranda," Walt persists. "That's barely one, one point five dollars you've got on your tray there."

"I'll steal some silverware, okay?"

"Y'all take some dishes, too."

"No respect." Walt shakes his head again and turns his attention to a large half-eaten piece of meat, the animal source of which I don't care to guess at, that rests on his plate gleaming with an obscenely brown sauce. "Pass the salt, please."

Michael complies, then pushes back his imaginary ten-gallon, smiling at me. "How goes it, kitten?"

"The usual." I shrug, listening to a girl behind me saying, "Every time I'm in France I get sick. Isn't it funny?" Sipping my coffee, I keep my eyes fixed on Michael's face. "What's new with you?"

"Well now, funny y'all should ask. My latest Cobol program just about blew up the Science Center, an' my professor's gonna string me up the next time I show my red ol' face in class. 'Course I got three hundred pages of tutorial readin' due tomorrow, an' I've gotta run over to the phone company first thing in the mornin' an' beg 'em not to disconnect my phone just because my roommate used the phone money to buy marijuana. But other than that, not much to report." An eyebrow arches, sleek and orderly. "Oh, an' my folks are threatenin' divorce again."

"Oh."

"All very well and good," Walt chimes in. "But what are you planning to wear to the Spee's pajama party?"

There is a tremendous sound of phlegm-rattling wheezing and then Andrew descends upon us, his cheeks blazing with an alarming red flush. "Hi, guys." Breathlessly he leans his palms on the table. "Anybody got a cigarette?"

"No, asshole." Walt glares at him. "Bug off."

"Shit." He whirls and clatters off, leaving a pungent scent of Gitanes in his wake.

Walt stabs his fork into his meat. "Dirty son-of-a-bitch bastard."

"Well, gal, I thought I'd wear pajamas." Michael winks at me again.

"What a concept."

"No-good rotten stinking moron," Walt goes on, bitterly. "Decaying scum-of-the-earth douchebag."

"Now Walt." I repress a smile. "It's not nice to talk about your roommate like that."

"He's a putrefying baboon and I hope he drops dead from lung cancer. The sooner the better."

"Then you really should keep a supply of cigs around for him, don't you think?"

A voice rings out from the end of the dining hall: "Panty raid!" Somebody cheers, and the master's baby starts crying again. Sighing, Walt inserts a large chunk of meat into his mouth.

A brilliant flash of crimson catches my eye, and I twist around in my chair to watch Robbie and Adolfo gliding out of the kitchen wearing handsome red frocks—new Kamalis, if I'm not mistaken. Their earrings, necklaces, stockings, and pumps are all charmingly coordinated in varying shades of red.

Robbie and Adolfo are certainly among the most prominent Adams House residents, although it's hard to say whether it's because of their tireless activism for gay rights or because of their exquisite taste in clothing. Nobody bats an eye at them, from Master Ackerman on down; after a few days of confusion, the incoming sophomores catch on too. Even Virginia remains unfazed, sometimes cooing over a particularly dazzling outfit. I eye them speculatively, wondering if it's true, as rumor will have it, that the boys are just good friends. Really.

"There." Walt drops his fork onto his plate and leans back with another sigh. "Six dollars and forty-two cents."

I tear my envious gaze away from Robbie's superb Italian shoes. "As opposed to six and a half."

"Every penny counts, Miranda."

"And a hundred or so makes a dollar."

"That's right."

"Maybe I should have been a math major."

"Why?"

I blink at him. "Hey, you want my apple for dessert? I'm not going to eat it."

"No thanks, Eve." He grins. "Get it? Eve?"

Michael touches my shoulder. "Eat something, gal."

I look at him. "Don't you know this is Oxfam night?"

"Yep." He is unmoved.

"Don't you see? I feel too guilty to eat."

A fourth tray is planted on the tabletop, nearly pushing Michael's tray off the edge into his lap. He steadies the tray with a quick hand. "Hey now."

"Oh, I'm so sorry." Anne Devereaux sits down, and I smell L'Air du Temps. "It's such a crowded little table."

"Isn't it though?" I stand up. "Luckily, I was just leaving."

"Really?" Walt says in surprise.

"Oh well." Anne sidles her chair an inch or two toward Michael. "I just love your belt buckle. Is that a cow's head? I didn't know cows had horns."

"Bye guys." I pick up my tray.

"It's a steer." Michael grits his teeth at me and scoots his chair closer to my vacated spot. "Ain't y'all ever been to a feedlot?"

On my way to the garbage bins I manage to avoid speaking with another former roommate of mine, Melissa, who used to and for all I know continues to dissolve into baby talk when under stress, an irritating habit that contributed little to the general morale of an already volatile rooming situation. Feigning sudden interest in my sneakers, I am able to sidestep yet another tortuous encounter with Nevill Barth, the house English tutor, who keeps asking me out for coffee so we can talk about Hemingway and poststructuralist criticism over *baba au rhum*, undeterred by my chilly assurances that I have an antipathy for sweets. Next, executing a subtle pirouette around a little yapping cluster of Eurofags in their handsome black overcoats, I relinquish my tray, and finally stalk toward the exit. Bryan and Carlos are standing by the salad bar, laughing. As I pass by them Carlos calls out: "Hey, surfer girl!" I catch a glimpse of Bryan's suddenly frigid face and I say *"Qué pasa, guys?"* and keep moving.

Nursing my shinsplints as I walk up the four flights to my room, I tally up the varying sensory offenses of six blaring stereos, one screaming match, two whiffs of pot, and the frenzied clatter of a popcorn-maker. At the door to C-45 I hear an electric typewriter and the Dazz Band. In the living room, Jessica is sitting perfectly straight over her typewriter, the stereo tuned to her favorite funk station.

"Hi, honey, I'm home." I toss my books and jacket onto the couch. "What's for dinner?"

She doesn't turn her head from the keyboard. "What's another word for *repressed?*"

"Suppressed, restrained, constrained, inhibited." I sprawl on the couch and pick up the *Crimson.* "Stifled, curbed, subdued. Why do you ask?"

"Guess," she says sourly.

"You're doing the crossword puzzle?"

"Very funny." She taps a few keys and then sighs hugely. "Hey, d'you think I can get away with implying that Jane Austen was bisexual?"

"Why not? You live in Adams House."

"Oh, Christ." She leans over and rests her forehead on the typewriter. "Lord help me."

"I'm serious. You'll get an A for sure."

"Goddam fucking son of a bitch."

"I hope you're referring to your thesis."

"I'm sure you do."

Tossing the *Crimson* aside, I get up and stroll over to where she sits. I place my hands on her shoulders and start massaging her deltoids.

"Harder harder," she murmurs. "Faster faster."

"Don't be disgusting."

When I sense that she's about to slide onto the floor, I give her neck a final squeeze. "Try to relax." I return to the couch and pick up *The New Yorker.* Jessica subscribes.

She's typing away with renewed vigor. "You're an animal," she tells me, cheered.

"Call me Fido," I say absently, in the middle of another unintelligible *New Yorker* poem. Finally I throw the entire magazine into the empty fireplace. "God, I hate this pretentious crap. I know several monkeys who—"

"Hey, speaking of crap." Jessica reads aloud from her notes: " 'Jane Austen as social critic. Early feminist writings reveal precocious awareness'—"

The phone rings from underneath my coat. "I'll get it," I say loudly, poking around for the receiver. "Hello?"

"Hi, is Jessica there?"

"Hi, Steve. How's everything?"

"Fine, thanks. Who's this?"

"Bella Abzug. It's Bella Abzug."

"Oh, I guess I have a wrong number."

"I was only joking, Steve. Bella Abzug lived here last year."

"Oh. Who am I talking to then?"

"Here's a little hint. Seven letters, sounds like veranda. Tall gal who lives with Jessica, blue eyes, dishwater-blond hair—"

"Oh, hi, Miranda. Is Jessica there?"

"Just a minute." I bring the receiver right up to my mouth. "Jessica," I scream, "it's for you."

Jessica takes the phone and sits at the other end of the couch. "Well, hi, Steve." She rolls her eyes at me. "I'm fine, thanks. How are you?"

"Be nice to him," I whisper, standing up. "He can't help it if he's a peabrain."

"What did you say, Steve? I couldn't hear you. Miranda was telling me something."

Abandoning her to Steve, I go into the bathroom to brush and floss my teeth. Then I dispose of the floss by flicking it out into the air shaft, which has wonderful acoustics and makes for some stimulating eavesdropping now and again. A couple of floors down someone is singing "Misty" in his bathroom. His voice, a wistful tenor, floats dreamily upward, and I turn away from the mirror, checking the impulse to tilt close and see if I've gotten any blemishes since the last time I looked.

Jessica now occupies the entire couch and is using my coat for a pillow. "Well, it's nice of you to ask, Steve. Really. But it's the Radcliffe Senior Soirée, you know. The girls are supposed to ask the boys." I lift up her legs and reclaim my place, settling her feet in my lap. She wears a white crew sock and a sagging pink anklet. "Right. Like a Sadie Hawkins dance." She rolls her eyes at me again. "Well, to be honest with you, Steve, Miranda and I have already asked two football players from Kirkland House to go with us. They're very sweet boys. Varsity." I start playing "This Little Piggy Went to Market" with her toes and she kicks back at me. "Listen, Steve, I've got to run. We're having our Wednesday-night fire drill over here. Thanks for calling. Yes, I enjoyed talking to you too. Really. Bye now." She hangs up the phone and drops her jaw into her neck, reminding me irresistibly of a disgruntled carp. "Why do these graduate students keep bothering me?"

"Jessica?"

"What?"

"Are they buying us corsages?"

"Who?"

"The football players."

"Oh, Christ. My life is falling apart, and you're pestering me about corsages."

"Why is your life falling apart?"

"Do you want an itemized list?"

"It might be helpful."

"Okay. In no particular order: Steve, my thesis, the Radcliffe Senior Soirée, Yale Law School, and a Coop bill for three hundred dollars."

"That's all?"

"Do you mind if I slug you?"

"Couldn't we talk about your thesis instead?"

"But what I'm really worried about is the Soirée."

"Your thesis. I insist."

"God, you're a bore."

"Now, Jessica." I clear my throat sententiously. "As I hope you realize, this thesis represents a truly magnificent educational opportunity, a once in a lifetime chance to contribute in a meaningful and lasting way to the prestigious academic community we know and love—"

"Do you mean Harvard?"

"Not to be confused with Princeton, say, or Stanford," I affirm. "You should be grateful. Think of all the starving children in Africa."

"I'll send them my meal card. Let them write my thesis."

"Come on, buck up." I give her instep an encouraging little squeeze. "You've been at the typewriter for three days. How many pages have you written so far?"

"Four."

"Four?"

"Well, four and a half. If you count the outline that makes a grand total of six."

"Sweetheart," I say delicately, "when is it due?"

"A week from Friday. Oh Jesus, Miranda." She sits up and grabs my wrist. "Anything yet?"

"Did I say *due?* Whoops." I smirk at her. "I can hear Freud spinning in his grave."

"It's ten days already, isn't it?"

"Twelve. But who's counting?"

"Have you been to UHS yet?"

"You know how I feel about bunny rabbits."

"Miranda—"

"Now let's see." I disengage my wrist from her grasp. "Who's the lucky guy who gets to pay for baby carriages and child support? Anthony, maybe? Or Danny, the waiter at Soup 'n' Salad who took me to a Celtics game during spring break?" Tim's name hangs in the air between us, although technically speaking he can hardly be classified as a candidate. "Or Guillaume, my one-night stand from the romance-languages party?"

"Guillaume? You mean the kid who spilled sangria down your back?"

"Maybe." I shrug, thankful that she's accepted the omission. "I'd rather it be Anthony, though. His parents are rich." I smile crookedly at her. "I wouldn't mind hanging out in Coral Gables watching my stomach get fat."

"Jesus, Miranda."

"I hear Florida's a nice place to raise kids."

"Aren't you going to take your sweater off?" Anthony whispers.

"No, it's too cold." Absently I pat his shoulder, mentally retracing the steps that have led to this unexpected little Tuesday-night tryst. It seems to have begun with a casual discussion at dinner about the Brattle Theatre, which led to a 7:35 showing of Breathless. *Next was Pamplona and two double espressos apiece, followed by a quick detour to the Hong Kong for a couple of Scorpion Bowls, which somehow resulted in an impromptu excursion to his room to look up a favorite Yeats passage, and now here I am in Anthony's rumpled futon with my underwear*

shut into Volume 2 of the Norton Anthology of Poetry. "You're a swan, a swan," he murmurs, mouth at my hipbones. His hands are moving over my body with an urgency I find somewhat unnerving, and I am in fact about to politely ask him to stop kneading my quadriceps when suddenly he is thrusting against my left leg, the flesh of his buttocks shimmering smooth and pale in the moonlight. He's breathing with what strikes me as unnecessary loudness. I look over at the door to the living room, wondering if any of his roommates are in. "Miranda," he whispers hoarsely, sinking onto my pelvis, still shaking a little. My kneecap feels sticky, my back is starting to hurt, and it occurs to me that I was never all that crazy about Yeats anyway.

"You're taking this very well," Jessica says dryly.

"Will you stop? I don't even know for sure." I toe off my sneakers and begin flexing my ankles. "Which reminds me. Why did the Valley Girl take two birth-control pills?"

"You must be kidding."

"Come on. Be a sport."

"Jesus. Why."

"She wanted to be fer sure, fer sure." I poke her in the ribs but she merely frowns.

"Have you been checking your diaphragm for holes?"

"Now who's kidding who? Do you check *your* diaphragm for holes?"

"We're not talking about my diaphragm," she snaps.

"Don't you think they look like giant contact lenses?"

"No."

"Screwy little things. So to speak."

"Don't be disgusting."

"Fallible loops, you might call them. Note the oblique allusion to fallopian tubes."

"Jesus, Miranda. Will you stop joking for once?"

"I thought I told you to relax. Would you kindly remove my notebook from underneath your lumbar region? I want to write this down. When you get a chance, of course." I reach for the phone and start dialing.

"Hi, is Dean there?"

Jessica flashes her cynical fish face at me and climbs out of the couch to go back to the typewriter.

"Hi, Miranda."

"Hi, Kevin. How's everything?"

"Really shitty. How about with you?"

"Oh, I can't complain."

"You can't complain?" he says aggrievedly. "What do you mean, you can't complain?"

"Speech defect. Darling, is Dean around?"

"Miranda, why don't you go out with me instead? I don't already have a girlfriend."

"It's sweet of you to offer, Kevin. But I'm afraid I'm just not good enough for you."

"Oh." There is a short silence. "But still. I just don't think you're using your energies constructively here."

"I beg your pardon?"

"Let's face it, Miranda, Dean's a tough nut to crack."

"Watch your mouth." I open my notebook.

"Look. He spends a good twenty, twenty-five percent of his time with Jennifer, right? Drinking, screwing, and arguing."

"Not necessarily in that order, I hope."

"Right. Then, what with meals, watching TV, and going to Advocate meetings, that doesn't leave much time for outside activities, like cheating on his girlfriend or going to classes." Kevin speaks with the oily reasonableness of an economics major. "It's really a matter of simple arithmetic."

I'm hunting through my jacket pockets for a pen. "What's your point, Kev?"

"Miranda, can I be honest with you?"

"Why bother?"

"Have you and Dean slept together?"

"Why don't you ask Dean? He's your roommate, after all."

"That's kind of a personal question to ask someone, isn't it?"

"I suppose you're right." I find my favorite Bic fine-point in an inner pocket, along with a couple of pieces of sugarless gum and a lipstick I thought I'd lost weeks ago. "No, Kev, I'll tell you the truth. It's Jennifer I'm after. Is she around, by any chance?"

"You're so wild, Miranda. I need that in a woman."

"Don't start flattering me now. I take it Dean's not there?"

"And smart too."

"Yes, but I can't cook and I hate housework. Do you still want to marry me?"

"Well, thanks, Miranda, but really I just want to get you into my room to show you my bar graphs."

"Forget it. I go for anemic stringy-haired intellectual types, not great big M.B.A. bruisers like you."

"Oh, Miranda." He sighs breathily into the receiver. "What are you doing tonight?"

"Staring at a blank page. Where's Dean?"

"Having dinner with Jackson."

"My, what a small world it is."

"They're probably talking about you right now."

"It's a lovely thought, Kev, but more likely they're discussing the next issue of the *Advocate.*"

"Give yourself more credit than that, Miranda."

"I'm not sure the Registrar would go for it." I snicker.

There's a silence at the other end of the line. "Do you want me to leave a message for Dean?"

"Yes, tell him that I called to ask him a question about *Lady Chatterley's Lover.*"

"Wait, I'm writing it down. Can I borrow your copy when you're through?"

"I'm not sure you're ready for it."

"How do you spell 'Chatterley'?"

"Never mind. Maybe you could just tell him I called."

"Sure. But I already wrote down 'Lover.' "

"That's what I like about you, Kev. You always get to the heart of things."

"Thanks."

"I'd chat some more, Kev, but we're having a little fire drill over here just at the moment."

"I guess you'd better go then."

"I guess so. Nice talking with you."

"You too, Miranda. I'll leave the message on Dean's bed."

"Good thinking. Thanks, Kev."

We hang up, and I write *fallible loops* in my notebook.

Jessica speaks without turning her head from the typewriter. "Fascinating."

"I assume you're referring to your thesis."

"What else would I be referring to? Gosh, I just can't put down this book on Jane Austen's political views. Did you know she was an avid proponent of agricultural reform?"

"Wow."

"I don't suppose you can come up with something a little more articulate than 'Wow'?"

"Jessica, I'm trying to write a poem here. Do you mind?"

"That's your problem." She goes back to her halfhearted typing.

The telephone rings, and I start at the noise, dropping my pen on the floor. "Shit."

Jessica leaps up. "I'll get it."

I hand her the receiver. "A cheap diversion."

"Hello? Oh, hi, Sutter." She listens for a moment, then jabs at my calf with her big toe. "Sutter wants you to know that he's not cheap."

"Ask him how much." I lean over the arm of the sofa and retrieve *The New Yorker* from the fireplace. Settling back, I start to turn to the book-review section but am distracted by a Bulgari ad.

Jessica stretches out on the floor, using my running shoes for a pillow. "A special on PBS?" she is saying. "Sutter, I'm trying to write a thesis over here."

I snigger at her over *The New Yorker* but she ignores me. "What's that? A Jacques Cousteau documentary?"

Yawning, I switch to the movie listing.

"Oh, all right. You know I can't resist Jacques Cousteau. D'you have any beer? Fabulous. See you soon. Bye." She hangs up. There is a brief silence. "Miranda?"

"What."

"Your feet stink."

"I beg your pardon," I say, not lowering the magazine. "I believe you mean to tell me that my *shoes* stink."

"Don't worry about it." She stands up. "Jane Austen's feet smelled too."

I flip over to "Talk of the Town." Jessica switches off the typewriter and starts gathering up the crumpled paper that litters the floor in a chaotic white jumble. "I know what you're thinking."

"Madame Jessica knows all, sees all."

"Shut up. You're thinking I should stay here and work on my thesis."

"Did I say anything?"

"No, but I could tell you were thinking it." She's putting on her shoes. "Your lower lip is sticking way out."

"I'm just trying to figure out this goddam cartoon, that's all." Sighing, I toss *The New Yorker* back into the fireplace. "Just go and have a good time, okay? Drink beer, look at the whales, ogle Jacques Cousteau's skinny little French bod." I'm trying to find my pen again. "I'll stay here and watch your thesis. What time does it usually go to bed?"

She stoops and picks up my pen from where it has landed not ten inches from my right foot. "This your gun, *hombre?*"

"What keen eyes you have."

"Yep." She cackles and disappears into her bedroom. When she returns she's wearing a tight-fitting imitation leopard-skin jacket that has shiny black plastic buttons the size of small pancakes. "I'm off. How do I look?"

"Very *National Geographic.*"

"Hey," she says, pausing in the doorway. "What are you doing tonight?"

"Oh, I don't know. Stuff for poetry class." I slouch lower on the sofa. "I should do laundry, I guess. I'm down to underwear I'm embarrassed to be seen in."

"You've got Sutter's number, don't you?"

"Well, I haven't actually memorized it, but he's in the directory, isn't he?"

"It's taped to my lamp too."

"Thanks." I look up at her quizzically. "Have fun tonight."

"Don't work too hard, okay?"

"Me? Well, listen, since you're so concerned about my school-work, I'd like to point something out to you that you may have overlooked."

"Well?"

"The longer you stay here, the less likely it seems that I'll get anything done at all."

She grins. "Is that a hint?"

"No, but I wish you'd get the hell out of here already."

"Bye."

When I hear the door slam, I stand up and go over to the radio and switch it off. I stand for a moment by the window, looking out at the Charles and at people going in and out of Harvard Pizza. Then I go into my room and sit at my desk with my notebook open in front of me.

The phone rings, but I don't move from my chair. As I'm closing my notebook I notice that I'm a little hungry, and I contemplate going downstairs and across the street to Tommy's. But no. The way the day is going, I just don't think I could stomach it.

THURSDAY | 2

|||||||||||||||||||||||||||||||||||||||||||||||||||||||||||||||||||

Something is tickling my hip. I roll over: a soft crackling noise. Now it's lodged just underneath my kidneys. Sleepily I wonder what it could be. A candy wrapper? A pencil? Then again, maybe it's just a cockroach.

"Shit." I jerk myself upright and peer around. Then I see that there's a little piece of paper crumpled up among the sheets.

A note! I snatch it up, but am disappointed to see that it's my own handwriting. I lean back against the pillows and close my eyes, but now there are soft moaning noises coming through the wall from next door in C-41.

Oh, shit. Not again. I get out of bed, hitch up the waistband of my pajama bottoms, and scuff into the living room. Bright morning light pours into the room. Grimacing, I sit in the armchair and limply cross one leg over the other. Is it my imagination, or do my feet look blue? As usual they are freezing cold.

Slowly it dawns on me that I'm still holding the scrap of paper in my hand. Too enervated to reach over into the fireplace for a

27

magazine, I smooth out the note and blink a couple of times to get my eyes to focus.

1. UHS
2. buy lucky rabbit's foot (ha ha)
3. laundry (?)
4. career services (?)
5. Mug 'n' Muffin 4 pm Angela
6. Robbins 6–10 pm
7. Dean (?)

The telephone rings, catching me in mid-yawn. "Hello?"

"Have you gone to UHS yet?"

"Hi, Jessie. How's everything?"

"Well, have you?"

"I'm still in my pajamas, so I guess that means I haven't."

"Miranda, the lab closes at nine."

"Really? What time is it?"

"Eight forty-five. You haven't gone to the bathroom yet, have you?"

"God, you're nosy."

"Goddam it, Miranda. Get the hell over there. *Now.*"

"I love it when you talk dirty."

She screams. "Will you go?"

"Can I change into my clothes first?"

"Just shut up and go."

"Jessie?"

"What, for god's sake?"

"Thanks for calling. I'll save some urine for you."

"Don't be disgusting." She hangs up.

I yawn one last time, and do a few neck rolls. Then I jump up and dash into my room, which is now blessedly quiet, and waste a few more seconds scrabbling around for a pair of clean underwear. I pull on the same clothes I wore yesterday: a man's extra-large white shirt, a favorite black sweater, baggy black pegged trousers, white socks and sneakers. One earlobe with a tiny diamond stud, the other with two gold hoops, followed by a dab of the Paco

Rabonne that I swiped from Michael. I can't seem to locate my hairbrush just at the moment, and so by default my toilette is complete.

I slip into my jacket and I'm off down the stairs at a good clip, this time counting four stereos and only one whiff of pot. In the foyer by the mailboxes I run into Dean's girlfriend Jennifer. Her hair is wet, presumably from her morning shower.

"Aren't you the early bird," I say affably, poking around in my pockets for my sunglasses. "How's everything?"

"Just fine, thanks." As she smiles at me I notice that she's got lipstick smeared on her front teeth. "How about with you?"

"Me?" Actually, I muse, she's a rather nice girl aside from an erratic tendency to speak with a British accent, a habit I find a trifle confusing as I understand that she grew up in Rhode Island. "Oh, I can't complain." I nod.

"That's good." She nods also.

"Yep." Nodding one last time, I saunter along the foyer, step outside, and viciously kick the door shut with my heel. "Ow."

It's a brilliantly clear Cambridge morning, with the kind of cool, invigorating breeze that makes my nose run. In the five-minute walk along Mount Auburn Street I'm forced to recycle both of the two little dried-up wads of Kleenex I've found jammed into my jacket pockets. By the time I reach UHS my nose is raw and the urge to pee is ferocious.

The staff is brisk and casual about the whole business; they hand me various forms and ask questions about my sex life I'd just as soon not answer. I notice that my hand is shaking as I sign the consent papers, and for a moment I'm tempted to run through the waiting room tearing at my hair and screaming for Ryan O'Neal. Instead, five minutes later I find myself quietly handing over my urine sample. The technician, a marvelously sickly-looking specimen himself, accepts the warm little plastic cup with a distinct look of nausea on his face.

"You can call after four-thirty for the results." His gaze is apathetically fixed on my right ear.

"Great. Thanks." I give him a big insincere smile. "Have a nice day."

"You too." Holding my urine sample at arm's length, he lists off down the hallway. There is a large greenish stain on the back of his lab coat.

I walk back down Mount Auburn Street muttering reassurances to myself. *Cheer up. You lead a charmed existence, remember? The best and the brightest, right?* All at once I catch myself thinking about those big grainy posters in the subway, the ones showing a sad-eyed teenager with a football under her dress. Sniffing damply, I wrench open the door to Adams House. *Bloody good cheering-up job. Maybe you should become a Planned Parenthood counselor.* I slink into the dining hall singing "Life During Wartime" under my breath, breaking off only when I get into the kitchen and pick up a tray, a grapefruit half, and some yogurt.

A pale, pear-shaped junior whose name I don't know looks at me strangely as I pass him by the pastry tray. I nod at him but he immediately turns his wall-eyed attention back to the chocolate twists.

Frowning, I go into the dining room and look around. Jessica is at a table with John, Clark, and Roald, three juniors who share an enormous A-entry suite in which they often throw loud, successful parties, notorious for the way in which their respective girlfriends somehow seem to end up in the wrong bedroom at the end of the evening. Of course, I remind myself as I move toward them, *wrong* is rather a subjective term. Nobody else seems to be complaining.

"Good morning, gang." I sit down between John and Roald. "Isn't it a glorious day to be alive?"

"Oh, Jesus." John jabs his fork into an egg, bursting the yolk all over his toast. "Never a moment's peace."

Roald smiles at me. "Good morning, Miranda."

"Good morning, Roald. How's everything?"

"Just fine, thanks. And how are you?"

"Can't complain."

"That's good. Uh, Miranda?"

"Yes, Roald?"

"Can I have your grapefruit half?"

"Get your own grapefruit half, Roald."

"That's not very generous of you, Miranda."

"That may very well be true." I nod judicially. "Pardon me while I dig into this luscious pink grapefruit here."

"After all I've done for you, Miranda."

"What have you ever done for me, Roald?"

"I brought you a cup of coffee once."

"I asked for tea."

"All right, Miranda." He rises and starts dragging himself off to the kitchen. "I'll get my own grapefruit."

"Bring me some coffee, will you?" I call after him. "Cream, no sugar."

"Jesus, Miranda." John wipes grapefruit juice off his cheek. "You almost got me in the eye."

"Sorry." I lift another spoonful to my mouth. "My aim's not very good in the morning."

Jessica clears her throat. "Did you have a nice little walk, dear?"

"Yes, thanks. There's nothing I like better than leaping out of bed and going for a hearty stroll first thing in the morning. And I don't mind saying so."

"Keep it down, Miranda." Clark frowns at me. "People are looking at us."

"I'm from California, remember?" Gently I spit a grapefruit seed onto my tray.

"Oh yeah." He nods and jams an immense forkful of waffle into his mouth.

Jessica slopes forward over the tabletop. "Hey."

"Hey what?"

"You're not lying to me, are you?"

"About what?"

"Yes, I think I will slug you after all."

"No, no, that won't be necessary." I brush a few drops of grapefruit juice off my shoulder. "Listen, I made it with three minutes to spare. I have the deposit slip to prove it, too. Time-stamped and everything. It even smells like—"

"Oh, shut up. Good thing I called, or you'd have slept till noon."

"Possibly. By the way, your hair is dangling into your coffee."

"Shit." She tilts away. "Why didn't you tell me?"

"I just did."

"Sooner, dope, sooner."

"Oh, look," Clark says thickly through a mouthful of waffle and syrup. "Katherine got her hair cut. Looks awful, doesn't it?"

"I guess Halloween came early this year."

"Who's that she's with?"

"I'll bet he's from Lowell. She always goes out with guys from Lowell."

"I hear she had mono last fall."

"Really? Somebody told me it was herpes."

"Goodness," I say genially. "You boys certainly have your ears to the ground, don't you?"

"She told everybody it was anemia." Chuckling, Clark opens a box of Cocoa Puffs and pours it into his bowl. "Hey, Miranda. Didn't you just get a haircut too?" He sprinkles three packets of sugar into his cereal and adds milk.

"Me?" My maladroit self-barbering tends to result in odd little spikes and asymmetrical lines. People are constantly asking me where I get my hair done; most often I tell them that my haircutter is an East Village acupuncturist–cum–graffiti artist named Popo who also repairs Vespas on the side. Though I embellish the story more and more outlandishly in the expectation that someday someone will actually challenge me about it, no one has, but I'm cherishing high hopes based upon Popo's recent appointment as Secretary of State. "A haircut? No." I shake my head. "I got them all cut."

Clark laughs uproariously, pounding the tabletop and making the dishes rattle. "God, you're a scream, Miranda," he gasps.

"Prettier than the painting, don't you think?" Out of the corner of my eye I spot Dean coming into the dining hall. He shows the checker his ID card and goes into the kitchen.

Clark wipes his eyes with his napkin. "What painting?"

Roald returns with his grapefruit half and a cup of coffee. "Here's your coffee, Miranda. Cream, no sugar, right?"

"Right. Thanks." I stand up. "Anybody want anything?" I turn and go off without waiting for a reply.

In the kitchen Dean ponders the pastry tray. He's wearing Levis and his bright-red windbreaker. His hair is damp and slicked close to his head in dark waves that will lighten to blondish brown as they dry.

"I recommend the crullers."

He turns. "Oh, hi," he says in his low, somehow silken voice. "But I think I'd rather have one of those chocolate twists."

"I hear they're fabulous too."

"Oh, really?" He hesitates, and then takes one and puts it on his tray. "Okay."

"Good choice. Oh, by the way."

"Hmm?" He's looking at the pastries again.

"I tried calling you last night."

"I know. Kevin left a message." He puts the chocolate twist back and takes a bran muffin.

I find myself noticing a large jagged patch of cheek where he didn't shave. "So did you have a nice dinner?"

"Yeah, nothing special. Went to Charlie's."

"Talked Advo over cheeseburgers?"

"The usual." He glances nervously over his shoulder. "Well, I guess I'd better be—"

"Yes." I turn to look at the cereals. "Enjoy that bran muffin. It's good for you."

"Hey."

I swivel around by forty-five degrees. "Yeah?"

"I tried calling you back, but you weren't home."

"Oh?"

"Is tonight still okay?"

"Tonight?" I arch an eyebrow. "Oh, that's right. We were going out for a drink, weren't we? The Ha'Penny, did we say?"

"Yeah."

"Okay."

"When?"

"I get off work at ten. How about ten-thirty or so?"

"Cool. See you later."

"Yeah, *ciao*." Discreetly I remain behind, whiling away the proper interval by trying to picture him and Jenny without their clothes on.

"Corn flakes, darling." Jackson speaks softly into my ear, and I jump. "Ever seen them before?"

"Christ." My heart is pounding. "You scared me."

He's smiling down at me. "Did I?"

"No, I was only faking it." I draw an unsteady breath. "I suppose you've just been waiting to creep up on me?"

"Wouldn't you like to know."

"Not really."

"Why? Is there something you'd like to hide?"

"Why would I have anything to hide?"

"Just trying to keep you on your toes, Randa."

"I still wouldn't be tall enough, would I?"

His smile fades a little. "What's that supposed to mean?"

"Nothing."

"Christ, I hate it when you're cryptic."

"Maybe you should have been an archeology major." Swiftly I turn away.

John shoots me a look as I sit down. "Just window-shopping?"

"Shut up." Jessica points her fork at him. "I'm about to tell a joke."

"Oh, no," moans Clark. "Please don't."

"Shut up." Jessica thrusts her fork in his direction. "I know I have problems with my delivery—"

"Delivery?" I say.

"Oh, Christ. I'm sorry." She lowers the fork.

"I couldn't resist."

Clark looks back and forth between us. "Am I missing something, girls?"

"Didn't I just tell you to shut up?" This time Jessica reaches for her butter knife.

He leans back in his chair. "How about that joke, eh?"

Jessica rolls her eyes. "The only reason I'm going to tell this joke is because it's really too good to keep to myself."

"I know that one." Roald waves his arms. "There's a Jew, a Catholic, and a black guy, see—"

"Roald, will you be quiet, please?" Jessica fingers her butter knife.

"Sure."

"Good. Is everyone ready?"

No one says a word. I hear a cup dropping in the kitchen.

"Okay. Why did the elephant fall out of the tree?"

The silence drags out for a few more seconds.

"To get to the other side."

"Ninety-three."

Roald is waving his arms again. "Oh, about ten inches."

Jessica looks triumphantly around the table. "Because he was dead."

"Dead!" I give an appreciative yelp of laughter.

The others, however, are quiet. Roald slurps his coffee, frowning into his cup.

I laugh again. "Dead."

John raises his hand. "Jessica?"

"What?"

"I'll be brief." He lowers his hand. "I wish you'd kept your joke to yourself."

"Who asked you?" she snaps.

"Come on, gang. Just a minute here," I intervene. "What Jessica told is a riddle, not a joke. So let's have some cooler heads prevail, okay?"

"Riddles, jokes," John says impatiently. "Don't be so damn technical, Miranda. It's still stupid."

"You think so?" I notice that he's got little glutinous particles of cereal stuck between his teeth.

"It doesn't make sense," complains Roald. "How did the elephant get up in the tree in the first place?"

I blink at him. "He was born there."

"Oh, I see." He nods.

"Miranda?" Stephanie Kandel is standing by the table with her tray. "Hi, sorry to bother you—"

"No bother," John interrupts. "Have a seat."

"No, I really can't." She glances at him and then back at me. "Uh, I missed English C this week and I was wondering if you got the assignment?"

I watch her flip her long, rather lank brown hair off her shoulder. She's always pleasant to me, and is doubtless one of the nicest, brightest sophomores in the house. Tipping my chair back, I ponder why it is I don't seem to like her very much.

"Miranda?"

"Yeah?"

"He gave us an assignment, didn't he?"

"Yep." I look up at her. "After he finished taking attendance."

Her brows crinkle. "He's taking attendance now?"

"I guess. He was muttering something about the final grade being based on class attendance."

"Oh, no."

"But listen, you know how he is. He's always muttering about this or that. I'm sure he didn't mean it."

"Oh, I hope so."

"You know, it's like him saying he's going to penalize people for having long brown hair."

"He said that?"

"No, no, no. I just meant that it's exactly the kind of thing he would do."

"Oh, no." She fingers the ends of her hair.

"Anyway." It looks to me like she's got about a million split ends. "Weren't you asking me something about the assignment?"

"Uh, yes." Now her fingers play over an inflamed-looking pimple at the corner of her mouth. "Was I assigned to read one of my stories for next week?"

"Nope. Guess you lucked out this time."

"Oh, okay. Great. Thanks."

"Come on, Steph, pull up a seat." Clark smiles at her. "Plenty of room." He smashes his chair up against Roald's.

"Ow," Roald says faintly.

"Thanks, but I'm with somebody. Thanks again, Miranda."

John stares at her as she walks toward the sunny tables down by the windows. "Cute girl."

Jessica looks at me. "The great Oz has spoken."

"Oh, not in a flashy way, like Miranda here." John points at me with a grubby forefinger. "Or in a more understated way, like Jessica, but in a—in a—"

"I think it's time to go back to Kansas." Jessica stands up. "Let's go, Dorothy."

"Okay." Hastily I swallow three spoonfuls of yogurt and stand up too. "I'm ready."

"So long, boys," Jessica says, waving her silverware at them. "Try not to fall out of any trees today."

"Thanks for the advice." John rips a jelly doughnut in two.

As Jessica and I near the end of the dining hall, Roald gives a sudden bray of laughter. "Dead!"

"Sad, isn't it," she murmurs. "And to think he scored sixteen hundred on his SATs."

"Yes, but I hear his father still had to pay off the admissions office."

When we reach the foyer Jessica touches my arm. "Listen. About the test. I'll be in the history library all afternoon."

"Okay."

"History library, got it?"

"That's H as in hangman, right?"

"Jesus, Miranda."

"Jessica?"

"What?"

"I think you're going to be late for your ten o'clock class."

She checks her wristwatch. "Oh, shit."

"Have fun."

"Call me."

"Bye." I wave and head for the stairs.

I try telephoning Michael to see if he wants to go to the Coop with me, but there's no answer. I lean back against the sofa and something crackles familiarly at the base of my spine. It's my little note from this morning. Stifling a yawn, I cross my legs and squint down at my spidery handwriting. It seems that there are only two options open to me this morning: I can either go to OCS-OCL or I can do my laundry.

"Hmm," I say aloud. I *could* go outside and make the ten-minute trek to the Career Services building. There, crowded on all sides by every known species of job hunter, internship seeker, med-school applicant, potential fellowship nominee, and other equally unsavory types, I'd sooner or later end up in an ill-lit corner sifting through a stack of outdated job listings, too overwhelmed to even think of trying to approach one of the ostentatiously harried counselors, most of whom are austerely dressed Wheaton College graduates with tight chignons, who in the past have been less responsive to my courteous little questions such as *How do I select an appropriate grad school?* or *Where's the bathroom?* Now, folding my arms under my head and staring up at the ceiling, I remind myself that one outdated job listing is pretty much indistinguishable from any other outdated job listing.

Then again, I could carry about a hundred pounds of laundry up and down the narrow Adams House stairwells, hoping to god I don't meet anybody in transit. And of course there's the matter of quarters and detergent, of which I have neither.

"Hmm," I say again, peering at my list. Then I crush it into a tiny ball and pitch it into the fireplace. Sighing, I kick off my sneakers, plump up the end cushion, make the appropriate mental adjustment to my schedule, and curl up on the sofa.

Angela is late. Closing my Roget's, I mull over the words *generate, propagate,* and *procreate,* poking at the remaining half of my blueberry muffin until finally it's reduced to a drab, distinctly unappealing little pile of crumbs.

Making a face, I wipe my fingers on a napkin and push my plate away. Within seconds the waitress arrives to take the plate and pour more coffee into my cup. "Thanks," I say with a polite little smile. She ignores me and I watch her whisk off in her brown apron, coffeepot held like a truncheon. Then I look back down at my notebook, contemplating some lines that came to me this afternoon while I was running.

"Hi, am I late?" Angela sits down in a cataclysm of jacket, beret, shoulder bag, books, and an enormous canvas tote. "I'll have a bran muffin, please," she says to the waitress, who's already pouring her a cup of coffee. "Toasted. Extra butter."

Then Angela turns to me, her lip gloss shimmering in an anticipatory smile. "Wanda, did you know that bran muffins have fewer calories?"

"Fewer calories than what?"

"Than the other kinds."

"Ah." Suppressing a sigh, I try to remember exactly how she fell into this little habit of addressing me as Wanda.

"Listen, I stopped in at Ann Taylor on my way over and they had these discount coupons for John Dellaria. Wouldn't it be fun if we hennaed our hair?"

"No thanks. I'm not the redhead type."

"No, no. I don't mean the red henna. There's this neutral henna that just enhances your own natural color. Want to?"

"I think I'll pass."

"How about a pedicure? I'm getting one done tomorrow morning."

"Well, I can't say I'm not tempted, but—"

"And then there's a sale at J. August we could go to afterwards."

"I'd love to, sweetie, really, but—" I sit with chin in hand, wondering why it is that she keeps pressuring me into these little get-togethers. Beyond the fact that we both live in Adams House, our sole mutual interest seems to be a certain attachment to the Coop's cosmetic counter. I sip at my coffee and look at the clock hanging on the wall in the smoking section. "But I'm way behind on my work."

"This place has eyelash tinting too." Angela leans forward. "I thought we could get our lashes tinted at the same time we were getting our pedicures done."

"Forget it. They'd probably clip my eyelashes and tint my toenails."

"Oh Wanda." Her face droops. "I just thought it would be so much fun for us to do together."

"I know, but look, sweetie, is this a study session or what? Get out your nudie photos of B. F. Skinner and let's get cracking."

"Wanda," she says reproachfully. Clucking, she sorts among the books and papers contained in her various impedimenta. Eventually she extracts a single textbook and places it on the table in front of her. As she's uncapping a yellow highlighter her muffin arrives. "Oh god." She pushes the book aside and reaches for her plate.

I curve over my notebook, my right hand meditatively twisting a spiral of hair between my fingers. *Genesis, fertility, proliferation . . .*

A spray of brown crumbs scatters on the page. "Hey."

"Oh, sorry, Wanda." With the pads of her fingers Angela plucks up the crumbs, which leave behind little amebalike grease stains. She smiles, sucking on a forefinger. "Delicious."

"Your teeth are rotting, even as we speak."

"God, you're morbid. What have you been writing?" She pulls my notebook toward her. "I'll bet it's really depressing."

"I really don't—"

She pushes my hand away and bends her head over the page. "You're always so secretive about your work, Wanda." She reads my half-dozen lines, mouthing the words to herself, and then she closes the notebook and returns it to me.

"Oh, Wanda."

"It's just a little something I'm throwing together for poetry class. D'you think it's literary enough?"

"Well, I—I mean, it really is kind of morbid."

"Morbid? Me?" I fold my arms over my chest.

"It's just that—" She hesitates, then leans forward. "I guess the part about not sleeping really hit home."

"Oh?"

"I haven't been sleeping well lately." Her breasts lie on the table in two neat cashmere-encased spheres. "I haven't been sleeping well at all."

"I'm sorry to hear it."

"And I'm tired all the time."

"Maybe you should go to UHS."

"Wanda, can I tell you something?"

"Sure."

She fidgets with her pearls. "It's about Philip."

Oh shit. "What about him?"

"Well, you know we've been having some problems lately."

"Sure, but almost everybody has problems." I take a big swallow of coffee. "I'll bet even B. F. Skinner has a problem every once in a while."

"I know, but—"

I'm trying as surreptitiously as I can to signal our waitress for a check. "But what?"

"Well, it's about our sex life."

"Oh?" *Please look. Please turn and look at me right now. Yoo hoo. Check, please.*

"Well." Angela takes a deep breath, which makes her chest appear to miraculously inflate on the tabletop. "Last night we're making love, right? The usual stuff. And then he starts saying,

'Please come, please come.' Over and over again." She's capping and uncapping her highlighter pen, click-click, click-click. "It was so horrible, Wanda. I didn't know what to do. The more he kept saying it, the worse it all got. So finally—well, I—" Now her voice sinks to a whisper. "I faked it."

"Oh?"

"Then he starts asking me all these questions again, after I told him a million times they embarrass me. No, he's got to get his little checklist out and find his favorite Cross pen. Do I like it this way, would I prefer it if he did it that way, should we try it in weird positions I know he got from some awful book somewhere. I swear I just wanted to scream." Click-click, click-click. "I haven't had a good night's sleep in days." Click-click, click-click.

"Have you tried taking naps?"

"I tell you, Wanda, I feel like I'm at the end of my rope."

"Oh?" Where the hell is the goddam waitress when you really need her? I sneak a glance around.

"Sometimes I really wonder about this relationship." Click-click.

"Well, sweetie." Gently I remove the pen from her grasp. "Is everything else okay?"

"Oh god yes. We spend all our time together." Now she tinkers with her knife and fork. "I had to tell somebody, though. My shrink appointment's not till tomorrow, and I thought I'd go crazy if I kept it inside another minute."

"What are friends for?" I stand up. "Excuse me for a minute, will you?" I walk toward the telephone, repeating the UHS number in my head as I extract a dime from my pocket.

"Yes, can I help you?"

"I'm calling for the results of a pregnancy test."

"Did you bring your sample in this morning, hon?"

"Yes." I loosen my hold on the receiver. "They told me I could call after four-thirty for the results."

"What's the last name?"

"It's Walker. W-a-l—"

"Hang on a minute, hon." She puts me on hold.

While I'm waiting I hear the toilet flush in the men's room. Seconds later a man emerges with a hand at his crotch, having not quite finished zipping his fly. He sees me and glares, sinking his jowls into his collar.

I nod. "Nice day, isn't it?"

"For you maybe." He stumps off, wiping his hands on his pants.

"Yeah." I grimace rudely at his bald spot, and then the phone clicks.

"Hello?" says the voice.

"Yes?"

"Your test came out negative, Mandy."

"I'm Miranda."

"Oh, right. Let me look at this again." In the background I hear a voice saying, "Leukemia, I guess." Someone laughs. "Miranda? Walker, right?"

"Yes, that's me."

"Right. Sorry, hon. I was looking at somebody else's chart."

"Ah." Do I know anybody named Mandy?

"Anyway, your test came out negative too."

"That means I'm not pregnant, right?"

"That's right, hon."

I let out my breath, softly. "That's great."

"But only as much as can be determined within the first two weeks."

"Oh."

"If you still haven't gotten your period in the next week or so, you might want to come back for another test."

"Oh?"

"Just to be sure."

"I see. Thanks." I hang up.

Back at our table Angela is back to capping and uncapping her pen. "Wanda, I feel fat. Let's go play squash."

"No thanks."

"Why not?"

"I hate squash."

Click-click. "How about racquetball then?"

"I hate racquetball too."

"There's a five-thirty aerobics class at the IAB."

"I wouldn't be caught dead in an aerobics class."

"All right, we'll go jogging." Click-click.

"Can't." I take the pen away from her again. "I'm due at Robbins by six."

"But Wanda, we'd have so much fun zooming around together. Besides, I just bought a new Gloria Vanderbilt jogging suit at the Coop."

"Sweetie, you hate to exercise."

"That's true." She brightens. "Oh well. I tried, didn't I?"

"Yep. Hey, do you know anybody named Mandy?"

"Mandy? No. Why?"

"No reason." I slip a dollar bill under my coffee cup and start gathering up my belongings. "Let's go."

As we walk along Mass Ave I feel myself pierced by the soft keen melancholy of impending Cambridge twilight. The sidewalk is crowded with late-afternoon traffic, mostly students streaming in and out of the copy shops and ice-cream stores.

"I don't suppose some course or another had a paper due at five o'clock?"

"Fine Arts 13." Angela looks over at me. "How did you know? Philip's been upset about it for days."

"He should try to relax more."

"He just wants to do well, that's all."

"Well, sure, don't we all?" Neatly I avoid stepping in a small mound of dog shit.

"God, for a double-double chocolate cone." She's waving at somebody inside Steve's Ice Cream. "I can't though. I'm saving myself for dinner."

"You know, if you really want to get some exercise, Jessica's been taking tennis lessons. You could play a few sets with her."

"That's okay. I don't feel like it anymore."

"She's probably home by now. Why don't you give her a call?"

"No thanks." Her face is set in lines of such rigid civility that I remember anew the conspicuous lack of rapport that exists between them, although Angela is always scrupulously affectionate whenever they're in the same room together. Jessica ignores her. "I'm not in the mood."

"Really? I'm sure she'd love to get out there and have a few rollies with you."

"Rallies."

"Whatever. Why don't you give her a buzz? She's probably sitting by the phone just waiting for something fun like this to come along."

"I'm really not in the mood anymore."

"Oh well." Smiling, I picture Jessica's features going completely blank, her eyes shuttering to pale empty blue discs. "She's not very good yet anyway. Mostly she goes to stare at the instructor's legs."

"Oh look, there's Philip." Angela tugs at my arm. "And Bryan too."

My smile dissolves. "Where?"

"They just went into Schoenhof's."

"Speak of the devil."

"I want to make sure he got his paper in all right, okay?"

"Go right ahead."

"Oh Wanda, do you mind?"

"Look, I've got a million things to do." I pull my arm away. "You just run along."

"Thanks, Wanda." Her lip gloss is glimmering again in that breathless smile. "I knew you wouldn't mind. I'll see you later, okay?"

"Sure, okay." God, I hate it when she calls me Wanda. Shaking my head, I walk on toward Robbins.

"Excuse me," someone whispers, "but do you have the reserve reading for Phil 169?"

"Huh?" I look up from my notebook. *Jesus, this guy's posture is even worse than mine.* Languidly I flip through the manila folders on the shelf next to the desk. "Sorry. It's checked out."

"Uh, do you know when it'll be back?"

I'm at my notebook again. "No, sorry."

He shifts his feet for a few moments. Then, with a scarcely audible sigh, he turns and leaves the library, closing the door quietly behind him.

I've had at most five minutes of peaceful concentration when somebody returns the Phil 169 reading and shows me the contents of his backpack to be checked, which receive the briefest of inspections from me. After nearly eight semesters of working in the philosophy library, I've adopted a somewhat laissez-faire attitude toward my role as desk attendant. What thief, I ask myself, stows the books where he knows perfectly well they'll be examined on his way out? In the finest spirit of Rousseau, I rarely waste my time in lengthy scrutiny; and now with an imperious nod I permit still another patron to depart more or less unchallenged. God only knows how many books Robbins has lost because of me.

I squirm in the chair, the bones in my derriere aching, and look up at the clock. It's nine-thirty: in another quarter-hour or so I can start ushering people out. It's far too late into my shift to begin reshelving books, and anyway it'll give Charles something to do tomorrow morning. Charles is a student at the Divinity School and seems to feel obliged to actually do some work while on duty here at the librarian's desk. Carefully I straighten the stacks on the cart next to the desk, figuring that he'll be bound to appreciate my little contribution to his spiritual growth.

" 'Scuse me," a voice whispers. "Y'all got any books on the meanin' of life?"

"Michael." I finish aligning *Plato's Republic* on top of *Nausea*. "It's only the philosophy library."

"An' I thought I'd come to the right place." He walks around the desk and pulls up a chair close to mine. "What's doin', kitten? Metaphysically speakin', of course."

"Oh, the usual. Nothing but angst, angst, and more angst." I close my notebook and look at him. "After last night's suppertime tragedies, I'm sort of afraid to return the question."

"It ain't too bad."

"Really?"

"Try me."

"Okay. How's everything?"

"I wouldn't know. But my baby brother got himself into Yale, Brown, Princeton, an' Columbia."

"You're right. That's not too bad."

"There's more."

"That's what I was afraid of."

"Harvard wait-listed him, y'see, an' my mother's about ready to curl up an' die. Speakin' of angst. Guess I came to the right place after all."

He laughs, and someone over in the nonsmoking area makes

a loud shushing noise. Robbins is another one of those tiny obscure departmental libraries, so small that it's divided into three sections by means of two massive bookcases that do little to ensure auditory privacy. Smirking at Michael, I roll my eyes and rattle the keys to the front door, another of my crass tactics to close up the place as near to ten o'clock as I can possibly manage.

"Am I makin' too much noise?" Michael whispers. "I don't wanna get you in any trouble."

"Are you kidding?" I say loudly. Then I lower my voice and lean close. "Hey, I heard this great joke today."

"Y'all gonna try'n cheer me up?"

"I know you'll love this. Why did the elephant cross the road?"

"I dunno. Why?"

"Because it was the chicken's day off."

Our laughter is hushed from the next section over, whether by the same sourpuss as before it's hard to tell. As I'm reaching for the keys again, the door opens and the stooped Phil 169 student steps diffidently up to the desk. "Sorry to bother you," he whispers, "but has the—"

"As a matter of fact it has."

"Oh, good. May I—"

"Sorry, we're closing in a few minutes. Reserve readings don't go out for overnight circulation."

He looks at his wristwatch. "It's only twenty till."

Michael nudges me. "That's enough time to get it Xeroxed, ain't it?"

"Eh?" I frown at them both. "Oh, all right." I shove the folder at him. "But bring it back before closing time."

"I will. Thank you." Holding the folder close against his concave chest, he turns and scuds out into the hallway.

Three people straggle by, their bags receiving the idlest of glances from me. "I know what you're thinking, Michael," I say, smiling crookedly. "It's a dirty job, but somebody's got to do it."

He doesn't return my smile. "You know, darlin', you can be kinda ornery now'n again."

"Oh, Michael, it's a jungle out there. Believe me, I know." I take his hand and hold it to my cheek. His skin is warm and smells faintly of Paco Rabonne. "Hey, have you been buying cologne behind my back?"

He just looks at me, and after a little while I let go of his hand. "I mean, you smell nice."

The door opens and the Phil 169 chap returns. "The department copier is working again," he says, in the tone of one who has just witnessed a healing at Lourdes.

"Well, that's good."

"Yes." Tenderly he hands me the folder. "Thanks again for your help."

I feel an odd stab of—what? Remorse? "You're welcome."

"Well, good night." He starts to open his satchel for me but I wave him away. "Thanks, miss. Have a good evening."

"You too." I stand up and start rattling the keys again. "Closing time, folks," I call out. Prowling through the other two sections I find only Raphael Manini, star philosophy graduate student, celebrated wunderkind of the department, ace teaching fellow and already a published author of several articles on postmodern existentialism. "Hey, Raphael. It's closing time."

Using his folded arms for a pillow, Raphael snores peacefully with his head face-down on the tabletop.

"Hey. Wake up. It's time to go." I tap his shoulder.

"Wha?" Abruptly he bolts straight up in his chair, unfocused eyes blinking in terror. "Jesus," he gasps. "Why'd you creep up on me like that?"

"It's my job," I explain. "It's closing time."

"Oh." Still batting his eyes, he twitches his shirt into place. "I guess that means you're kicking me out."

"There's a Holiday Inn a few blocks away."

"That's okay. I can take a hint." Slowly he collects his books, papers, pens, pencils, slide rule, Scotch tape, compass, rubber bands, eyeglasses, cigarettes, lighter, and miniature stapler and stuffs them into a crisp white Lord & Taylor shopping bag and stands up. Yawning, he takes a comb out of his back pocket and runs it through what's left of his hair. "You a philosophy major?" he asks me for the twentieth time.

"No, I'm an East Asian–studies major." Last time I was majoring in folklore and mythology. The time before that, as I recall, it was biology.

"No wonder I never see you in any of my courses."

"Well." I clear my throat. "I'll just be closing up now, I guess."

"Interested in auditing Phil 180? I know it's a little late in the semester, but I'll help you catch up on the reading list."

"Maybe next term." I drift back to my desk, where Michael is stamping the desk blotter with the ROBBINS LIBRARY OF PHILOSOPHY ink stamp, humming under his breath.

"Having fun, darling?" Perching on the arm of his chair, I breathe in the warm familiar scent of his neck.

"Simple pleasures, gal."

The phone rings, and I reach over Michael to pick up the receiver. "Robbins. Can I help you?"

"Well?"

"Hi, Jessie. How are you?"

"Well?"

"Well what?"

"Well, are you?"

"Well, am I what?"

"Don't be a dope, Miranda," she says crossly.

"Oh." I nod farewell to Raphael, who furtively grips his Lord & Taylor bag to his abdomen. "No, I guess I'm not."

"Well, thank god. You dumbshit."

"Hey," I protest. "You've already called me a dumbshit today." I snatch my hand away from Michael, who's begun stamping my forearm with the date stamp which he has set for June 24, his birthday. "Can't you think of another nasty name to call me?"

"You're absolutely right. I apologize."

"Apology accepted."

"Thank you. Shithead."

"Derivative, but it'll have to do. Why am I a shithead?"

"Thanks for letting me know, shithead. What do you think I've been doing all day, out shopping for little pink booties?"

"Oh dear." I clamp a hand across my forehead. "I'm sorry, Jessie. I'm really sorry."

"It's okay, jerk."

"It won't happen again."

"Ha."

"At least not this week."

"That's more like it. Hey, cut that out." I hear Sutter giggling in the background.

I let go of my forehead. "Tell Sutter I'll scratch his eyes out if he so much as lays a hand on you."

"Miranda says hello," she says loudly.

"I hate it when you translate."

"Look, I've got to run. The commercials are over."

"I understand."

"Hey, are you still going out with the boy wonder tonight?"

"I guess so." I steal a glance at Michael, who's now carving his initials into the desktop with his Swiss army knife.

"Well, have fun. If you can call it that."

"What's that supposed to mean?"

"You know I think he's boring."

"I don't see what—"

"Different strokes, though, I always say."

"Don't be disgusting."

"And speaking of scratching eyes out, hope you don't run into Jennifer on the way over."

"Thanks for the good wishes."

"You know it, dope." She hangs up.

Michael's back to the date stamp, imprinting the back of my notebook with June 24, working his way downward in neat vertical rows. "Hey, are you trying to tell me something?" I lean forward to breathe at his nape again. "How many more shopping days is it, anyway?"

"Anythin' wrong?" He doesn't look up from my notebook.

"No, why?"

"Are you okay?"

"I'm fine."

"Yeah?" Now he turns his head to look at me. His face is very close to mine, and I find myself studying the mossy green-brown of his eyes and the fine silky arch of his brows.

"Of course I am." I stand up. "Can't complain. What time is it?"

"Ten-fifteen."

"Darling, will you stop staring at me? I've got to run. I'm not paid for overtime, you know."

"I was gonna ask you if you wanted to mosey over to Piroshka's with me for a cappuccino."

"I can't tonight, Michael." I'm twitching into my jacket. "But I'll take a raincheck, okay?"

"Sure, okay." He stands up too.

I'm tossing my notebook, pens, and thesaurus into my bag. "Let's get out of here." I wait at the door while he places the stamps and ink pad in a corner of the blotter and then pushes in the desk chair. He comes toward me and I hold the door open for him to pass. Instead, he pauses in front of me.

"Are you really okay?"

"I'm really okay, Michael. But I'm sort of late for something. And I just totally blew off a whole evening's worth of Soc Sci 33 reading."

"*You're* worryin' 'bout Soc Sci 33?"

"*You* don't have a two-hundred-pound section leader breathing down your neck, do you?"

We walk into the hallway and I lock the door behind us. We're silent as we leave Emerson and descend the steps into Mem Yard.

"Michael."

"What."

"Knock knock."

"Who's there?"

"Kant."

"Kant who?"

"Canteloupe's always better than watermelon." I look up into his face, trying to see if he's smiling. "Get it? Kant-elope?"

"Yeah, I get it."

"Funny, huh?"

"Yep."

"It's okay. You don't have to laugh if you don't want to." There's a full moon tonight. Fat and pearlescent, it casts a spectral white light that shimmers off Widener's immense proscenium and smooth high creamy-colored columns. "Hey, I've been telling all the jokes tonight." I touch his sleeve. "It's your turn now."

"Sorry." He moves his shoulders restlessly. "Don't feel like it."

"Michael?"

"Yep."

"What are you doing tonight?"

"Oh, not a whole lot. Gotta make a few phone calls, I guess."

"Yeah?"

"Yeah."

"Can you be a little more specific?"

"Sure. Somethin' like, No Ma, I don't know anybody in the admissions office, but if you want, I'll try sleepin' with the Dean's wife to see if it'll get Daniel off the waitin' list."

"Michael."

"Yep?" His smile is unnaturally bright, and all at once I'm assailed by the feeling that I'm forgetting something. *Shit. What is it?* Somebody over in one of the Yard dorms is playing "Stairway to Heaven" at full volume on his stereo. A couple passes by us, hand in hand, and then I realize that I'm supposed to be meeting Dean right about now. *What time is it?* But I seem to have missed a beat or two; already Michael is turning away.

"Well, so long, gal."

"Michael."

"What?"

His skin looks pale and luminescent in the moonlight. The sockets of his eyes are flooded with blue-black shadow and I can't make out his expression.

"You're coming to the master's tea tomorrow afternoon, aren't you?"

"Hadn't thought 'bout it."

"It'll be a gas," I say, cajolingly. "I hear there'll be brownies."

"I'll think about it."

"Good. I'll see you there."

"Maybe."

"Oh, come on. Cucumber sandwiches, and we can see and be seen by the beautiful people."

"Now I'm changin' my mind."

"Don't." I still can't see his face clearly enough to read his intent. "So I'll see you tomorrow, okay? And don't forget you owe me a cappuccino."

"No'm," he says. "I won't forget."

————

I tiptoe down the tiny cramped steps into the Ha'Penny and see Dean standing in front of the jukebox, looking at the song titles, his head bent over the arched glass panel.

Softly I say: "Got a quarter, buddy?"

"Oh, hi." He looks at me with his quick enigmatic smile.

"Play 'Brass in Pocket,' will you?"

"I was just looking."

"Oh." A rush of childish disappointment floods my chest for a second. "Me too."

"Sorry I'm late."

"Are you? I thought I was." I look at my watch and laugh airily.

Dean glances down too, and then he bends closer. "How come your watch says twelve-thirty?"

"It's broken."

"Those real sapphires?"

"I guess so."

"Nice. Birthday present from your parents?"

I keep the smile fixed on my face. "No, my grandmother gave it to me. She said she liked her Timex better."

"Oh. Can't you get it repaired?"

"I don't know. I never tried."

"Oh."

We take a table in the very back. "God, I love this place," I say, slipping into my chair. "The cute little tables, the candles." *The convenient amnesia of the cocktail waitresses.* "The ambience."

"Yeah." Dean takes a pack of Camels from his blazer pocket, taps one free, places it between his lips and lights it, accomplishing this all in one graceful motion. He takes a deep drag, and coughs. "Shit, my bronchitis." He inhales again, more delicately.

"What can I get you?" Our waitress, a ponytailed brunette wearing pink-trimmed Tretorns, stands before us with her tray poised.

Dean looks at me. "You go ahead," I say, unable to make up my mind.

"Dewar's and water," he says. "Twist. Three cubes." Then they both look at me again. Dean's knees, I note, are touching mine under the table.

"I—I—oh, well." I smile weakly. "How about a greyhound."

"Sure thing." She winks at me and goes off.

In her wake there is a brief silence. I press my lips together, wondering if I've recently applied lipstick, and if so, what shade it might possibly be. *God, I hope it's not that loud fire-engine red I pilfered from Jessica's desk last week.*

"Did that girl just wink at you?"

"Did she? Oh, it's probably just a nervous tic."

"Yeah?"

"It's a very high-pressure job here, you know." I'm picturing the worn blue denim of his Levis against my own black trousers. Caught between a delicious sensation of clandestine exhilaration and doubt as to whether he's even noticed, I'm afraid to move my body from the waist down. I slide the pretzel basket his way. "Pretzel?"

"No thanks." He's looking at me, his hazel eyes almost violet in the light, and my fingers stay curled around the basket. We remain like this for what feels like a long time. When somebody calls out my name I jump in my chair, and look around to see Pablo Esperanto coming toward us at full lope.

"Well, hi!"

Dean reaches for another cigarette, and I let go of the pretzels.

"Hey, hey." Pablo waves as if we were in fact twenty paces apart. "What's going on, kids?"

"Hey, Pabs." I show my teeth in a barbed smile. "What's up, dude?"

"Oh, just finished another silly rehearsal for a concert in Mem Hall I promised to do." He sighs. "And the New York Philharmonic won't stop pestering me."

"Really? Do you owe them money?"

His lips thin. "They want me to join."

"Ah." He's certainly got the physique for a concert pianist, I muse, with his tall slender body, fiery dark eyes, and long tapering fingers. Less attractive is his proclivity for describing in brain-numbing detail both his royal Castilian lineage and the contents of his parents' loft on Spring Street. "Why?"

"Maybe they think I'm good."

"Ah."

"So Deano. What's new?" Smiling now, Pablo looks down at me. He knows I know he's a good friend of Dean's girlfriend Jennifer. "Tell me everything."

When Dean does not reply, I tilt back in my chair, gazing up into Pablo's swarthy face. "Oh, we've just been sitting here criticizing the English department." Once again I'm trying to figure out exactly why Jessica dated him for all of three weeks. "What else do English majors talk about?" It occurs to me he might look awfully good in tails.

"Good question. You guys talk about grammar? Punctuation? Conjugating the verb?" He leers, revealing a set of large, rather yellow teeth.

"I like to think we're a little more highbrow than that."

Just then our waitress muscles her way to our table, and with a superbly aimed elbow forces Pablo to step back a pace.

"Here we go. A greyhound and a Dewar's water." She smiles at me as Dean pulls out his wallet. "New haircut?"

"Huh?"

"Oh." She takes Dean's five-dollar bill. "I mean, I like your haircut."

"Keep the change," I say loudly.

"Thanks." She plows off, dislodging Pablo by another good foot and a half in the process.

"Is she a bulldozer or a cocktail waitress?" he complains, rubbing his arm.

"Well, Pabs," I say, before he can regain his balance, "it's been fun. But if you'll excuse us, we were right in the middle of a structural analysis of *Moby Dick.*"

"Oh yeah?"

"Melville. Herman Melville."

"Thanks." He flexes his hands a few times. "Well, I'll leave you two to your little extrapolations. And Deano. If I see Jenny tonight, I'll be sure and tell her you're in out of the rain."

After Pablo has gone back to his table, Dean leans forward and looks at me. "Miranda?"

"Yes?"

"You owe me two dollars for the greyhound."

"I beg your pardon?"

"I said, you—"

"How about a toast?" I raise my glass high. "To structural analysis."

"Yeah."

He drinks, but I merely brush the rim of my glass against my lips. Then he's leaning forward again, and our elbows touch.

"Oh," I say, feeling strangely flustered. "I mean, I love your leather patches."

"Thanks."

We fall silent, and suddenly I wish I'd ordered Perrier. I pluck an ice cube from my drink and slip it into my mouth. "So anyway." The ice cube rattles against my teeth.

He sighs. "Yeah?"

"How's everything?"

"Oh, okay, I guess." His voice is soft, moodier now. Impulsively I reach across the table and touch his throat.

He leans away, flashing me a startled look. "What was that for?"

"Sorry." I lace my fingers together in my lap. "It's just a nervous tic."

He lights a cigarette and inhales with a little whooshing noise. "I thought you were going for the jugular or something."

"I'm sorry," I say shrewishly. "It won't happen again."

He coughs. "I was kidding. It was a joke."

"Oh." I'm trying to remember which movie actress I've just quoted. It would be nice if it was Katharine Hepburn, or even Barbara Stanwyck. Virginia Mayo, though, would be a drag. *Jackson would know.* Wincing a little, I brush my bangs out of my eyes.

"—and that's just the way I feel about it, Miranda."

"Mmm."

He sighs again. "Miranda, Miranda."

"Yes, that's my name," I say encouragingly, although I wish he'd stop pronouncing it with a soft *a*.

"Eddie Hacker wants me to help him start a new humor magazine."

I am silent for a moment. "Isn't the *Lampoon* more than enough already?"

"He says the Lampoon snobbishness makes him sick."

"Maybe he's disappointed he didn't get in."

"Yeah, well." Dean stubs out his cigarette in the ashtray. "He wants me to be managing editor."

"My. You accepted, of course."

He hesitates. "I told him I wanted to talk to Jennifer first."

"Does she sign your checks too?"

"Sorry?"

"Go on."

"Well, you know she's sort of my unofficial Advocate adviser." Although only a junior, Dean's long been considered a rising star on the Advocate staff. There's talk he may be elected to an officer's position before the semester is out. "She understands politics better than I do."

"I'm sure. And what did she tell you to do?"

"She never really said. We ended up arguing."

I try to keep my eyes from lighting up. "Oh?"

"Yeah, we were just sitting there talking about it calmly, and then Kevin comes in and wants to know if I got the message from you he'd tucked under my pillow."

"Well, that was nice of him."

"Then all of a sudden she starts going on and on about how working on Eddie's magazine would probably make the board veto my series on F. Scott Fitzgerald, and fuck up my chances for making fiction editor next year."

"Why?" By the time Dean is or isn't fiction editor, I muse, I'll have been out of college for a whole year.

"She thinks it would be seen as a conflict of interest."

"You mean like spreading yourself too thin?" I smirk at him but he's busy inhaling on his cigarette.

"Exactly. But I think it'd look good on my résumé."

"Résumé?"

"She knows that Eddie and I prepped together. You'd think she'd understand that it's hard for me to turn him down."

"Stuffy of her, isn't it?"

"And he wants me to start right away. He's already lined up the backers."

"Really?"

"Well, his father, mostly."

"I see."

He's smoking rapidly. "So I think it'd be a good thing to do."

"And Jenny doesn't."

"No." His gaze flickers. "We fought about other things too."

"Oh?"

"Yeah." He looks away and then down at the table, his eyelashes drooping in a mannerism that Jessica once uncharitably described as an obvious emulation of the ailing Keats.

"What about?"

"Well, if you must know, we fought about you."

"Me?"

He leans back in his chair and exhales a stream of smoke just over my head. "She's jealous of you, Miranda."

"Why? We haven't done anything for her to be jealous of. You've been nothing but respectability itself."

"Have I?" He looks pained.

"You bet."

"But still—"

"So we took a lit class together last semester. So what?"

"Yes, but—"

"So we hang out in cozy little bars till the wee hours. What's the big deal?"

"Well, I guess she's worried about—"

"*What* a little worrywart she is. Maybe she should try to relax more."

"She wants me to stop seeing you."

"Try closing your eyes."

"What?"

"Surprise, surprise, Mira—I mean, surprise, surprise." It's our cocktail waitress again, placing a glass in front of me.

"What's this?"

"From an admirer. A double greyhound. He said he thought you could use it."

"An admirer?" I gape past her beyond the bar, where I see Pablo grinning our way and lifting his glass in salute.

"Oh," Dean says. "It's our friend the pianist."

Frowning, I look away. "Big of him."

"You'd think he could order a drink for me too."

"I guess he's not that big." I take a sip of my first greyhound and it catches in my throat. Coughing, I press a hand to my chest.

Our cocktail waitress leans down. "Are you okay, Mira—I mean, are you all right?"

Sputtering a little, I nod up at her. "I'm fine."

"You sure?"

I notice Dean eyeing us and I nod more vehemently. "I'm fine. Really. I think somebody over at the next table needs you."

"Okay. I'll be back." She pats my arm and careens off.

There is a short silence, and then Dean gives a wheezy chuckle. "That Pablo. What a slimy bastard."

"Yes," I say, my voice still a bit ragged, "I can see why Jenny would be attracted to him."

His smile fading, Dean picks up a swizzle stick and pokes at the misshapen little ice cubes in his glass. "Oh yeah?"

"Birds of a feather and all that." I take my hand off my chest. "And while we're on the subject, where did she pick up that phony British accent, anyway?"

"Jesus, you're a bitch, Miranda."

"You think so?" I gaze back at him, my body very still. "So why do you go out with me?"

"I don't *go out* with you."

"Oh? Then what's this? Gathering material for your little humor magazine?"

"We get together for a drink now and then." He drops his voice to a fierce whisper.

"Oh, really? Then why do you go sneaking around behind your girlfriend's back?"

"I don't go sneaking around behind my girlfriend's—"

"Would you mind speaking up? You're cringing into your drink."

"Jackson was right." Dean grips his cigarette lighter. "You're a manipulative, neurotic bitch."

I swallow, once. "Jackson said that?"

He hesitates. "Only the manipulative part."

"Ah."

"The neurotic-bitch part is mine." He drops his eyes to the tabletop, lashes fluttering.

"I see." I feel a pinching tightness in my chest. "Well, you can't both be right, can you?"

In the silence that ensues I rattle the pretzel basket back and forth, trying to see if there's a single unbroken one in the lot.

"God, you're pretty," Dean says.

"I beg your pardon?"

"You're so pretty, Miranda."

"Well, thanks." Now I'm staring at him over a red-and-white-checkered tablecloth littered with glasses, cigarette butts, soggy cocktail napkins, and a basketful of pretzels that aren't perhaps as fresh as they should be.

"I mean it."

"So do I." Sighing, I push the basket away, all at once dampened by the *déjà vu*.

*E*lbows digging into the arms of her chair, Mary props her fingertips together, making a little temple of her hands. "Well, you know, Miranda, sometimes our inner wounds can fester, just like actual wounds."

"I'm not sure I follow you."

We sit facing each other in brightly colored UHS chairs, Mary as usual eschewing her desk in the interest of fostering interpersonal rapport. Between us is a shimmeringly polished coffee table decorated with recent issues of *New Woman* and *Art in America* and a yellowing asparagus fern.

"Well, if not treated properly and allowed to heal, a wound can become raw and inflamed. That's why we have these weekly meetings, Miranda. I'm here to help you with your troubles, your inner wounds."

"So you're sort of like a mental-health disinfectant."

"That's an interesting interpretation."

"Pine Sol, for example."

She takes up the little notebook that's been resting in her lap,

61

and I eye her warily. Once, after I commented upon her steno-grapher's pad, she flipped it open with a steely little smile and began asking me questions about the time Jackson slept with his roommate's younger sister who was visiting Cambridge for the spring crew races on the Charles. "He'd just finished a paper on *Lolita*," I'd riposted, and then diverted her by inventing a dream, liberally peppered with Freudian imagery and obscure references to the collective unconscious.

"Now Miranda." Mary crosses one leg over the other, nylons hissing. Her calf bulges hideously. "A few sessions ago you mentioned feeling alienated from your parents."

"Did I?"

"Why don't we talk about that."

I arch my foot and gaze at my sneaker. Soon, my shoelace will need to be tied again. "I got a letter from my mother the other day."

"Yes?" Mary looks expectant. "And what did she have to say?"

"I can't really summarize it. I didn't get past the first paragraph."

"Oh? And why is that?" she asks happily. I look over at the small plastic sign on the wall next to her diplomas, which I can only assume is a clue to her therapeutic philosophy: NO PAIN NO GAIN.

"It was boring." I shrug. "I really don't have the time to waste reading such shit. I've got a lot of work to do."

"I see." Wrinkling her brow, Mary taps her chin with the eraser of her pencil. "Well, let's try approaching this from another angle, shall we?"

"Should I turn my chair in a different direction?"

"I don't think that will be necessary. You're fine just as you are."

"Well, thanks. Then why am I here?"

"Miranda." Now she's grinding the eraser into her chin. "When was the last time you wrote a letter to them?"

"My parents?"

"Yes." Maybe she's trying to give herself a dimple.

"Thanksgiving. I sent them a Hallmark card with a picture of a turkey on it."

"That's the most recent word your parents have had from you?"

I slouch a little lower in my chair. "Well, Phi Beta Kappa sent them a letter of congratulations. Does that count?"

"Since Thanksgiving." She's scribbling rapturously in her note-book. "It's April now, so that means it's been, let's see—"

"That's two P's in Kappa."

"Now, what about phone calls?" she persists.

"No, I don't think Phi Beta Kappa telephoned them."

"I mean phone calls between you and your parents."

"A few. I make Jessica answer the phone whenever the rates are low in California. She tells them I'm out playing video games."

"Every time they call?"

"That's right."

"Even if they call on—oh, Sunday morning, for example?"

"Especially on Sunday morning."

"Mmm."

"Sometimes I have Jessica answer the phone even when the rates aren't low in California," I volunteer. "I have her tell whoever it is I'm out playing video games."

"Mmm."

"Even if it's somebody I might actually want to talk to."

"Mmm."

"Unlikely as that might be."

"Miranda, let's talk about this feeling of alienation." She speaks casually, too casually, and it is with a mixture of resignation and suspense that I watch her reach over for a file folder on her desk. She pulls out a sheet of paper and hands it to me. "I've had some time this week to take a look at your poem."

Oh shit, I think, cursing myself for finally relenting and giving her one of my poetry assignments, after weeks of pleasurably idle promises. I look at the lines I typed on Jessica's typewriter. With a pink highlighter Mary has marked a stanza near the bottom of the page.

> *playing to no stage, I hear the applause,*
> *the viscous fingered hiss of*
> *grinning phantoms*
> *their teeth glitter untouched white perfect rows*
> *smiling on me damp and sure*

———

"It's not one of my better efforts." I hand it back to her.

"Miranda, your work isn't being graded in here." She returns my poem to the file folder. "I'm interested in your writing from a psychological viewpoint, for what it tells me about how you feel about yourself. There's a morbid theatricality here which is pretty striking."

"Well, I had to turn something in for poetry class, didn't I?"

"I think your choice of words here is quite significant."

"Really? Professor Tidwell found my language obfuscatory and confusing."

"Do you often have the feeling of being on stage?"

"I'm not sure we can really discuss a stanza out of context."

"You once mentioned that you felt as if you were masquerading somehow. I believe that was the word you used."

"Did I?" *Goddam that little notebook.* "But don't all Harvard students secretly believe they're the admission office's one mistake?"

"You've also told me that you felt as if you were fooling people."

"Mmm."

"This constant sensation of performing, Miranda."

"D'you think I should've taken more drama classes?"

"Of fooling the world. This is the kind of thing I mean by 'inner wound.' "

"Mmm." I'm staring at the asparagus fern, wondering yet again why anybody in their right mind would choose to work at UHS when they could go into lucrative private practice and have real patients instead of whining college students complaining about homesickness and academic pressure. Once I asked her this very question. She countered by asking me why I had chosen to come to UHS, and all I could think to tell her was that it's free.

"Miranda?"

"Inner wounds," I say hastily.

"Miranda, something tells me that you might want to evaluate your reasons for being in therapy."

I look at her. "Would you care to expand upon that?"

"Well, I'd explain myself further—" Here she pauses to check her watch. "But I'm afraid our time is up."

"Oh, come on, give me a hint."

She allows herself a tiny inscrutable smile. "Think about it until next Friday."

"Okay." I stand up and put on my jacket.

"Have a good week."

"Yeah."

I'm in the Coop's record department, flipping through the "S" bin in search of the latest Squeeze LP, when I come across an album by Soft Cell. I lift it out and stare at the cover, my fingers tightening against the cool, smooth plastic. Despite myself, I start hearing the warped giddy rhythms of "Tainted Love" playing in my mind.

I'm running up the stairs of the Lowell House bell tower on my way to a Eurofag Quaaludes-and-Cointreau party, pleased with myself for having closed up Robbins a whole hour early in my own private celebration of Thanksgiving break. Whistling, I skim up the sixth flight and vault around the corner onto the landing, where I literally stumble into Jackson and Wendy Hughes kissing in the stairwell. Steadying myself against the wall, abstractedly I note that Wendy's sleeveless blouse reveals a pair of rather flabby white triceps. My mouth twists into a smile as I look up into Jackson's face. "Sorry," I say clearly. "I told you I'd be here at midnight, didn't I?" I turn and go downstairs and over to a party at Dunster House, where I introduce myself to Richard Amidei, the lead singer in a new campus band called White Bread, and compliment him on his handsome leather tie. We trade stories about the horrifying number of papers we each have due, the workloads escalating with each shot of tequila, and then he gently brushes the little pieces of lime pulp from my face and asks me to dance. We spend the next hour or so slow-dancing in the middle of the room, determinedly oblivious to the tempo of whatever song happens to be playing. I remind myself to keep focusing on how lightly my hand rests in his, and how his fingers feel as they curve against my waist. We move apart so he can go off to the men's room; he is gone for what seems like such a long time that eventually I wedge myself in a corner of the room with a tall, dark-haired graduate student named Henry, who turns out to be a proctor at Weld, my freshman dorm. We gossip about some English professors we both know, and then switch over to nineteenth-century poetry for a while, but in the middle of a passionate discussion of "Ode on a Grecian Urn" I find myself too nau-

seous to continue. Henry walks me back to Adams House, and when we finally make it up the stairs, we come across Jackson sitting with his back against my door, smoking a cigarette. I am too miserable to be greatly surprised that he and Henry know each other through the history-and-lit department, and wait for them to finish shaking hands before I go into C-45 and into the bathroom, where I proceed to retch for what seems like hours.

"He's a nice guy," Jackson says presently, holding a wet washcloth to my forehead. "I'm glad you got to meet him."

"Me too," I say faintly.

"Listen, Randa." His voice is less steady now. "About tonight—"

"Shut up." I close my eyes. "Please just shut up."

"I just wanted to tell you—"

"Tomorrow you're taking me to the movies. And you're paying."

"Okay."

"And you're buying the popcorn."

"Okay." He runs a hand down my spine. "How're you feeling?"

"Fabulous." I open my eyes and brace myself for another spasm. "Thanks for asking."

"I love you."

My stomach heaves again and I lean forward into the toilet bowl, thankful that the dorm crew has been by recently to clean, and that for once they did a good job of it. Although I expect that next time around they will probably be less enthusiastic about the task at hand.

I drop the album back into its bin and look around. Teddy Anson, the only person I know on the *Lampoon* staff who seems even remotely anthropoid, is pawing through a sale carton a few aisles away. I slip up behind him and clap my hands over his eyes. "Guess who."

"Marquis de Sade? Jimmy Connors? Adelle Davis? Charlton Heston?"

"Oh, never mind." I take my hands away and step around next to him. Sighing, I start poking through the albums.

Teddy remains inert, eyes squeezed shut. "Walter Mondale? Bella Abzug? Virginia Woolf? Peter and the Wolf? Kaye Ballard?"

"Will you stop the goddam free association already?"

"Okay, sure."

"Theodore, it's me."

His eyes are still shut. "Me who?"

"Miranda."

"Is it really? Miranda Walker, you mean?"

"Yes. Feel free to open your eyes anytime you want."

His eyes pop open, swiveling in my direction, and instantly he breaks into a smile. "Hi, Miranda. How are you?"

"Can't complain. Yourself?"

"Just dandy. You're looking great as always."

"Thanks. What's new?"

"Oh, nothing much. Just doing a little shopping for my mother's birthday."

I look down at the album he's been holding on to all this time. *The Best of the Dave Clark Five*? I had no idea your mother was so groovy."

"You bet she's groovy. She was the first one on the block to get a rotisserie microwave."

"Theodore, you overwhelm me."

"Why do you keep calling me Theodore?"

"Say, don't your folks pay your Coop bill?"

"Yep." He nods benignly. "I thought maybe I'd get Mom the cast recording from *Hello, Dolly*. Something nice and sappy. She'd like that. She's groovy but she's also a little sentimental."

"Oh?"

"Every year she sends me a big red card on Valentine's Day."

"How sweet."

"So's the candy she sends me." He snickers.

"How about *Oklahoma?* Where the corn grows as high as an elephant's—"

"She's already got that one. Maybe *My Fair Lady?*"

"Are you sure she doesn't already have that one too?"

A look of doubt clouds his features. "Maybe. Or is it *Hello, Dolly* she already has?"

"Maybe it's *Fiddler on the Roof* you're thinking of."

Now he looks at me suspiciously. "Hey, you don't even know my mom, do you?"

"No, but I'm sure I'd love anybody who's lucky enough to have a rotisserie microwave."

"So how could you know what albums she has?"

"Theodore, I've got to run. I've got a class to go to."

"Why do you keep calling me Theodore?"

"You're just full of questions today, aren't you?"

"Well, sure." Teddy gestures grandly. "Isn't that what the university environment is all about?"

"Been rereading our old college prospectus, eh?" Waggishly I poke him in the general region of his upper intestine.

"Oh, you're jabbing at me," he laments. "Why are you picking on me, Miranda?"

"Picking on you? Teddy, don't you know when someone's extending a hand in friendship?"

"Huh?"

"Don't you like to be touched, Teddy?" I give him another prod in the gut.

"Ow." He retreats a step. "What's your point, Miranda?"

"Can't you take a hint? Don't you know when somebody's trying to reach out to you?"

"Really?" He comes two steps closer. "Want to go out for a cup of coffee?"

"I've got a class to go to, remember?"

Teddy steps one pace backward, then does a little side feint to avoid a tweedy Cambridge matron barreling toward the classical-music section. "Miranda," he says plaintively, "how come I've never actually seen you inside a classroom? Or leaving one?"

"Poor timing on your part."

"You really take courses? You're actually enrolled here?"

"Of course I am." I'm sifting lazily through a jumble of discounted cassettes. "I'm just not ostentatious about it."

"Oh."

"Besides, taking classes isn't what Harvard's all about."

"No?"

"Of course not." I hold up a Led Zeppelin tape and then toss it back into the pile. "I'd stop poisoning my mind with that silly old prospectus if I were you."

He takes half a step forward. "Then what *is* Harvard all about?"

"Who am I, Alfie?"

"And now you're calling me names."

"Teddy, I've really got to run."

"Where?" he asks suspiciously.

"Warren House."

"Who house?"

"Warren House. English department building over by the Freshman Union."

"Oh. Well, I'll walk you to Lamont. Guess I'll go read magazines for a while before lunch."

As we make our way across Mass Ave and through the Yard, Teddy's telling me about Fools Week at the Lampoon. "I videotaped a whole bunch of new members jumping into the IAB pool fully clothed. During team practice," he says proudly.

I try to think of something pleasant to say, and failing that, I change the subject. "I see the new *Lampoon* is out."

"Yep."

"Are any of your pieces in it?"

"Pieces of what?"

"Pieces of eight," I snap. "Yo ho ho."

He whoops and goes off into a strangled paroxysm of laughter. "Oh god," he gasps. "That's too funny. Yo ho ho." He laughs again. "You should be on the *Lampoon*."

"Icicles in hell."

"God, you're funny *and* bitchy," he says, fawningly. "You're perfect for the *Lampoon*. Are you sure you don't want to join?"

"Teddy, I'm graduating, remember?"

"A mere technicality. Why don't you comp for us?"

"I'd rather die."

"See? You have the perfect attitude." As we climb the steps past Pusey Library, Teddy chuckles. "Speaking of dying, somebody almost did at the IAB the other day."

"Don't tell me. One of your initiates had an anchor tied to his leg."

"Close. Somebody on the swim team got tangled up with the inflatable shark and almost drowned."

"My, that *is* funny," I say evenly.

He's still chuckling. "No, what's really funny is that their coach started hyperventilating, hit his head on the bleachers and had to be rushed to the emergency room. Twelve stitches." Grinning, he wipes his eyes.

We halt at the long shallow steps leading up to Lamont. Just inside the double glass doors, the afternoon-shift guard, a thin old man in a maroon blazer, stands at the security kiosk, nodding blindly at the people streaming past, waving IDs and books at him.

"Well," Teddy says brightly, "this is my stop."

Huddled in my big down coat, I come along the path in time to see the Lamont guard leave the library and walk down the steps toward Quincy Street. In the bitter wind his trousers, flared at the cuffs, flap wildly around his thin ankles, revealing dark socks and garters. I stand watching him, my nose buried in my scarf, and then I turn around and go back to Adams House. Slowly I walk up the stairs to Michael's room, where I've just spent the afternoon helping him prepare for his French final, and when he opens the door to let me in I go over to the big La-Z-Boy with the Peanuts throw pillows and sit down, still in my coat and scarf. I lean forward with my face in my hands, shivering.

"Gal?" Michael says, coming over to squat on his heels next to me. "What's wrong?"

Shaking now, I curve more tightly into myself. I feel him loosening my scarf, and then he places his hands over my ears to warm them.

"Whatcha doin'?" he whispers, taking his hands away. "Kitten?"

I keep my face buried in my palms. "Trying to cry. Do you goddam mind?"

"Sure. I mean no." He touches my hair. "You go right ahead. I got plenty of Kleenex."

"I can't, goddam it."

"How come?"

"I don't know."

"Honey," he says, "it's okay. I'm pretty sure I'm not gonna flunk my French exam. D'accord?" He pronounces it dack-cord.

After a while I raise my head, sniffing. "I could use a tissue."

He goes into his bedroom and returns with a box of pink Kleenex. I take one and blow my nose. "How come you have such sissy tissues?"

"I like pink."

"So do I." I shove the damp Kleenex into my coat pocket. "Thanks."

"Gal?"

"Michael?"

"Y'all mind if I ask you a serious question?"

"Yes, but now's as good a time as any."

"Is there a reason why we ain't gone to bed together?"

For a moment I am silent. Then I look up at him, feeling my eyes start to sting. "I think I like you too much."

"Kind of ass-backward logic, ain't it?"

"That's the way I operate."

He crouches next to my chair again and takes my hand. "I kinda wish it weren't that way."

"I know. I mean, we could try it, I guess, but—"

"Yeah." He sighs. "Why mess up a good thing."

"I know it seems stupid." I'm trying to keep my voice even. "I'm sorry."

"No, it ain't stupid." His fingers tighten on mine. "It's fine, honey."

There is a silence, and then I sigh in a long soft breath. "Michael."

"Gal?"

"There's no heat in this goddam room. Let's give Kurt a call, okay?"

He looks at me and smiles. "Ma chère," he says, "ma chère." He pronounces it maw-shair, *drawling out the* shair *until it sounds like a four-syllable phrase.*

"Michael?"

"Yeah?"

"While I'm calling Kurt," I tell him quietly, "you'd better get out your Larousse. We have some more work to do."

"Well," Teddy says again, with undimmed cheer, "this is my stop, I guess."

"What?"

"I said, I'll see you later."

"Okay," I say absently. "Good luck with getting your mom's birthday present."

"Thanks. It was last week, so there's no rush." He dissolves into burbling laughter. "Yo ho ho. God, that was funny." As I turn away, he cries: "Wait."

"What."

"Which party will you be at tomorrow night?"

"Which party?" I feel a keen ache behind my eyes.

"Spee or Advo?"

"Aren't you guys having your usual Saturday-night bash?"

"Oh, sure. But you know us, we love to crash parties. Break a few glasses here, break a few glasses there."

"All in a night's work."

"Yep." He starts giggling again, and I wave at him and start walking toward Quincy Street. When I reach the crosswalk, I'm overtaken by a vociferous knot of freshmen bent for lunch and enthusiastic over the prospect of ratatouille. I pause, letting them pass me, and then all at once I decide to skip class and go back to C-45 for some aspirin and a nap.

I'm sitting cross-legged on Henry's couch, holding an immense bouquet of irises in my arms as I watch Henry pace back and forth, a Ronald McDonald glass half-filled with Miller Lite dangling in his hand.

"Miranda," he's saying, "I just don't understand." Back and forth, back and forth. "I just don't understand this at all."

"There's nothing to understand."

"Nothing to understand?" He glares. "There's plenty not to understand. Like why I'm not supposed to see you anymore, for example."

"We can't, Henry."

"Why not?" Back and forth. "Tell me why we can't."

"Because I'm going out with Jackson."

"I know that," he says impatiently.

"So why don't you understand?"

"Thanks for reminding me. I also don't understand why you're going out with him."

"We're not discussing my relationship with Jackson."

"Maybe we should."

"I'd rather not."

"Finally, something I can understand." He grins sardonically.

"Bully for you." My mouth tight, I watch him as he strides to and fro in his noiseless black Converse hightops.

"Look, Miranda, can we stop this goddam running around in circles? We're not getting anywhere."

"No, but it's good exercise."

"You don't want to talk about your relationship with Jackson, you

don't want to talk about your relationship with me." He runs a hand through his already disheveled hair. *"Maybe you'd like to talk about the weather?"*

"We don't have a relationship, Henry."

"Will you stop with the goddam semantics?"

"Shh." I point at the door. *"Your kiddies."*

"Whoops. Thanks." He takes a long swallow of his Miller Lite, and then holds the glass out to me. *"You want some?"*

"No. Thanks."

He resumes his pacing. *"Let's try and talk about this honestly, okay? I'll start. Ready? Okay. Now, I'm perfectly aware of the fact that you're going out with Jackson."*

"Look, Henry—"

"Although why you're doing it is beyond me."

"I don't want—"

"If you ask me, it doesn't seem to be making you particularly happy."

"Nobody's asking you."

"The point is, Miranda, I'd just like to spend some time with you."

"It's not that simple, Henry."

"Why not?"

"What happened the last time we saw each other?"

"Miranda, nothing happened."

"I beg to differ," I say coldly. *"That was not nothing."*

"So we kissed each other. It was nice, right?"

"Yes, but—"

"And we left all our clothes on, right?"

"I—yes—"

"And I didn't even try to unhook your bra, did I?"

"I—what?"

"Oh, sorry. You don't wear a bra, do you?"

My face is burning. *"Screw you."*

"Coward, coward," he taunts me.

I jump to my feet and throw the irises at him. They flutter against his chest like slim violet-plumed birds and fall rustling to the floor. Henry takes another sip of his beer, and looks over at me. *"I'm sorry,"* he says mildly. *"I thought you liked irises."*

I stoop to pick up a flower that's landed near me. Gripping the stem in my fist, I straighten up, feeling a little dizzy. He stands watching me *as I come near, and timidly I put my arms around him. Closing my eyes, I rest my cheek against his sweater, which smells faintly of Miller Lite, Liquid Paper, and my creme rinse. "I'm sorry too," I say, dropping the iris.*

His arms encircle me. "I guess that makes us even." I can feel the Ronald McDonald glass against my shoulder blade, chilly even through my shirt. "Next time I'll get you roses, okay?"

"Okay." I press my cheek harder against his chest. "Henry?"

"Miranda?"

"Please don't spill your beer all over my shirt." I don't see any reason to tell him that it's Jackson's.

The light ashen shadows of late afternoon are spilling into my room, silvery and mysterious. I look over at my clock-radio. It's nearly five-thirty, which means that the Adams House tea is doubtless in full swing by now. Yawning, I picture the prim dark rooms at Apthorp Court, jammed with the usual assortment of physical-sciences nerds, house tutors, classical musicians, overweight political activists, social climbers, zealous sophomores, unidentified kindly-looking adults dressed in what appears to be their Sunday best, and a sprinkling of glammie types prowling ecstatically around with a particularly offensive air of being deliberately out of their milieu, the whole lot of them eating and drinking as if there's no tomorrow, rattling teacups and standing around making half-hearted conversation while busily scanning for fresh trays of brownies and puff pastries.

On the whole, I'd rather go running.

Shit. In the middle of another yawn I remember that I told Michael I'd be there. I roll over onto my back, fingers laced together behind my head. Pondering, I start flexing and pointing my feet. Left, right, left, right.

By the time I hear the front door slam, I've degenerated into mindless absorption in my foot-flexing. Left, right, left, right. "Jessie?" I call out.

There is no reply. I get up and peer into the living room. "Jessica?" Nothing. I go into the hallway. "Jessica?"

"No, dope, it's the Queen of England," she screams from the bathroom.

"You're squeezing your face, aren't you," I scream back and dart into the bathroom, where indeed, she stands before the mirror with forefingers poised like pincers. "Hey!"

"Hey what."

"Stop that."

"Go away." She starts pinching her chin.

"Jessie, stop for a second. Please, just for a second. Pretty please? Pretty please with an olive on top?"

Without turning her head she rolls her eyes in my direction, rendering her absolutely carplike for a brief, magical second. "I hate olives."

"Well, I know you don't like cherries, so I thought I'd substitute olives."

"I hate olives, cherries, and Melba toast."

"Yes, but you'll like this." I lean against the towel rack. "Knock knock."

"Oh Christ."

"Come on. Just this once."

"Christ."

"Thank you. Knock knock."

"Who's there?" She keeps her fingers at her chin.

"Olive."

"Olive who?"

"Olive you."

She gives a brief mirthless smile and begins scrutinizing her forehead. "Hilarious. Will you go away now?"

"Not until you leave your face alone."

"It's my face. I can mutilate it if I want to."

"Will you at least tell me why you're doing this?"

"Because my complexion sucks. Isn't it painfully obvious from twenty feet away?"

"Jessica, your complexion is fine."

"Easy for you to say. I'm the one looking at all these zits."

"You're crazy. Now look, what's the real reason for all this?"

She grips a piece of flesh between her fingers. "I'm a horrible, disgusting person. Is that a good enough reason?"

"Can we please talk about this in the living room? You know how I hate these little tête-à-têtes in the bathroom."

"I can't leave now. My face is all red and blotchy."

"We'll put a paper bag over your head, okay?" I take her hand and draw her into the living room, where we settle into opposite ends of the sofa. I unlace her shoes and slip them off her feet, blinking at her socks. Today she wears a black-and-white-striped glitter sock and a brown cableknit knee-hi.

"Righto then." I start massaging her insteps. "What seems to be the problem?"

"Nothing. I have no problems." She sighs, leaning her head back against the sofa. "That feels great."

"Look, I give footsie, you spill guts. Deal?"

"A little harder on the arch, please."

"How's this?"

"Fabulous."

"Good. Now talk."

"Well, my first mistake was going to the tea."

"Foolhardy girl. Hey, did you see Michael there?"

"Michael?" She thinks for a moment. "No. But I did see Beverly Stinson."

"Mistake number two?"

Jessica nods, then drops her chin and rolls her eyes in a single coordinated gesture of woe. "Beverly," she says darkly, "has not only finished her thesis, she's had it typeset and bound in a blue leather cover."

"That's the most ridiculous thing I've ever heard."

"Pigskin," Jessica moans. "Hand-tooled Spanish pigskin."

"Jessica, Beverly Stinson has a face like a scallop. What are you worried about?"

"I'm worried about her blue pigskin thesis."

"Twenty years from now, your thesis won't mean shit." I switch to her other foot. "And Beverly Stinson will still look like a scallop."

"That's true." Jessica brightens a little.

"An aging scallop."

"Yeah," she breathes.

"Good. Now, is there a mistake number three?"

Her face droops again. "Melba toast."

"Oh, right. Olives, cherries, and Melba toast."

"After talking to Beverly, there was only one thing to do."

"The buffet?"

"What else."

"It's always the victims who blame themselves."

"I ate about ninety hors d'oeuvres, mostly cream cheese on Melba toast with little olive slices on top. I'm about to explode. Don't bring any pins or other sharp objects near me."

"I thought you said you hated olives."

"Now I do."

"Ah."

"Besides, they ran out of brownies."

"I see."

"So I spent an hour stuffing the goddam Melba-toast things into my mouth waiting for more brownies to arrive."

"Look at it this way. If you hadn't been busy eating olives on Melba toast, you might very well have been cornered by some social misfit wearing chukka boots."

"Yes, but—"

"But what?"

"Don't you know how fattening olives and cream cheese are?"

"But they were on Melba toast." I'm gently bending each of her toes in succession. "Melba toast isn't fattening."

"But olives and cream cheese are."

"So that makes up for it."

"Huh?"

"Don't you see? They cancel each other out."

"They do?"

"Of course. I thought everybody knew that." I give her metatarsals a final knead and stand up. "It's simple yin and yang. Olives in, Melba toast out."

"Fine." She wiggles her toes. "I'm just not eating for the next three weeks."

"That's my girl." I put one leg in front of the other and bend forward, touching the floor with my palms. "Now listen. I'm going running. If you squeeze your face while I'm gone I'll beat your nose in."

"Promises, promises."

"Don't be disgusting." I reverse my legs. "Hey, it's Friday night, isn't it?"

"So what?"

"So it's time to start having fun."

"Says who?"

"What glamorous schemes have you cooked up for yourself?"

"Don't say cooking."

"Sorry."

"My plans for tonight? Three guesses."

"Starts with T? Six letters? Rhymes with—"

"Right."

"That's glamorous."

"So what are you doing tonight?"

"Me?" I stretch lower, grunting a little. "Hot date in the Widener reading room." Carefully I straighten up. "I haven't done any reading for Soc Sci 33 all semester, and my section leader's getting huffy about it."

"Right, so you started skipping classes."

"It seemed the logical thing to do."

"Hey." She turns onto her side and looks up at me. "What'd you get on your last paper? The one on surfing subcultures."

"An A," I say indifferently, and go into my room to change.

My run is long, and fast, and as I walk down the entryway steps into Adams House I'm still breathing hard, flushed and damp with sweat. I'm leaning against the wall next to Kurt's office, shaking out my left calf, when Jackson saunters down the steps, singing to himself: *"I know this world is killing you . . . Alison, my aim is true . . ."*

He sees me, and stops. "Your leg okay?"

"The usual." I look down at my shin. "Still bothers me on the last mile or so."

"You don't warm up properly."

Involuntarily I smile a little. "I know."

"You'll injure yourself someday."

"Probably."

"I mean seriously injure yourself."

"I've been lucky so far."

"Then why does your leg hurt?"

"Because I don't warm up properly."

There's a brief silence. I shake out my other leg, even though it isn't actually troubling me at the moment.

"Want a rubdown?"

"Pardon me?"

"I said, d'you want a rubdown?"

"Oh." I glance at him. "Really?"

"Really."

You're buzzed on endorphins. Your glycogen supply is exhausted. Your nervous system is completely haywire. Say no. "Sure."

He crouches down before me and takes my ankle in his hands. "How are you, sweetie?"

"I'm okay."

"That's good."

"How are you?"

"I'm fine." Lightly he kisses my knee, and it's all I can do to keep from jerking away in surprise. "Cinderella."

"Yeah. In size-nine Nikes."

He's rubbing my calf with a steady touch. In the white light of the entryway lamps his hair shines a rich ashen brown, and I reach down to wind my fingers through the wave of hair that sweeps down across his forehead. He looks up at me, no smile. I am quiet, watching him, and then I withdraw my hand.

His fingers stop, curving around my leg just beneath the knee. "Feel better?"

I flex the ankle. "Yes. Thank you."

"You're welcome." He straightens, and now he stands looking down at me. "I'm on my way in to dinner. Care to join me?"

"I'm all sweaty."

"You look beautiful."

"Thanks." I swallow. "But I'd like to shower first, and dinner'll be over by then."

"Okay."

He's about to turn away, and swiftly I say: "How about dessert?"

A half-smile curves his lips. "Okay."

———

Jessica's in more or less the same position she was in when I left. I pull up the bottom of my sweatshirt and swab at the sweat on my face. "How's the thesis coming along?"

"I've been *thinking*." She doesn't open her eyes.

"Thinking about alpha waves," I say genially. I lie down on the floor, hook my feet under the bottom of the sofa, and start doing my sit-ups.

"Eighteen, ninety-three, forty-seven, twelve."

"Cut that out," I gasp.

"Just trying to help." She rolls onto her stomach and buries her face in a cushion. I finish my sit-ups, then do a few push-ups and leg stretches; after I shower and get dressed again I return to the living room to find Jessica prone as before. I perch on the edge of the sofa and pick up the phone, dial Michael's number, and as I'm listening to the rings I gaze at the smushed sliver of her face that's just barely visible among the pillows. First her nostril flares a couple of times. Then she breathes adenoidally through her mouth for a while. Finally she yawns and a pale-blue eye opens sluggishly. By this point I've long since hung up the phone and am sitting chin in palm, elbow on knee, legs crossed, studying her.

"Mighty fancy for the Widener reading room," she remarks in a muffled voice. "Why are you wearing so much eye shadow?"

"Your nose is turned up like a pig's. I can see straight up your nostril."

"Well, why don't you read my fortune in the cilia, dope?"

"I can see a tall, handsome stranger."

"Goody."

"I see romance, passion, intrigue. Intimate dinners in poorly lit bistros."

"Don't stop," Jessica murmurs. "D'you want to see the other nostril?"

"No, that's okay. There's plenty of hair in this one."

"Fuck you."

"Do you want me to finish your fortune or don't you?"

"Sorry."

"I see a big house in Scarsdale. I see a big green lawn, hibachis. A golden retriever. Canasta parties. I see weekly facials and enormous bills from Bloomingdale's."

"Wait a minute." Jessica sits up. "What about the handsome stranger?"

"That's what your husband wants to know."

"What? Oh."

We're still snickering when there's a knock at the door. Jessica leaps to her feet, suddenly energetic. "It's the handsome stranger, I know it." I remain perched on the couch, listening. "Oh. Hi."

"Hi, Jessie. How are you?"

"Me? Oh, I'm fine, Jackson," she says in a loud warning voice. "What's up?"

"Well, I was just wondering if Miranda's around."

"Maybe. I'm not really sure."

"Mind if I have a look?"

"It's really messy. We haven't vacuumed since we moved in."

"That's okay. I doubt I'll be looking under the chairs anyway." He comes strolling into the living room with Jessica sharp upon his heels, and I see that he's changed his shirt. "Hi," he says, smiling. "Here you are after all."

"Yep."

"Ready to go?"

"Let me just get a jacket." As I stand up I watch Jessica's eyes flying from me to Jackson and back again to me before abruptly narrowing into blue slits. She follows me into my room and shuts the door behind us.

"What's going on?" she hisses.

I pull on my jacket, dab on more lipstick, run my fingers through my hair, and finally turn to face her glare. "I'm not sure," I reply, mildly.

To my horror, she suddenly looks as if she's about to burst into tears. "Don't squeeze your face, okay?" I whisper, giving her a quick hug before plunging back into the living room and whisking Jackson out of C-45, thereby forestalling what almost certainly promised to be a dampening performance on Jessica's part.

"It was Katharine Hepburn who said that." Jackson takes a swallow of his Beck's. "Why do you ask?"

"No reason." I'm gazing past the dance floor toward the bar, which is jammed with the usual eclectic Oxford Ale House crowd:

the long-faced leather-jacketed townies, some multicolored punkers, the Cher-haired girls in skintight jeans, a couple of Hell's Angels showing off their tattoos, and a few brave Harvard types idling about self-consciously, darting nonchalant glances at the mohawks and studded belts and bracelets. In fact, I think I recognize a kid from my Soc Sci 33 section, wedged in between two black-haired Amazonians wearing Cleopatra-style eye makeup and hobnailed boots, who ignore what appear to be his vivacious attempts to strike up a conversation. I can't help laughing softly as I take a sip of my beer.

"What's so funny?" Jackson says.

"Nothing."

"My, you're inscrutable tonight." He takes a hank of my hair and tugs upon it. "What are you smiling about?"

"Am I smiling?"

"Yes." His hand slides through my hair, and rests lightly against the curve of my neck. "Tell me. What's the joke?"

"It's just this place. I love the ambience."

"What ambience?"

"I enjoy thinking about Caroline Kennedy being tossed out of here on her face."

"You don't believe that silly story, do you?"

"Some kid from Winthrop House told me it was true."

"Freshman week, right?"

"Yes, but how—"

"They tell it to all the freshmen." He's signaling for another round. "You shouldn't have been so gullible."

"I'm not sure the Oxford Ale will ever seem the same."

"Truth is vulgar, darling."

"I thought truth is beauty."

We sit silently for a while, not looking at each other as we drink our beers. Presently Jackson lights a cigarette and offers it to me.

"No thanks."

"Really? You've quit?"

"I never started."

He blows a smoke ring over my head. "You know, I used to think Jessica liked me."

"Well—"

"She's a good egg though. A bit hard-boiled, but nice." He laughs. "Or should I say a little cracked."

I arch an eyebrow. "I beg your pardon?"

"But I've always admired that mother-hen instinct of hers."

I give my empty beer bottle to the waitress, who in turn places fresh ones on the table. Jackson hands her a five-dollar bill. "Keep it," he says to her.

Lowering my eyebrow, I take a sip of my beer. "I think it was my turn to pay."

"Don't worry about it."

"Well, thanks."

"No problem."

We're silent again for a while, and then Jackson looks over at me.

"Hey."

"Yeah?"

"You never told me."

"Told you what?"

"What's for dessert?"

"Dessert?" I feel myself starting to smile. "Maybe they sell beer nuts here."

"That's not what I had in mind."

"I think there's a candy machine by the bathrooms."

"No, that's not what I had in mind either."

"Mmm."

The big black speakers are blasting out the Romantics' "What I Like About You." Jackson touches my arm. "Dance?"

"Okay."

He takes another drink of his Beck's and helps me slide out of the booth, and then all at once we're dancing on the Oxford Ale's tiny uneven dance floor. Right next to the kid from my Soc Sci 33 section, in fact, and one of the Amazon twins, whose hobnailed feet can really dance up a storm.

SATURDAY | 4

||||||||||||||||||||||||||||||||||||||||||||||||||||||||||||||||||||||||||

*T*he phone is ringing.

I am in bed, evidently, and my feet seem to be propped on my pillows somewhere down past my knees.

"Ick," I murmur, stirring. A series of more or less unpleasant sensations stickily unfurl onto my consciousness:

My mouth and brain feel as if they've been stuffed with rotting cotton.

The bed smells like Jackson.

Jackson is gone.

It seems to be daylight outside.

The phone is still ringing.

And I am developing a tremendous headache.

I tuck the covers more securely about my shoulders, grimly aware that if I don't get coffee soon I will probably die.

The phone stops ringing.

My clock-radio reads 3:07.

I see that I am wearing Jackson's t-shirt. I peek under the covers to assure myself that I'm not wearing his underwear too.

My next-door neighbor in C-41 suddenly screams out *"Dios mío"* and then there is silence again.

Over in C-45 I turn my radio on to a classical-music station. Folding my arms underneath my head, I stare up at the ceiling, wondering how many brain cells I may have destroyed last night.

Dear god.

Coffee. I must have coffee.

I creak out of bed and shuffle into the bathroom, where I splash a little cold water on my face and dribble Visine into my eye sockets. Then I yawn a couple of times and slope toward the mirror. My hair, I note clinically, is spiking wildly, my complexion looks a little dull, and I have a large violet hickey on my neck. I'm still gazing at myself with limp interest when I hear the front door open and then slam shut.

"Jessie?" I call out. "Is that you?"

There is no answer. I go into the living room, but it's empty. "Jessica?" I knock on her bedroom door.

"What do you want?"

"Uh, did I get any mail today?"

"No."

"Jessica?"

"What?"

"Can I come in?"

"No."

"Why not?"

"I'm busy."

"Doing what?"

"Mind your own beeswax."

"Oh. Okay." I go back into the living room and lie down on the couch, wincing at the light. Seconds later, Jessica storms out of her room. Through half-closed eyes I notice that she's still wearing the clothes she had on last night, and her hair is almost as frowsy-looking as mine is.

"What," she asks icily, "are you doing?"

"Resting," I explain. "My head is throbbing."

"Must you lie around half-naked?"

"Don't you mean to say half-dressed?"

"Do I have to bear this?" she entreats the ceiling. "Am I being punished for something?"

"Jessie." I struggle up into a modified slump. "What's wrong?"

"What's wrong? I'll tell you what's wrong." She proceeds to count off on her fingers. "One, I went out with Sutter last night, which means no work on my thesis. Two, I wake up with the biggest hangover since the invention of gin—"

"You too?" I say commiseratingly.

"Will you shut up?"

"Sure, okay."

"Three, Sutter tells me at lunch that he's afraid he's gay. Four, I come crawling back into Adams House and who do I bump into but our mutual friend Tim, who's looking even more dog-eared than usual." She pauses to catch her breath and glare at me.

"Is there more?" I say, warily.

"Five," she snaps. "A letter from Yale Law School. A goddam summer reading list three pages long. I haven't even finished the goddam Monarch Notes for my thesis and they want me to start worrying about goddam torts?"

I clear my throat. "I thought you said there wasn't any mail."

"Not for you." Her tone could disintegrate steel.

"Oh."

"Six."

"Uh oh."

"*Someone* seems to have borrowed a pair of my underwear."

"Oh?"

"My *best* pair of underwear."

"Well, now that you mention it—"

"And if you'd care to look down at yourself you might guess who I'm referring to."

"Whom."

"Did you have to take my black lace bikini from Frederick's of Hollywood?" she screams.

"It was on top."

"Why me, God?" She's addressing the ceiling again. "What have I done to deserve this?"

The telephone rings and she snatches at it. After listening for a moment she drops the receiver on the floor. "It's for you," she announces with a distinctly unpleasant look on her face. "It's your boyfriend."

I reach down and pick up the receiver. "Hello?"

"Hi, Miranda," Tim says. "It's me."

"Sorry, wrong number." I hang up.

Jessica stares at me, tapping her foot on the floor. "You're unbelievable. Do you have any idea of how unbelievable you are?"

"No, but if you want to tell me I'll listen." Actually, I think I'd really rather close my eyes and go back to sleep. "But would you please stop pounding your foot like that? It's making my headache worse."

"You're really unbelievable."

"Jessica, I've asked Tim a dozen times to please leave me alone."

"That's not the point."

"Fine. What's the point?"

The phone rings again and this time I answer it. "Hello?"

"Miranda, why did you hang up on me?"

"Sorry, I think you have—"

"I'm downstairs. Can I come up?"

"No."

"Why not? Miranda, I've got to talk to you."

"Tim?"

"Yeah?"

"Kindly leave me alone. Your cooperation in this matter will be greatly appreciated." I hang up on him again, and look over at Jessica. "Make that thirteen times."

She screams. "I can't bear it, I just can't bear it." She goes into her room and slams the door. In a minute or two I hear her throw open her door, and then the front door slams shut.

With a long sigh I slide back down on the couch until I am completely horizontal. I close my eyes and watch the purple and yellow flashes that dance against my eyelids in perfect rhythm to my racked temples.

The telephone rings again. Without moving from my prone position I pick up the receiver. "Hello?"

"Can I please come up? I really need to talk to you."

"This is it," I say. "I'm calling the police." I hang up and let my arm dangle on the floor. My limbs feel as if they're about to drop off my body at the slightest provocation. In the meantime I keep watching the color show on my eyelids, although it does seem to be making me somewhat dizzy.

When I open my eyes again, the afternoon light appears to have waned a little, and my craving for coffee, if not food, has grown more urgent. I lean over and reach for the phone.

"Darling."

"Gal?"

"Do me a favor?"

"Sure. What?"

"A muffin and a cup of coffee from Tommy's."

"Y'all lost motor capabilities since the last time I saw you?"

"Sort of. No butter on the muffin, please."

His voice sharpens. "You okay?"

"I'm fine. Really. I just can't leave my room."

"Why not?"

"Why not." I'm smelling the rich bitter scent of coffee, picturing one of Tommy's huge, dark, dense, puffy-topped muffins just pried out of its old-fashioned metal baking tin. Too enervated to plead a sudden attack of agoraphobia, I find myself telling Michael the truth. "—so it's really just a simple case of lesser evils. Can I have extra milk in my coffee?"

"Honey," Michael says, gently, "get it yourself." Quietly he hangs up the phone.

I give the receiver a look of anemic shock and replace it in its cradle. "My stars," I say aloud. Then I hang my head over the edge of the couch, eyes fixed on a crack in the ceiling, and do some chin exercises, opening and closing my jaw like a suffocating fish.

At a loss for anything better to do, I've been at my chin stretches for quite some time when the phone rings again. Hoping it's Michael, I answer it with my head still drooping off the couch. "Yass?" I say through a stuffed-up nose.

"Mira? Is that you, honey?"

"No," I mumble, pinching my nostrils shut. "I'm afwaid you hab a wong number." I hang up and roll off the sofa onto the floor, which is chilly but surprisingly refreshing. And so, when the phone rings again a few minutes later, I succumb to a false sense of rejuvenation. "Hello?"

"Mira? Is that you, honey?"

"Can you speak up? We have a bad connection."

"Mira? Can you hear me?"

"What? I can't hear you."

"Can you hear me now?" she shouts.

"Hi, Ma. What's new?"

"We haven't heard from you in so long."

"I've been working hard. Phi Beta Kappa and all that."

"Yes, we know about that already. They wrote us."

"Why are you shouting at me?"

"Oh. You can hear me okay now?"

"What?"

There is a brief silence, during which I hear remnants of someone else's conversation, as if two telephone lines have been spliced together. "—and then," comes a tiny far-off female voice, "the straw that breaks the camel's back, he straggles in at three in the morning—"

"How's Jackson?"

"—drunk as a skunk—"

"He's fine."

"That's good. How's your health? Are you eating right?"

"—she's as big as a house and they only got married in January—"

"Honey? Can you hear me?"

"So how was Mexico?" I shout.

"Just wonderful. The Taggarts send their best to you."

"That's nice."

"—how they're going to pay for that new car I don't know—"

"Are you getting enough fruits and vegetables?"

"What? I can't hear you."

"—and then they buy a fancy waterbed on credit—"

"Are you getting enough roughage?"

"Ma, don't gross me out."

"What, honey? I couldn't hear you."

"There's another party on the line," I say loudly. "Sounds like a nosy old busybody boring some poor soul to death."

There is utter silence for a few seconds, and then the little voice says: "Will you *look* at the time? I'm going to be late for my dentist appointment."

"Yeah, right," I shout. "You're not fooling anybody."

The line crackles in the sudden hush.

"Hello? Mira? Are you there?"

To my regret, the connection is now much improved. "Why are you screaming at me, Ma?"

"What? Was I screaming?"

"How's the weather out there?"

"It's wonderful. Honey, any news from Columbia yet?"

"No."

"Honey, I hate to bring this up—"

"Done any golfing so far this spring?"

"A little. But honey, have you given any thought to—"

"How's your handicap?"

"Same as usual. But have you thought about what you'll do if they don't accept you?"

"What?" She's probably sitting at the kitchen table, I muse, with her mid-afternoon cigarette and cup of coffee, yellow Trimline balanced on a hunched-up shoulder, drawing invisible patterns on the tablecloth with a restless forefinger. The dishwasher's probably going full blast, and I'd wager there are three or four avocado pits sprouting in old Laura Scudder peanut butter jars on the shimmeringly clean windowsill that overlooks the backyard.

"Mira? Did you hear me?"

"Sure I heard you. You want to know what I'll do if I don't get into Columbia."

"Well?"

"No problem. If it doesn't work out with Columbia, I'm going to be a singer in a rock band."

"What did you say?"

"I said, my second choice is to be a rock singer."

"Is that a joke?"

"Why would I be joking?" I prop my feet up on the sofa. "It's got a lot of things going for it, Ma. No typing, and the chance to travel."

"I don't appreciate your sense of humor."

"The way I figure it is, it shouldn't take more than a year to learn how to play the bass guitar. I mean, it's only got four strings, right?"

"I don't appreciate it at all."

"I guess it really depends on my finding a good guitar teacher."

"Miranda."

"Yes, Ma?"

"I think you'd better call me back when your attitude improves."

"Don't hold your breath."

"What did you say?"

"What? I couldn't hear you."

"When you call, let the phone ring for a while."

"Pardon?"

"Your father and I'll be in the backyard weeding the lawn."

"Okay."

"We'll be expecting your call."

"Okay."

"Do you have anything else you'd like to add?"

"Yes, tell Dad not to strain his back on those weeds."

"Remember to let it ring for a while."

"What?" I hang up and let out my breath in a soft rush of air. Then I scramble to my feet and lurch into my room for my clothes. Within seconds I'm dressed and am on my way downstairs. It's only as I reach the ground floor that I realize that I've forgotten to brush my ludicrously tousled hair. "Oh, shit," I say aloud. Then I shrug, and stop to check the C-45 mailbox. There's something in there. *Mail.*

But it's just a little note for me, scrawled on the back of a mimeographed GREEN TORTOISE TO PHOENIX advertisement, doubtless ripped from a nearby bulletin board.

Miranda,
    I've got to see you. Please call.
                         Tim

Carefully I tear the note in two. The part with my name on it I stick into my trouser pocket underneath a damp shred of Kleenex. The other part I fold and slip into the C-16 mailbox, which I happen to know belongs to a suite of lonely juniors, at least one of whom isn't more than ten pounds overweight.

The dining hall is quiet and dimly lit in the pre-meal lull. In the kitchen the staff bustles about, bantering among themselves and clattering metal bowls and serving trays as they get ready for the start of dinner. Nobody bothers me as I slip in before official opening time to take two cups of coffee; Serge tosses me an orange and compliments me on my hair. I smile at him and go back into the dining hall, where I sit at the end of a large rectangular table that seats the French Club on Tuesdays and the Italian Club on Wednesdays. I stare at the tabletop, trying to remember every single Italian verb I've ever memorized.

Abruptly overcome by a yawning fit, I've decided to try the French verbs instead and have almost finished my second cup of coffee when an indolent voice speaks nearby, making me jump a little: "Early bird for dinner, aren't you?"

"Huh?"

Jackson's roommate Gerard stands next to my chair. His eyes are puffy and ringed with dark circles and he looks as if he hasn't shaved in a few days. His chin sparkles with sparse golden-reddish stubble. "I said, you're an early bird, aren't you?"

"You bet." I pull off a long piece of orange skin. "I hear they're serving worms tonight."

He laughs and sits down next to me. "God, I miss you. How come I never see you anymore?"

"I guess it's not that small a world after all."

"Well, I feel abandoned," he chides, wagging a nicotine-stained finger at me. "Can I have some of your orange?"

"Sure." I give him half.

"Thanks. Love your hair."

"Thanks. Trying to grow a beard, I see."

"Somebody finally noticed." He preens, turning his face left and right so that I can examine his profile. "Like it? It's very Robert Frostish, don't you think?"

"It's wonderful, Gerard." I wink at him. "In a year or so you may have a full-blown goatee there."

"It's only been five days, Miranda," he says defensively through a half-chewed section of orange. "Give it some time."

I'm stretched out on Jackson's bed, clipping my fingernails, when I hear the front door open and close.

"Hello?" Gerard calls out. "Ollie ollie outs'n free!"

Bending my head over my hands, I cut the nail on my forefinger dangerously close to the quick.

"Jackson?" The door to his bedroom swings open.

I look up. "Haven't you ever heard of knocking first?"

"Hi, Miranda." Gerard stands in the doorway smiling at me, hands in his pockets. His baggy khakis and oversized flannel shirt emphasize his wiry thinness even more. "How are you?"

"Fine, thanks, and you?"

"I'm fine, thanks. What are you doing?"

"Cutting my fingernails. Isn't it obvious?"

"Didn't you do that just a few days ago?"

"You're probably wondering why I'm here."

"No, not really. You're here a lot."

"I'm here because Jessica's entertaining someone in our room."

"Entertaining?"

"You know, Gerard." I wink at him in a grotesquely exaggerated expression that distorts most of my face. "Entertaining."

"Mmm." He shuffles his oxfords. "Where is Jackson, anyway? I stopped by Boylston Hall and got his Camus reserve readings."

"Do you want to come in?"

"Sure." Still blushing, he leans against the edge of the dresser. "So where is he?"

"He's at a dinner party at his thesis adviser's."

"That's nice."

"Speaking of entertaining."

"Mmm." Gerard shifts nervously. "So why aren't you there? Didn't they invite you too?"

"Of course I was invited. I'm Jackson's girlfriend, right?"

"Right. So why didn't you go?"

"Have you ever gone along with Jackson to one of his dinner parties?"

"No, he usually goes with—"

"Right." I push myself a little higher on the pillows.

"I mean—" Gerard runs a hand through his hair. *"I mean, he always seems to have a good time."*

"Have you ever had to sit through a five-course meal listening to people argue over where the best restaurants in Provence are?"

"Well, I can't say as I—"

"All the while wondering which fork you're supposed to use next?"

"Well, no, not—"

"And then have Jackson rag on you for two hours afterwards for not contributing to the party?"

"Contributing?"

"You know, Gerard." I wink again. *"Contributing."*

"Mmm."

"So Jackson and I decided that maybe it would be better if he went by himself."

"Oh."

"We decided this together, of course. We had a long discussion about it, and together we decided that this would be the best thing for all concerned."

"Sure."

There is a silence, during which I trim an already short thumbnail.

"Charlie Chaplin festival at the Brattle," Gerard says suddenly. *"If we hurry we can catch the beginning of* The Kid.*"*

"When does it start?"

He looks at his watch.

"Ten minutes."

"Okay, I—" Then I shake my head. *"No, I can't go."*

"Why not?"

"I left my wallet in C-45."

"That's okay. I'll take care of it."

"I don't have a jacket either."

"Borrow one of Jackson's."

"I'm not wearing any makeup."

"You look fine."

"I've got a lot of work to do."

"Are you going to come along peacefully or do I have to sling you over my shoulder?"

"Oh, Gerard." I swing my feet onto the floor and reach for my sneakers. "You really know how to handle a woman."

"Do you want me to pick out a jacket for you?"

"Sure. Thanks." I tie my shoelaces and stand up, noticing out of the corner of my eye that he's blushing again.

Gerard waves at somebody over by the checker's desk. I follow the direction of his wave and see Jackson and Stephanie Kandel, the girl in my writing class who was so anxious about missing the assignment, standing in line and looking our way. At this distance it's hard to tell if they're smiling or not.

"My stars," I say quietly. "Isn't that Jackson over there?"

"Yeah, we're having dinner together." Gerard slides his chair away from the table. "Then we're going over to the Advo to set up for the party tonight. You're coming, aren't you?"

I pick a tiny piece of orange pulp off my sweater. "I didn't know Stephanie was on the *Advocate*."

"She's not."

"Ah."

"Come sit with us." He stands up. "I never get to see you anymore."

"Thanks." I stand up too. "But I'm on my way out."

"Come to the party, okay? You owe me a dance."

"Listen, will you give Jackson a message for me?"

"Sure. What is it?"

I turn away. "Nothing. Never mind."

"Bye, Miranda," he calls after me. "See you tonight, okay?"

Walking out of the dining hall I am careful to keep my gaze on the floor in front of me. I'm mechanically climbing the C-entry stairs when I nearly collide with someone coming down. "Sorry," I murmur, flattening myself against the wall.

"Baby."

There's a touch to my shoulder, and I lift my head. Richard Amidei is leaning against the railing, looking down at me with his great deep-set dark eyes. He's wearing his old black leather jacket tonight, which has a tiny white Sex Pistols button pinned on the pocket over his heart.

"Richard."

"Babes." He takes my hand and raises it to his mouth.

"I like your button."

"Thanks. I like yours too."

"What? I'm not— Oh."

He's begun sucking upon my forefinger. "Orange," he says softly. "Your hair looks great. So why do you look so sad?"

"I thought I looked embarrassed."

"No, you look beautiful."

"Will you please stop doing that to my hand?"

"Why?"

"Because."

"Because why?"

"Because I haven't washed my hands in three days."

"Better and better."

I tilt against the wall, gazing at his strong sharp features and the smooth muscled curve of his jaw and throat. His dark hair, long and curly, is tied into a small ponytail that brushes artlessly against his nape. When finally I pull my fingers away, he steps a little closer and holds out his own hand.

"My turn?"

I take him by the wrist and hold his palm to my cheek. He smells of sweat and smoke and another, subtler musk.

"Baby," Richard whispers, lightly touching my face. "Your skin's so smooth." His fingertips glide across my mouth and as I start to sway toward him there's the clattering of what sounds like a hunting party tearing downstairs in hot pursuit.

" 'Scuse us!"

"Coming through!"

Richard and I step apart to let my next-door neighbors, the Bicknell twins, skitter past.

"Hi, Miriam," Beth squeaks.

"Cute hairdo," Stacey adds enthusiastically. They bubble on downstairs, dressed in matching floaty off-the-shoulder gowns. *Is there a prom tonight,* I wonder sleepily. *Why aren't they wearing corsages?*

Richard pulls me to him. "Miriam."

"What."

"We're playing at the Spee tonight."

"Yeah?" Closing my eyes, I let my head droop onto his fragrant leather-covered shoulder.

"I want you to be there."

"I'm so tired," I whisper into his jacket. "I should get some sleep."

"But don't you want to come see me?"

"Of course I do. But I'm so tired, Richie."

"Let's go upstairs."

"I'm waiting for the elevator."

"You'll wait a long time, baby."

A strain from "Stairway to Heaven" drifts through my head, and I look up at him. "Isn't that why they call it higher education?"

He smiles. "Let's go on up."

I let him take my hand and lead me up the remaining two flights of stairs to C-45 and into my bedroom, where he sits at my desk and waits while I dig my Estée Lauder mirror out from under a pile of clothes next to my bureau. Then I sit on my bed, propped up on pillows, watching him. His lips are parted in concentration as he bends expertly over the mirror.

"Looks a little messy in here," he remarks without looking up. "Haven't had time to do your spring cleaning yet?"

"I've been busy." I sink lower against the pillows. "My workload's unbelievable this semester."

"Yeah, mine too." He hums to himself for a while, then rises and comes over to the bed, mirror balanced on the palm of his hand. "Miriam?"

"Richie?"

"The elevator's here." He looks at me, his dark eyes shining. "Which floor did you want?"

"I don't know." I sit up, making room for him next to me. "You decide."

Now the mirror is on the floor somewhere, as are my shoes and one of my socks. Richard is kissing my neck. It's tickling me, and I squirm and sit up.

Richard gives me a heavy-lidded look. "You okay?"

"Be right back," I say, sliding off the bed. In the bathroom I stare at myself in the mirror for a minute or two, noting with perverse interest the traces of last night's makeup rimming my eyes.

Back in my room Richard is lying on his back, legs crossed at the ankle, eyes closed and humming to himself. One of his feet jiggles back and forth.

"Hi." I sit on the edge of the bed. "Miss me?"

He doesn't open his eyes. "Miranda blue," he sings softly, experimentally. "Miranda blue, Miranda blue." He keeps trying out different combinations of notes, all of them in a minor key, until finally I lean over him and take him by the shoulders.

"Call me Miriam."

At last he opens his eyes. "Miranda blue," he says, sliding his arms around me and pulling me close.

"Richie?"

"Relax," he whispers.

"I hate blue," I whisper back.

"No you don't." He's giving me that heavy-lidded look again. "Color of your eyes."

"Is it?"

"Blue like the sky."

"Really?" I touch my lips to his throat.

"Yeah," he whispers. "Yeah."

"Richie?"

"Miriam?"

"I just—will you—" I notice that his foot is still jiggling. "Just kiss me, will you?"

It's a little past nine and here I am by the Charles, running swiftly even though my legs are a little numb and my skull feels oddly hollow and silvery. My breath comes rapidly, synchronizing itself to the rhythm of my stride.

Left, right. Left, right.

The river glistens black and sinister, reflecting the yellow pinprick lights of the Harvard Business School twinkling from the opposite shore. I find myself wondering if it's true that they dredged up the body of a young woman in a business suit last weekend. They say she was still clutching her briefcase.

"Hey, Legs!" A bottle-green Plymouth cruising by on Mem

Drive slows alongside me, and a grinning dark-haired head emerges from the window. "Run over here, why doncha?"

"Hey!" I call back without breaking stride. "Drop dead, why doncha?"

The head looks surprised and retreats inside the Plymouth, which picks up speed and roars off into the darkness, red taillights gleaming.

One, two, three, four.

My head is pounding. Or is that my heart?

I'm trying to remember what it feels like to be tired. Instead I keep seeing Richard's face smiling at me in the dim light of the desk lamp he's covered with his jacket.

Already I've reached the Weld Boathouse, which overhangs dark and foreboding above the river, reminding me as ever of the Haunted Mansion at Disneyland. I turn around and begin running back toward Weeks Bridge. A double circuit tonight.

One, two, three, four.

One, two, three, four.

Wait a minute, I tell myself. *Is this an E-ticket ride?*

I lope past Winthrop House and then turn up Plympton Street, passing Leverett, then Lowell and Quincy House, dodging the usual clumps of people hurrying about with that loud, boisterous Saturday-night intensity that ordinarily tends to drive me into the library right after dinner. Better to tuck myself in a solitary corner of the Widener reading room where I needn't be forced to witness these vivacious, back-slapping, bug-eyed pursuits that always leave me feeling like I'm a hundred years old. *C'mon, Miranda, let's go out and have some fun.*

Fun. I hawk up a little phlegm and spit it into the gutter.

I've just negotiated crossing Mount Auburn Street against the light when a blood-rattling scream comes pouring down from the open windows of the Lampoon building across Plympton Street. Leaping over an empty beer bottle, I turn my head to sneer up at the party and jog straight into somebody standing in front of Harvard Pizza.

"Oh, shit!" a voice wails, and I look down to see a large slice of pizza lying at my feet, cheese side down.

"Gross," I exclaim, inspecting my sneakers to see if there's any tomato sauce on them. Or worse, some kind of animal matter. Sausage, say, or pepperoni.

"I didn't even get a bite of it," the voice goes on.

I lift my head, brushing the hair out of my eyes. "Hi, guys." Billy Collins lists against a street sign smiling loopily at me with an enormous hero sandwich jammed into his mouth. Lounging next to him, the collar of his Levi jacket turned up as usual, Skip Peterson dangles two teeth-marked crusts and a half-eaten slice in one tanned hand. Anthony lurks at the edge of the group, staring disconsolately at the doomed slice lying inert on the ground between us.

"Sorry about that," I tell him, restlessly shifting my weight from one foot to the other. "Extra cheese, wasn't it?"

He's shaking his head in sorrow. "Extra mushrooms too."

"Bummer."

"Hi, Miranda," Billy says, leering to the extent that he can through half a hero sandwich. "You're looking great tonight."

"Thanks."

"Yeah, nice legs." Skip grins at me.

"Of course it's cheese side down," Anthony says gloomily. "Murphy's Law, that's what it is."

Another scream from the Lampoon floods the street, followed by nerve-jarring sounds of chinaware being smashed and long whoops of laughter.

"Some party." Skip tosses his crusts and the rest of his slice onto the sidewalk.

"No, no," I say. "Murphy's Law was proven with peanut butter."

"Right, get technical." Anthony looks hurt.

"Peanut-butter pizza?" Billy's busily picking his teeth.

"Hey, big shot." Skip sticks a pointy elbow into Billy's side. "Why don't you be a gentleman and offer her a slice?"

He gulps. "Sure, okay."

"No, thanks." I can't stand still. "Cheese gives me zits."

"Me too." Billy points at his chin.

"Oh, gross me out."

"I don't see any zits." Skip shambles closer. "Where are they? Can I see?" He slides a hand down my arm.

"Get your mitts off me," I tell him, smiling. "Or I'll kick your teeth in."

He backs away. "Your skin looks great. Really."

I stand there for a moment looking at them, simultaneously wondering why I had once found Skip so amusing and whether Billy's father the ambassador really used to hide him in the closet during state receptions. "Well." I poke a strand of hair behind my ear. "It's been fun, gang."

"You're going?" Billy's picking his teeth again, this time with a toothpick.

"I'm afraid so." I turn away.

"Coming to the Spee?"

"Coming to the Advo?"

"I've got a lot of work to do," I call back, and start jogging up the street toward Adams House. As I reach the door it swings outward and I step aside to hold it open. The pear-shaped junior passes by, ignoring me. He carries three or four fat textbooks under his arm.

"Hi," I say. "How are you?"

He walks on without so much as a glance in my direction. Staring after him, I notice he wears tan chukka boots with thin navy-blue socks that are bagging a little over his ankles.

It's quiet in C-45. I switch on the living-room light and take off my running shoes. "Jessica?" I say, and then again, louder, "Jessie?"

There is no response. I knock on her door and then, cautiously, open it and peer into her bedroom. It looks the same as it always does—books on her dresser and clothing in her bookcase, with her desk impressively bare and neat—and so it's impossible for me to tell if she's been here recently or not.

Closing the door behind me, I return to the living room, where I pick up magazines and newspapers from the floor and arrange them in a tidy stack in the fireplace. For a second I'm even tempted to straighten the Matisse print hanging askew above the mantel.

Instead I sink into the sofa, pull the telephone close, and dial a number. On the fourth ring a voice I don't know answers.

"Hello?"

"Hi, is Michael there?"

"No, he's not. Can I take a message?"

"No, that's okay. Thanks."

"Sure."

I hang up. After a few seconds I dial another number.

"Hello?"

"Hi, is Henry there?"

"Henry?" There is a pause. "Oh. Henry. He's not here anymore."

"What?"

"He got a fellowship in New York. NYU, I think. So he finished up here a semester early and took off. In January, I guess it was."

"Oh."

"You want his new number? It's around here somewhere."

"No, that's okay. Thanks."

"Sure. Have a nice evening."

"Thanks." I hang up. From the nearby Lampoon comes a particularly resonant scream, thin and piercing. Jaw clenched, I reach for the phone again.

"Harvard Security," says a deep male voice. "Sergeant Manusco speaking."

"Yes, can you please send a squad car over to the Lampoon? I think they're slaughtering pigs again."

"Hello, Miranda. How are you tonight, dear?"

"Oh, I can't complain. And yourself?"

"A little bit of a cold, but otherwise I'm just fine. Thanks for asking."

"Sergeant, can't you please go over there and arrest them all?"

"I'm afraid I can't do that, Miranda."

"Why not?"

"We've gone over this before," he says, patiently.

"I know, but they're worse than usual tonight. Can't you at least get them put on academic probation?"

"It's not my jurisdiction, dear."

"Okay," I say in a small voice. "I'm sorry to have bothered you."

"Now Miranda—"

"You have a good evening, Sergeant. And take care of that cold."

"Miranda—"

"Try vitamin C."

"Miranda, will you—"

"And give my best to Mrs. Manusco." I slam the phone down.

Another scream, faint but prolonged, issues from the Lampoon. I get up, pull down the windowshades, and go back to the phone. I dial another number.

On the fifth ring somebody answers, laughing and breathless: "Hello?" In the background I hear "Roxanne" playing on the stereo, and what sounds like chairs being toppled over.

"Hi, is Jessica there?"

"Who?" the girl says, giggling.

"Jessica Hartsfield. She's a friend of Sutter's."

"Oh. Gee, I dunno."

"Well, is Sutter there?"

"Who?"

"Sutter," I say grimly. "He lives there."

"Oh." The volume on the stereo goes up, somebody yells *"Banzai!"* and the phone is dropped. A girl says, "Stop it, please stop," and then I hear more laughter. "Hello?" a male voice says politely, and I hang up.

I'm in the middle of cleaning out my closet when the phone rings. I hold up the green silk tie I've found underneath a stack of English 165 papers from sophomore year, and by the time I've torn the tie into two long narrow strips, the phone has fallen silent. I flip my clock-radio on to an oldies station.

In the very back of the closet, buried underneath tangled pairs of well-worn sneakers and my only pair of high-heeled shoes, I find a thermal undershirt, a Pierre Cardin dark-blue sock, a broken electric pencil-sharpener, two dead cockroaches, and, at the very bottom of the heap, a handful of dried-up leaves, their once-brilliant colors dimmed to dull brown and red. I stuff it all into a large plastic garbage bag I stole last semester when Kurt stepped out to investigate an overflowing toilet in E-entry. I include the strips of green silk as well as the cockroaches, which I gingerly transport using the Pierre Cardin sock as a glove.

I'm pawing through my few hangers of clothing when the phone rings again. This time I rush into the living room. "Hello?" I sweep the hair out of my face with a grimy hand.

"Hello," a cheerful, confident voice replies. "Is this—um, Miss Marian Walker, class of '82?"

"Miranda. My name is Miranda."

"Miranda," the voice repeats with unfazed good humor. "Good. Miranda, this is Ed Calhoun the Third. Winthrop House '82."

"So?"

"Miranda, I know you're busy—"

"Well, as a matter of fact—"

"—in your day-to-day life. But then, aren't we all?" Ed gives a low vibrating chuckle. "It's the constant round of lectures, seminars, hours at the library." There are sounds of papers rattling. "Now, I understand that you're an English major, um, Miranda. Lucky you the Adams House library has such a fine literature selection."

"I never go there."

"I just wonder, Miranda, in our daily rounds, from classroom to library, from dining hall to language lab, from dorm room to gymnasium, whether we ever stop to think—"

"I often wonder that myself."

"—whether we ever stop to think how fortunate we are to have all these magnificent resources available to us."

"You're selling magazines, aren't you."

"It's easy to take these wonderful opportunities for granted—"

"Do you have *Interview?*"

"Let me tell you why I'm calling."

"Oh god. You're not selling bibles, are you?"

"It's my pleasure and privilege to represent the Class of '82 Alumni Campaign."

"I *knew* you wanted money."

"Let me just explain this to you, Marian."

"Miranda."

"What we're doing is trying to establish a momentum here,

Miranda. A financial imperative to *keep* these wonderful resources available to future generations of Harvard students. Perhaps even your own sons and daughters."

"D. H. Lawrence. Very good."

"Beg pardon?"

"I haven't even graduated yet. Couldn't you at least wait until July?"

"What better time to join together with your fellow classmates, Miranda, as we together we—um." In the sudden silence I distinctly hear the sound of a paper being turned over. "What we're doing is trying to establish a momentum here, Miranda. A financial imperative to—"

"You've said that part already."

"What?" Another low throbbing chuckle. "Well, I'm glad to know that you're paying attention."

"What did you say? I wasn't listening."

"I said, What better time to join together with your fellow classmates, Miranda, as we together we share these last few exciting weeks before we spread our wings and start making our mark on the big old world out there. Miranda, your contribution assures your place in a growing network—um, community, a growing community of dynamic, far-seeing Harvard graduates—"

"It goes into the computer if I don't give you anything, doesn't it?"

"Well, naturally we maintain records of our contributions."

"I thought so."

"You'll be interested to know, Miranda, that from Adams House alone we've already collected over four thousand dollars in pledges."

"If I don't contribute, does it mean I won't get *Harvard Magazine* for the rest of my life?"

"Pardon?"

"I read somewhere that all Harvard graduates get a lifetime subscription."

"Well, gee." Ed clears his throat. "I'm not really quite sure about that."

"I should have known there was a catch."

"Well, anyway, Miranda, just to start wrapping things up—"

"About time," I interrupt. "Listen, don't you think it's a little strange to be sitting in your room on a Saturday night making weird phone calls to people you don't even know?"

"Pardon me?"

"I mean, why aren't you out partying, like every other normal person? Isn't there a movie you wanted to see? Couldn't you find any parties to go to? Why do you have to bother *me?* Don't you have any *friends,* for god's sake?"

In the sudden hush I hear my radio playing the Beatles' version of "Roll Over, Beethoven."

"I see your point," Ed says mildly. "So why were you there to answer my call?"

"A lucky coincidence." I claw a hand through my hair. "Listen, put me down for a pledge of five thousand dollars."

"What?"

"Payable in fifty-dollar monthly installments, so long as I keep getting *Harvard Magazine.*"

"You're joking, aren't you?"

"Why would I be joking? Did you get that all down on your little computer printout there?"

"I—um—"

"Good. Ed, I've got to run. I'm on my way to the Spee Club's pajama party. You've heard of the Spee Club, haven't you?"

"Can you hold on a sec?" He's rattling papers again.

"Well, Ed, it's been nice talking with you."

"Um, just a minute—"

"Why don't you drop by Adams House sometime? We do let Winthrop people in from time to time."

"I, um— What?"

"Bye now. Have a good evening." I hang up and glare at the Matisse print.

The phone rings again, shrilling noisily in my hand. "Shut up," I snarl, jumping up and retreating to my room, where I kick aside the big garbage bag and stand in front of my bureau. The phone keeps on ringing. "I'll kill you," I scream, and then the phone is quiet. Savagely I rummage through my bureau drawers, finally emerging with a faded flannel nightgown patterned with tiny purple flowers.

"Gag me, Laura Ashley." I pitch the nightgown on top of the garbage bag.

The radio launches into the Beach Boys doing "Good Vibrations" and I glance at the clock. It's almost midnight. I shove my bureau drawers shut. Skipping the post-run shower, rapidly I disrobe and change into jeans and Jackson's t-shirt. I find a comb underneath some books and tease my hair to make it look even frowsier, and dash some black mascara onto my eyelashes and add a little to my eyebrows. My reflection in my Estée Lauder mirror looks wan and unfamiliar. I show my teeth in a ferocious smile, drop the mirror onto the garbage bag, and reach for my jacket, feeling sufficiently uninspired to leave off my customary dab of Paco Rabonne.

"Love your *pajamas*, Miranda."

"Sleep in your jeans, Miranda?"

"Huh?" I've been peering around the ice sculpture to watch Robbie and Adolfo feeding each other canapés from the buffet. The two of them are wrapped in filmy champagne-colored peignoirs, and when I peeked under the table a little while ago I could see their feet in high-heeled mules with fluffy little pompoms on the toes. Now I drag my gaze away and twist around to face Beatrice and Alicia. The scent of their leather nightshirts is a bit overpowering.

"It's a *pajama* party, Miranda."

"Don't they wear pajamas in California?"

"Or do you sleep in the nude?"

"We do."

"Goody for you." I wheel around to stand next to Walt, who's reaching for a grotesquely large stuffed mushroom. "Is that your third or your fourth?" I ask, watching out of the corner of my eye as Robbie bends forward over the table, his peignoir falling open to reveal a smooth muscular chest.

"Sixth, but who's counting." Walt's diction is somewhat blurred by the pâté sticking to the roof of his mouth, which he struggles to dislodge with his tongue. Finally he swallows, and whispers, "I saw you looking."

"What?" I feel myself starting to blush. "Yes, well, who

wouldn't gawk at a life-size ice sculpture of Napoleon Bonaparte?"

"Yes, isn't it fabulous?" Walt nods and plunges a Wheat Thin into a bowl of taco dip. "But why Napoleon for a pajama party?"

"Notorious insomniac."

"Oh, really? That's interesting."

"I thought everybody knew that." It seems as plausible an explanation as any, I congratulate myself, taking another sip of my drink.

"Well, you learn something new every day."

"That's Harvard for you." Although Robbie's leaning forward again, inspecting the grapes, I'm diverted by the sight of Walt chewing away on his Wheat Thin. He grins at me, displaying flawlessly white, even teeth.

" 'S good," he says. "I call it Wheat Thin Olé. Can I make you one?"

"No thanks."

"How about a Sweet 'n' Sour Triscuit?"

"I'll pass."

"You're missing out, Miranda."

"Don't remind me."

"Golly, what a spread here." Beaming, Walt surveys the vast white-draped table. "Let me tell you something, Miranda." He bends conspiratorially close. "There *is* a free lunch."

"Don't you mean to say free buffet?"

"Will you look at all this food? What a great party."

I swirl the ice around in my greyhound. "Yep."

"I've eaten at least sixty-three dollars' worth so far," he boasts. "With luck I should break a hundred tonight."

"Is that retail or wholesale prices?"

He pauses in the act of spearing a meatball. "Oh, gee."

"Have you accounted for staff wages? Transportation costs? Breakage? Trash pickup?"

"Hmm." Walt chews with slow small bites. Then, as he's swallowing, his brow clears and he reaches for another meatball. "Oh, what the heck. It's a party, isn't it? I'll just eat till I'm completely gorged and ready to puke."

"That's using your noggin."

"That way I can be sure."

"Better safe than sorry, I always say."

"That's what I say too."

"Great minds think alike."

A tall, severe-looking girl passes by us holding a bottle of Moët. Squinting, I notice that there's a toothbrush dangling from the back of her coiffure.

"Heck. Why the heck not. It's a party, right?" Walt flips a meatball into the air and catches it in his mouth.

"Two points," I say. "Now wipe your hands and let's dance."

"Dance?" His eyes widen in alarm. "What do you mean?"

"Like dance. Boogie, cut the rug, trip the light fantastic, shake a tail feather. Let's go."

"Sounds like fowl play to me." He snickers but his face remains set in an expression of obstinate dread.

"Very funny." I take hold of his arm. "Come on, your dance card's not filled yet, is it?"

"But seriously, Miranda." He doesn't budge. "I've got work to do in here."

"Please," I wheedle. "Just one dance."

"That's what they all say. One dance, and the next thing you know, wham! Heroin addiction."

Sighing, I release his arm. "You're so dedicated."

"You bet. Have some fondue?"

"I'd rather die." I finish my drink and set the glass on the table next to a plastic tableau of little white sheep jumping over a fence. "*Ciao*. And good luck."

"You too," he says, already engrossed in twirling bread cubes.

They're playing Bowie's "Fashion" in the ballroom, and as I head for the high arched doorway I run into Dean and Jennifer emerging from the coat check. "Well, hi!" I waggle my fingers at them. "Some party, huh?"

"Yeah," Dean mutters, looking embarrassed. He's wearing baggy flannel pajamas and a long droopy red nightcap. I look over at Jennifer, who floats alongside him in a ruffled flannel nightgown sprigged with wee curlicued violets. Her hair is rolled up in big pink curlers and her face is smeared with what appears to be cold cream.

"My," I say, "aren't you just the cutest couple."

Jennifer tucks her arm through Dean's. "We like to think so," she coos.

"Maybe you two'll win the prize for best costumes," I coo back, and as I pass by them I wink coarsely at Dan. "Nice slippers."

He looks even more discomfited, if such a thing is possible, and as I pass under the arch I glance over my shoulder, long enough to see him shake off her arm. Humming along with the music, I enter the ballroom.

The vast domed ceiling is draped in mosquito netting and the walls have been completely covered with dark-red bedsheets. As I look around it seems to me that the cumulative effect is less that of a cozy boudoir than of an overblown parody of a padded cell. Turning my attention to the dance floor I note that it's the usual riot of PJs and nightgowns, along with a goodly sprinkling of night-shirts, kimonos, and long underwear, as well as the occasional housecoat. A number of girls have opted for the ever-popular French-chambermaid couture and are decked out in corsets, garter belts, fishnet stockings, spike heels, and a few well-placed feathers. The most daring males, of course, sport only boxer shorts. So far, though, I haven't spotted a single outfit in here that can hold a candle to Robbie's diaphanous little ensemble. Yawning, I'm con-sidering decamping to the bar and then popping into the screening room to see if *Pillow Talk* has started yet, and am in the middle of a tremendous second yawn when somebody bumps into me, el-bowing me in the ribs and almost causing my jaws to lock in surprise.

"Jesus Christ." The Spee's Vice President hurries past, his thin-ning blond hair flapping loose over his forehead. He wears a red pillowcase that's been ripped open and pinned shut in more or less the appropriate places. "Why don't you watch where you're going?"

Scowling and feeling my lumbar region for kidney damage, I lower myself into a loveseat covered with what seems to be a bearskin. But even as I'm examining the fur, I suddenly catch sight of Tim threading his way toward me through the crowds on the dance floor. I ricochet to my feet and begin a headlong retreat to the kitchen, where I know there are two cavernous pantries and a fire escape. But before I've taken more than a few steps, I'm halted by an arm clasping my waist. *Oh shit.* Bristling, I turn to face my captor.

"Miranda," Gerard shouts into my ear. "Hi."

"Thank god," I shout back over the music. "Let's dance."

We plunge into the throng, everyone convulsing to "Turning Japanese," and I samba us toward what I hope is an inconspicuous corner. We end up next to the makeshift stage, an immense wooden platform that's flanked by a pair of gargantuan sleep masks, at least six feet long, that hang from the ceiling by oversized velvet cords.

Thus concealed, I'm doing a subdued little equine two-step and am kept busy trying to indicate to Gerard that we're finished with the samba routine and he can take his hands off my hips. He's flailing zestily about, his bathrobe flying open in an exuberant display of boxer shorts and thin hairy legs. Finally I peel his fingers off me and start swinging my hands defensively in time to the beat.

"Come on," he shouts. "Get down."

I ignore him and keep a wary eye on the mob. My sedate finger-snapping shuffle is getting hard to maintain. Richard Amidei. Where's Richard?

"Oh baby." Gerard does a spin and almost bangs his head into one of the giant sleep masks. Grinning, he advances toward me, wriggling his hips like a crazed incarnation of Elvis Presley *en déshabillé.*

"Calm down," I shriek, threatening him with a clenched fist which I shake at his nose.

He drops to the floor and clutches at my ankles, helpless with laughter. "Kick me, beat me," he chokes.

I roll my eyes at the mosquito netting. My gaze descends onto what I think is Jessica in the middle of the dance floor doing one of her favorite routines from "Solid Gold." Isn't that her rainbow sock I see swinging high in a vivacious squat-kick?

"Come on, kick me hard."

"Oh, shut up." I scowl at him, noticing with dismay that his boxer shorts have little red hearts all over them.

"Please. Don't spare me."

"Miriam." In a rush of black leather and cigarette smoke, Richard kisses me without pausing in his pointy-shoed strut toward the stage, a guitar slung over his shoulder.

"Richard." I grab for him, trying to disentangle my feet from Gerard's hysterical embrace. "Wait a minute."

Richard squeezes my hand, crushingly hard, and keeps moving. "Later, babydoll." His eyes shine like onyx, dominating his face with their lush fringe of black lashes. "After the show." Then he's disappeared behind the stage, his musicians in impenetrable tow behind him.

Gerard's fingers are creeping up my leg. "Get off," I scream at him, frantically scanning the crowd in search of Jessica. Batting Gerard away, I'm almost sure I've located her underneath the strobe light, dancing with somebody in fireman-red long johns, and I'm about to dive toward her when a giant teddy bear steps in front of me, blocking both my view and passage. "Jessie," I wail, and the teddy bear twists around to look at me. Cornered, I shrink back against the wall, nearly squashing Gerard who's now crouching on top of a stack of bedspreads.

"Do it again," he urges me, slyly.

"Hi, Miranda," the bear says, his round glassy eyes boring into me. Monstrously, his muzzle doesn't move as he speaks. "How's it going?"

Aghast, I sidestep Gerard and plant myself more staunchly against the wall.

"It's me," says the teddy bear. "Don't you remember?"

"Me who?" Gerard inquires helpfully, as I remain mute.

"Loomis. Rolf Loomis. Winthrop '82." He extends a scabrous-looking paw.

"Get away from me," I snarl. "I don't shake hands with stuffed animals."

"But Miranda." His furry shoulders sag. "Don't you remember me?"

"Aw, now you've gone and hurt his feelings." Gerard pinches my calf in reproof.

"Ouch. Cut it out, Gerard." Glowering, I twitch my leg at him.

The bear takes a timid step forward. "We lived in the same dorm freshman year. Remember?"

"To the best of my knowledge," I say coldly, "there were no bears admitted to the class of '82. Now get away from me."

"But I was three doors down from you."

Clapping a hand to my forehead, I roll my eyes up to the mosquito netting again. "Why am I standing here talking to a stuffed bear?"

"Why are you talking to the ceiling?" says Gerard.

"Don't you remember? We went to dinner together once," the bear, Loomis, persists, taking another step toward me.

"Don't come any closer." By now I've drawn myself up to my full height. "I've got an elephant gun on me, and I won't hesitate to use it."

"Adams House bitch," the bear growls, then turns on his moth-eaten heel and lumbers off in a huff.

"You old grouch," I call after him. "Go hibernate for a few years, why doncha."

The music stops, and I crouch down next to Gerard on the bedspreads, shaking my head. "A talking bear, for god's sake," I whisper. "What next?"

"Hello out there," a voice booms over the sound system. "Is this on?" A hideously amplified thumping and crackling ensues as the Spee Vice President taps the mike. "We-e-e-ell, I guess so." He chuckles, and I notice some people holding their hands over their ears. "Good evening, everybody, and welcome to our annual pajama party. I'm Allan Richards, and you're not." He grins and smooths his pillowcase over his hips.

"There's your answer," Gerard whispers back. "Can I borrow your elephant gun?"

"A funny thing happened on the way to the Spee," Allan Richards is saying. "A guy walks up to me on Mass Ave and wants to know if I'm the Ty-D-bol Man. So you know what I said to him?" Even at this distance I can see that Allan spits when he talks. "I said, 'The Ty-D-bol Man? Are you crazy? Do I *look* like Mr. Whipple?'"

Throwing his arms wide, Allan mugs at the audience, but the response is lukewarm. There are even a few catcalls. "We-e-e-ell, okay then. We'll try something a little more sophisticated this time, okay guys?" Allan flips his lank blond hair off his forehead. "Okay. How many surrealists does it take to screw in a light bulb?"

An awkward pause follows. Eventually somebody calls out: "Ninety-three?"

Coyly Allan shakes his head. "Come on, guys, we all go to Harvard. Strain your brains a little."

There's another dispirited silence, finally broken when somebody else speaks up. "Ninety-three."

And then rapidly, with gathering force:

"Thirty-nine."

"Proust."

"Rock lobster."

"Any way he wants to."

"Because he was dead."

"Silly rabbi, trids are for kicks."

"Oh, about ten inches."

"Where's the bathroom?"

"Does anybody have the notes from yesterday's Ec 10?"

"I lost my keys somewhere."

"Anybody want to buy some pot?"

"I thought this was the Advocate."

"Mommy."

"Ninety-three."

"Hey, Allan, your slip is showing."

"All right already," Allan barks into the microphone, causing several people to sway backward against the noise. Arms akimbo, he surveys us for a few moments, and sulkily brings his mouth up to the mike again. "Okay, here's the band." He starts to move away, and someone waves a pink camisole in the air.

"Wait," a male voice calls out. "What's the answer?"

Allan pauses, glaring through the hair that has fallen over his eyes. "Well, if you don't know," he says, spitting visibly, "then I'm not going to tell you. Will the goddam band please start already?" He stalks to the end of the stage and clambers off, hampered by his pillowcase.

The crowd groans, and the camisole is pitched onto the platform. "I really need to know," someone says. "Where's the goddam bathroom?"

All at once the lights go off, and we are held in teeming darkness for what seems like an eternity.

"Jesus Christ," the voice exclaims. "I'm sorry I asked."

In our shadowy little nook I can hear Gerard snickering next to me. Two large spotlights have been trained upon the sleep masks and now are gradually illuminating them in a ghostly pink wash of intensifying sheen, making them seem, horribly, to be growing. Suddenly there's a dazzling flash as a bank of hot yellow lights flood the stage, and then Richard's striding up to his microphone and adjusting his guitar over his shoulder. "Hi, we're White Bread," he says in his low, thrilling voice.

A couple of girls up front scream, and Richard grins in my direction, although it's hard to say for sure if he realizes that it's me he's smiling at past the glare of the lights. The other members of the band have scrambled up on stage and take their places, the rhythm guitarist snatching up the camisole and draping it around his neck with a loud whoop.

This provokes more screams from the girls in front, and then the band crashes into an ardent rendition of "Honky Tonk Women." The dance floor resumes its kaleidoscopic convulsions, once again all shimmying torsos and flapping bath-towels under the twirling silver strobe light. Frowning, I turn my eyes to the small bevy of fans standing inert, worshipful, in front of the stage. I'm watching them smile and cry out when Richard executes a particularly voluptuous rock-star move—plucking a low, wailing note on his guitar, his body arching backward in an impassioned torque of leather and spine—when Gerard nuzzles me with his prickly chin.

"Here." He thrusts a small plastic squeeze-bottle of Afrin at me. "Have some."

I take the bottle. "I didn't know you had a sinus problem."

"I don't."

"You have a cold?"

"No."

"So what's this for?" I look at him suspiciously. "Do I sound stuffed up?"

"Miranda." He's snuffling with laughter. "What do you think's in there?"

I look at the bottle, then at him. "This is a trick question, isn't it?"

"I'm afraid so." He takes the bottle and unscrews the top. "Two little squeezes, and no more sinus problems. Watch." When he's done he gives the bottle to me again. "Here's to your health."

"It's Geritol, right?" Slowly I'm bringing the bottle up to my face. "Just tell me it's Geritol."

"It's Geritol. Three out of four dentists recommend."

"For their patients who—" I interrupt myself to inhale once, twice in each nostril. Then I give him back his Afrin. "Hey, Gerard."

"What?"

"Want to hear the answer to the riddle?"

"You know it?"

"Of course."

"Well?"

"No, you've got to ask me the question first."

"Oh, all right. How many surrealists *does* it take to screw in a light bulb?"

"Apple." Triumphantly I fold my arms across my chest.

His brows contract. "Is that it?"

"Yes," I snap.

Then he starts laughing. He's still flapping his bare feet in gleeful mirth when "Honky Tonk Women" ends to loud applause. The girls up front are actually mewing and a small red heart-shaped pillow is tossed onto the stage. "Richie, I love you," one of the girls calls out. The rhythm guitarist grabs up the pillow and stuffs it down the front of his pants, and the girls scream even more shrilly. Leering hugely, he unwinds the camisole from around his neck and shoves it down his crotch, displaying the result with a raucous pelvic thrust.

The crowd cheers. Richard laughs and says in one of his casual half-amplified asides, "Anybody bring his cucumber?"

"Ninety-three," somebody yells.

The rhythm guitarist swaggers to the edge of the stage. "Wanna suck me off?" he asks the girl who's just called out to Richard.

"What?" She takes a step backward.

"Sixty-nine, sixty-nine," someone shouts.

"Sure, okay." He starts to divest himself of his guitar. "How about doggie style, huh?"

"Woof!" Gerard hollers. With a cry, the girl bobbles around and begins pushing her way back into the crowd.

Leaning back against the wall, I grin and follow her with my eyes. *Serves you right, you little tramp.*

The rhythm guitarist resettles his guitar strap over his shoulder. "How come I can never get a date?" he complains.

A cool, husky voice replies over the PA system. " 'Cause you're a loser, man." It's Lyndon, the bass guitarist, speaking in his usual dispassionate tones, his pale handsome face devoid of all apparent emotion.

"Oh yeah?" the rhythm guitarist sneers. "And what makes you so goddam special, punk?"

"My tact, dick-face."

"Why don't you just suck me off?"

"Can't," Lyndon replies lazily. "Forgot my magnifying glasses." He looks at the audience over the rims of his mirrored aviator sunglasses, the violet streaks in his white blond hair glinting brilliantly under the lights.

"Oh yeah?" The rhythm guitarist glares. "Well, fuck you, you goddam fag."

Unmoved, Lyndon pushes his sunglasses higher on the bridge of his nose with a long white forefinger. "The next song," he says, "is an original. Yeah, I know, they wanted us to play all covers tonight." He looks around, his hair glimmering. "But we figured you clowns would be so fucked up by now we could sneak in a couple of our own tunes without anybody really noticing."

There's some scattered hissing at this, but for the most part people maintain a respectful silence, awed as ever by Lyndon's elegant New Wave apathy, the psychedelic flashes of color in his towering Retro pompadour, the conspicuously nurtured stains on his heavy dark hobnailed boots. Lyndon responds to the hisses with a contemptuous little smile. "Hey, signs of life." He glances over at Richard. "Maybe we should do all originals tonight."

More hissing, with some bolder groaning and booing. "Fleetwood Mac," someone calls out.

"Rod Stewart."

"Abba."

"Eat shit, freaks." Delicately, Lyndon runs a hand up and over his hair. "Jesus, you guys are almost better than TV." He reaches into his inside jacket pocket, removes a pack of Marlboros, taps out a cigarette and puts it into his mouth. Then he pulls out a lighter, touches it to his cigarette, inhales, and slowly, slowly, exhales. "Okay, kids. We get the message." He pauses for another languid drag. "One teeny-weeny original and then we'll go back to your jerky little Top Forty tunes. Okey dokey?"

There is some tentative applause.

"Terrific." Lyndon exhales a tremendous blue cloud of smoke. "Richard wrote this one, and he really tried to make the lyrics meaningful." He sneers, ever so slightly. "So the least you pinheads could do is pay attention."

More applause as Richard steps up to his microphone. "I wrote this song for a friend of mine," he says softly. "It's sort of a ballad."

The girls near the edge of the stage are moaning. From way in back somebody calls out: "I love you, Richie." My mouth tightens, and next to me Gerard twitches restlessly.

"Miranda, I'm thirsty. Let's go get a drink."

"In a minute." Absently I pat his knee. "I want to hear this song." My eyes are fixed upon the stage, which is now immersed in a faint bluish light that deepens into a bright rich aquamarine as the guitars begin, played neither fast nor slow, weaving a melody that seems at once melancholy and curiously elusive as the long, undulating notes keep slipping away, and disappearing into the momentum of the song itself.

Richard lifts his head and begins to sing.

> *Queen of woe*
> *Never lets go, never lets go*
> *Finding things that ain't lost*
> *Opening doors that ain't closed*
> *Sailing an ocean weeping*
> *Pretty queen*
> *Can you afford the cost*

Gerard jostles me in the strange, misty turquoise light. "This song is depressing me. Can we go?"

"In a minute." I'm gazing at Richard as if I've never seen him before. *Blue like the sky* . . .

Lyndon adds his flat, honeyed voice to the next verse.

Miranda blue
Lunar smile, crystal eyes
Can I see you, can I see you
You're lost, lone mermaid going higher
Lost in cool hearts
Cool hearts and sapphire

"Hey," Gerard whispers. "It's about somebody with your name."

"Imagine that," I say through dry lips. I sit frozen through another verse of Richard and Lyndon's mournful harmonizing, wincing in the painfully bright blue light. Finally, as I latch onto Richard's voice singing "Can you freshen a notion, reverse the automatic," I seize Gerard's hand. "How about that drink?"

We slip along the edge of the crowd. My heart is pounding, and glassily I stare at Gerard's pattering feet in front of me. When a big hairy arm blocks my passage, I release Gerard's hand and look up at Loomis the bear standing in front of me, a permanent smirk on his hoary muzzle.

"Ahoy there," he greets me, a paw jauntily resting where his waist might be. "Want to dance, *Miranda?*"

Numbly I reply with the first thing that comes to mind. "Suck me off, fuzzy-face."

"I beg your pardon?" He strains closer, and I utter a little panicky cry, feeling my knees start to tremble. Just then Gerard reaches around Loomis and takes me by the wrist, maneuvering me around the bear's paunchy middle. "She said," Gerard tells him genially, "to shove a beehive up your ass."

"Fuzzy-face," I prompt in a grateful mumble.

"Fuzzy-face." Gerard starts leading me away.

Loomis the bear stands there befuddled, scratching his armpit with a long-nailed claw. All at once I notice that he's wearing a pair of big, scuffed-up saddle shoes, one of which is unlaced. The skinny white shoelace dangles onto the polished wood floor.

"Hey, you old fleabag," I scream. "Tie your shoe. Don't you know you could get into an accident that way?"

After swiping a small pitcher of martinis from the bar we sneak into the kitchen, which is mercifully dark, and huddle in a corner next to the food processors, launching into our martinis with two shots apiece.

"Yuck. Too much vermouth," Gerard complains, and wipes his mouth with the back of his hand. He looks up and his eyes bulge. "Check it out, Miranda!" he whispers, nudging me. "Look at 'em go!"

"Huh?" I look around. The kitchen, as I knew it would be, is filled with couples twined in various postures of amorous entanglement. I shrug in the shadowy dimness and look down at my Dixie cup. "Just pitching woo."

"Is that what you call it? Jesus, look at those two over there on the butcher block."

"No."

"Oh, come on. It's like being at the movies." He nudges me again. "Look, she's unbuttoning his shirt with one hand."

"So what." I pour myself a refill.

"Oh, come on, Miranda. Lighten up, will you?"

"Don't call me Miranda."

"It's your name, isn't it?"

"I want a new one." I bolt down the contents of my Dixie cup in one swallow.

"What do you mean, you want a new one?" He turns to stare at me.

"I mean I want a new one."

"Terrific. So what should I call you then?"

"You go to Harvard. You come up with something."

"Oh, Jesus. This is supposed to be my day off." He screws up his face and thoughtfully eyes first the hanging copper pots, then the butcher block. "Wait. I think I'm on to something here."

"Well?"

"Roberta."

"Gross."

"Oh, come on. Why not?" He takes the olive from his cup and pops it into his mouth. "It's got dignity, substance, *My Ántonia* charm."

"Oh, I'm *sure*." With a scornful twist of my hand I flick a strand of hair off my shoulder.

"Wait. How about Ruth? Dignity, substance, *My Ántonia* charm."

"No way, dude."

"Miranda, will you cut the Valley Girl stuff? It's bumming me out."

"Don't call me Miranda." I grip his arm with soggy insistence.

"Ow. You're hurting me."

"Sorry." I let go, simpering. "Guess I don't know my own strength, huh?"

"It's okay. I mean, normally I'd be into it and all—"

"How about Tanya?"

"Sounds like country-Western Chekhov, if you ask me." He fills our cups and meticulously drops an olive into each.

"I guess you're right. Well, how about a nice androgynous name?"

"Better safe than sorry." He gives a rubber-necked nod of agreement. "Especially in these trying times."

"Okay then." I think hard for a moment. "Terry, Sandy, Robin, Bobby, Sue—"

"Sue. I love it." He raises his cup. "Cheers, Sue. To the new you."

"Cheers." I take a large sloppy gulp. "God, it's great to be alive, isn't it?"

"Sue?" Gerard says, tenderly.

"Yes?" I beam at him.

"Can I have your olive?"

"Of course." I hold out my cup. "I hate olives."

"Thanks, Sue." He plucks out the olive and swallows it with a little smacking noise. "Hey!" He's goggling over my shoulder. "Looks like she's about to go down on him now."

"Please don't tell me about it."

"Look, she's pushing up his pajama top. She's putting her tongue in his belly button—"

"Will you shut up?"

"And now he's putting his hands on her head—"

"I said shut up."

There is a silence, during which I sullenly listen to Gerard's rapid breathing next to me.

"Sue?"

"What."

"Someone's staring at you."

I lift my head from my drink. "What?"

"I thought you'd want to know."

"Know what? What did you say?"

"I said, someone's staring at you."

"What?" I straighten up in alarm. "Who is it?"

"Oh wow. She's down to his left hipbone."

"Gerard," I whisper. "Gerard."

"That's my name, don't wear it out." He snickers. "Ow! Why are you pinching me, Sue?"

"Who's staring at me?"

"Oh, some Malibu Ken type. He's standing in the doorway making puppy-dog eyes at you."

"Wavy brown hair? Little snub nose with freckles on it?"

"Well, I can't tell about the freckles from here—"

"Is it him?" I hiss.

"Yep. Friend of yours?"

"Is he coming any closer?"

"Well, he's sort of inching his way along." Gerard sips at his drink. "He keeps bumping into people and pissing them off."

"Oh, fuck." I finish my martini and then take a big swallow of Gerard's, feeling a bemused smile curving my lips. "Oh, fuck."

"Sorry?" Gerard crooks his head politely. "I couldn't hear you, Sue. You were talking into your Dixie cup."

"Oh, fuck." I turn and wind my arms around his neck. "Kiss me," I whisper, still smiling giddily.

"What?" He stares back at me wide-eyed.

"Put your arms around me, dope." I start nibbling on his upper lip, and before I know it we're hardly distinguishable from any other couple in the kitchen. Somewhat to my surprise Gerard isn't half bad at this, although when he blows in my ear I giggle and draw my face back a few inches. "Tickles."

Gerard loosens his embrace. "It's okay. He's gone now."

"What? Who?"

"Malibu Ken."

"What about him?"

"He stole two drinks on his way out, too."

"So?"

"It's a very bad thing, Sue, mixing your liquors."

I nestle closer. "Kiss me again, olive-breath."

"Who was he?"

"Oh, some guy I slept with one time. Now he won't leave me alone."

"Oh, that's Tim Lazare?"

Confusedly I lean back. "How the hell would you know?"

"Do you want me to let go of you now?"

"Oh," I say, trying to think, "don't bother."

"Whatever you say, Sue." He starts kissing my neck again.

"Mmm." As I'm wilting into Gerard's warm nappy clasp, my senses feel oddly warm and distorted. I find myself listening to the couple next to us, their voices unfolding in the semidarkness with a razorlike clarity.

"But what's the point of having birth-control pills," he's saying, "if you keep forgetting to take them?"

"Oh, don't be such a spoilsport," she says in a high-pitched singsong that's already getting on my nerves. "Just because I forget to take one now and again—"

"Every other day, Mandy?"

Mandy? I twitch in Gerard's arms and try to turn my head without his noticing.

"I know I'm a bit forgetful, but I don't see why you have to jump down my throat about it."

"It just seems rather pointless, that's all."

"You're the one who refused to wear a—"

"We chose the most mature method of—"

"And my mother keeps asking when we're going to get—"

"Two years of business school—"

She gives a little scream. "Will you look at those two on the butcher block?"

Gerard abandons my neck and whistles admiringly as he cranes over my shoulder. "Sue, look at this. It's better than anything I've ever seen on 'Wild Kingdom.' "

"I really don't want to know."

"They must be on the gymnastics team."

"Jeff," the girl next to us is saying, "I think we should call the police."

"Shake and bake!" somebody over by the microwave calls out.

"Jeff? Are you listening to me? I said—"

"I heard you. I was just trying to figure out how we could—"

"Jeff!"

"That's my name, don't wear it out. Ow!" he cries. "Why'd you pinch me?"

"I didn't pinch you."

I can feel Gerard shaking with silent laughter. "Come on," I whisper, twisting out of his arms. "Let's go."

"Sure, okay." He wipes his eyes. "Where to, Sue?"

"I don't know. Let's dance or something."

"Aren't you the sudden bundle of energy." He trails me out of the kitchen, still snuffling with little bouts of laughter. "Isn't Afrin just the next best thing to being there?"

"Almost."

Richard's band has begun a second set and is churning out "Heart of Glass," with Lyndon, now wearing two pairs of sunglasses, singing in deadpan falsetto. Gerard starts doing his favorite routines from West Side Story, paying minimal attention to the rapid-fire beat of the song. Gamely I try to keep up with him but my stomach is doing a better job than the rest of me, quivering and churning right along with Gerard's ebullient convolutions. Finally I give up and tug at his sleeve.

"Gerard." Suddenly I realize I'm sticky with a chilly film of sweat. "Gerard."

He's singing aloud to himself. *"When you're a Jet, you're a Jet . . ."*

"Gerard."

"Yes, Sue?" he shouts.

I notice that I've ripped his shoulder seam a little. "I'm going to the ladies' room."

"Aw, now?" He's glowing and pink, the very picture of healthy exertion. "I haven't done my Officer Krupke imitation yet."

"Yes. Now." I swallow. "You can stay if you want."

"You sure?"

"Sure I'm sure."

"Well, come back when you're done powdering your nose."

"Sure." I turn and weave my way out of the ballroom and up the big marble staircase. When I reach the top I pause for a moment, dizzily clutching the railing. Staring down at the floor, I find myself eavesdropping on the people milling past.

"Where's the bathroom?"

"Have you seen my date?"

"I hear there's a talent scout from Columbia Records here tonight."

"Got a joint?"

"Kind of a dull party this year, don't you think?"

"That dinky buffet. A hummingbird would've starved."

"Yeah, did you try those meatballs? I almost barfed."

"Let's go to the Advo."

"Forget it. We just came from there. It's packed."

"Couldn't move."

"Couldn't breathe."

"Great. Let's go."

I look up and tilt my head, listening to Richard's strong silvery voice singing "Watching the Detective." I stand there holding on to the railing for a little while longer, and then I smooth my t-shirt over my abdomen, run a hand through my hair, and start down the steps for the door.

There's a small crowd outside the Advocate, and as I'm edging forward I gape at Gino Larici planted with a hand firmly on the doorknob. "No, sorry," he's telling someone. "I can't let you in without an invite."

"An invite?" echoes the person on my left, incredulously. "Since when do you need an invite to get into an Advocate party?"

Gino shrugs, his small jagged features set in an expression of pious implacability. "New policy." His free hand creeps up to the collar of his leather jacket, turning it up more stiffly against his neck. "Like New York."

"Hey, Gino," my neighbor says. "Remember me?"

Gino's eyes are fixed upon a point some inches above my head.

"Rules is rules," he says, and suddenly I remember hearing about his recent election to the poetry board. "You want me to break a rule just because you're my roommate?"

An almond-eyed Eurofag wearing black penny-loafers pushes his way to the front. "Hey, Gino. Great jacket."

"Yeah." His gaze flickering almost imperceptibly, Gino opens the door a few inches. "Have a nice time."

As the Eurofag nimbly scoots in under Gino's leather-encased arm, Gino's roommate lets out an outraged puff of air. "You're a douchebag, Larici. A pus-filled, roach-infested douchebag."

"Now, now." Gino shuts the door and curls his fingers around the knob again. "There are ladies present." His eyes rest for a moment upon me, and without thinking I step forward.

"Hi, Gino," I say, trying to smile. Upstairs they're playing Lou Reed's "Sweet Jane" so loud I can feel it vibrating in my sternum. "How's everything?"

"Great." Gino appears to be studying my feet.

"Aren't these great sneakers?"

"Yeah."

"They're Keds." Twisting on one foot, I show him the label on the heel. "Classic Keds."

"Great."

"Say, Gino."

"Yeah."

"Mind if I come in?"

Gino doesn't raise his eyes. "Got an invite?"

"An invite?" My breath hisses in my throat. "Gino, I was dancing on the goddam Advocate mantelpiece while you were still in Riverdale prepping for your SATs and waiting for your voice to change."

"So?"

"Look, Gino." I take another step forward. "I have to find somebody. Then I'll come right back down again. Okey dokey?"

"Yeah, sure." He doesn't move a muscle. "That's what they all say."

"Gino baby!" Three strong-featured brunettes, all wearing swirling dark skirts and little tasseled half-boots, come shouldering their way up the steps, laughing and breathless.

"Sweetheart."

"Angelface."

"Sugarlips."

"Dunster House sluts," Gino's roommate jeers as the girls disappear inside, their heels clicking smartly on the doorstep. "This is it, Larici. Now you've finally pissed me off."

Gino shrugs again. "Life is tough."

"I mean it. I'm really starting to get angry with you."

"What do you want, Gino?" I blurt. Abstractedly I note that I am trembling a little. "Am I supposed to offer you money? Should I beg? Go down on my knees and plead? Is that it?"

"No tickee, no dancee."

"You douchebag." My voice is shaking. "You're a slime-covered, disease-ridden scumball."

"Don't forget the roaches," Gino's roommate encourages from the sidelines. "Toss in a reference to dog shit, maybe."

"Dog shit?" Now I turn my accusatory glance upon him. "If he's such a creep, why'd you room with him then?"

Gino's roommate looks surprised, and lifts his shoulders in a shrug. "I made a mistake."

"What?" I stare at him for a moment, and to my horror I feel my eyes begin to fill with tears. I'm about to start batting my way through the little knot of people lining the steps when a voice calls out above the music: "Miranda! Yoo hoo!" Pausing, I flash a look at Gino inert at his post, where apparently he's contemplating the stars above Kirkland House. As I'm taking another blurry-eyed pace forward, the voice calls out: "Miranda! Up here!"

Finally I look up. Rod, the *Advocate*'s managing editor, is dangling half his body out over the windowsill as he beams hospitably down upon me. "Did you have fun tonight?" he calls, his tortoise-rimmed spectacles flashing in the moonlight.

"No."

"Why not?" he cries, astonished.

"I haven't even been inside yet."

"Well, come on in, silly."

"I can't."

"Why not?"

"Because Gino won't let me in."

"What?"

We both look over at Gino, who now appears to be pondering his own shoes, and then Rod screams: "Let her in, enema-face!"

His features impassive, Gino looks up at Rod. "She doesn't have an invite."

"You half-wit overdressed turd!" Rod screams. "Let her in!"

"No problem."

"Rod?" I call up.

"Yes, Miranda?" He's smiling solicitously, now teetering by his hips from the window. "What can I do for you?"

"Can Gino's roommate come in too?"

"Does he have an invite?"

"No."

"I'm afraid not, Miranda. You know the rules."

The knot in my stomach is getting worse. "Never mind then."

"What?"

"If he can't come in, I'm not coming in either."

"But Miranda," Rod cries, swaying. "I just told that rancid sleazebag down there to let you in."

"Too bad." I turn away.

"Oh, all right!" Rod screams. "Let 'em both in, latrine-head!"

"Thanks, Rod," I call up. "You're a brick."

"Anything for you, sweetheart." Rod disappears from the window.

"Thanks a lot." Gino's roommate has come trotting up the steps, smiling at me. "I really appreciate this. I really do."

"Don't mention it."

"I really do appreciate this."

"Let's go on in."

"Thanks a lot. Really."

"After you."

We squeeze inside—Gino refuses to open the door more than a scant foot wide—and then Gino's roommate grabs my hand and shakes it vigorously.

"Thanks a lot. It's really nice of you." With a last radiant glance, he turns and plunges down the narrow, crowded hallway and vanishes left and up the stairs. Since I'm moving less adroitly in his wake, it takes me a while to shove my way through the crush, dodging cigarettes and beer bottles being waved about. Finally I make it up and around the last stretch of steps and am thrust roughly into the main room, where it's dark and noisy and over-heated and jammed with people dancing to the Monkees' "Last Train to Clarksville." I cram myself into a spot against the wall, squeezing close to a slight, scared-looking kid who retreats even more deeply into his oversized jacket. Over on the mantel ledge there's Rod doing the Twist with—I squint incredulously—yes, Molly, in her black polka-dotted miniskirt. I look across the room, and there on the oak table is Gerard, still in his bathrobe, flapping his arms to the beat and grinning at nobody in particular. My stomach gives a little churn, and I shut my eyes. The Monkees trail off, and now it's the familiar opening notes to "Wild Horses."

"Excuse me."

Warily I open my eyes. It's my neighbor, the skinny kid. I blink at him. "What."

"Sorry to bother you." We're lodged so closely together that he doesn't have to raise his voice much above a whisper. "Do you want to dance?"

He looks so miserable that I'm not even tempted to smile. "Uh, do I know you?"

"Well, no." Nervously he brushes a lock of dark hair off his brow. "But my girlfriend's dancing with somebody else, so I thought I'd ask you."

"Kid," I say, "they're playing a slow song. You just don't ask a total stranger to dance with you to a slow song."

"I know." He swallows. "But you seem like a nice person."

"What?" I look harder at him. "Oh, no. Don't tell me. This isn't your first Advocate party, is it?"

"I'm sorry," he whispers.

"It's not your fault, kid. Look, what's your name?"

"Victor."

"Victor, tell me a little something about your girlfriend."

"Well, let's see. She's a champion gymnast and she speaks four languages fluently. She plans to study international politics and—"

"Just the facts, Victor."

"She listed Adams House as her first choice in the housing lottery."

"Say no more." I lower my face right up close to his. "If I were you, I'd dump that bimbo and find myself a nice social-studies major from Mather House."

"Okay," he agrees. "Now will you dance with me?"

My stomach cramps and I give a little moan, closing my eyes again.

"I'm sorry," Victor says anxiously into my ear. "I didn't mean to be so pushy."

"It's okay." I keep my eyes shut. "Aggressive guys overwhelm me a little, that's all."

"Really?" He sounds pleased.

Mick Jagger's caterwauling soulfully over the sound system, his ragged, sensual voice suffusing the room. Dimly I wonder how many times I've heard this tape before.

"Miranda." Now somebody's whispering into my other ear.

"What," I mumble, not opening my eyes.

"Will you dance with me?"

At this my eyes start open. It's Dean, standing so close that his belt buckle presses against my hip. "Hi there," he says, smiling.

"Hi."

"Fancy meeting you here."

"Small world, isn't it?"

"You're admiring my shirt, aren't you?"

"Not really. I liked your pajamas better." I pinch myself closer against the wall.

"Did you?" He's still smiling. "Personally, I thought it was time for a change." His breath, warm and limpid, brushes over my face. He reeks of Scotch. "Let's dance, baby." He takes me by the wrists and draws me into the swaying press of dancers, his arms sliding around me as he begins to undulate us back and forth in a tiny seesawing shuffle, slowly circumnavigating an area the size of a large coffee filter.

I'm so taken aback that I allow myself to be thus oscillated for several shambling rounds before I finally address the side of his head which he has so intimately nestled against my jaw. "Hey."

"Hey what."

"I don't mean to be pushy, but—"

"You? Never." His embrace tightens.

"—but is Jennifer around, by any chance?"

"She went home."

"Ah."

"She wasn't feeling well."

"I'm sorry to hear that."

"Me too." His fingers are gently massaging my rib cage.

"When the cat's away."

"Yep." He laughs breathily into my neck.

I'm about to ask him to stop mauling my scapula when suddenly I sense that I'm being watched. I lift my head from Dean's shoulder to meet the bright unwavering gaze of Alicia, who holds Beatrice in a possessive grip as they gyrate together in the semidarkness. Pouting her mouth at me in a silent smiling kiss, Alicia runs the tip of her tongue over her upper lip.

I stare blankly at her for a moment, and as our respective convolutions rotate us apart I look up from an enthusiastic little dip on Dean's part to see Jackson and Stephanie over by the fireplace. Her arms are clasped around his neck and he is kissing her, her throat a pale arch meeting the bended curve of his head.

Wait. What's wrong with this picture. She must be standing on tiptoe, I reason dully, or is perhaps wearing high-heeled shoes. Dean starts nuzzling my neck as we lurch about, and twitching my head I catch sight of Gerard up on the oak table, dancing with a huge inflated plastic shark, which he is clutching familiarly just underneath the fin.

Mick Jagger finally fades away but Dean still holds me to him as the guitars to "Walk This Way" begin. People unglue themselves from each other and commence their solitary jiggling and writhing about. I struggle to lean away. "Hey."

"Hay is for horses." He gives me a flirtatious little squeeze. "Let's get a drink." He takes my hand and is hauling me toward the bar when all at once I feel a warm dampness in the back of my jeans.

"Goddam it." I stop, so abruptly that Dean, still grasping my hand, executes a loose-limbed boomerang that brings him swirling up close to me again.

"What's up?" He's still listing avidly toward the bar.

"Somebody spilled a drink down my back."

"Well, it's too late to cry about it now." He tugs at me. "Come on, let's get over there before they run out of booze."

"I'm going to look at myself in the mirror downstairs."

"Vanity, vanity." Fondly he clicks his tongue at me. "Go on then. I'll try to save you a cup."

"Thanks loads." I snatch my hand away, and without a second glance I set off, using my elbows for leverage. Dourly I keep my gaze fastened on the floorboards as I thread my way downstairs, where I find that the door to the bathroom is locked. I lean against the wall, listening to three contralto female voices talking inside.

"—and then I said, 'I can't believe you've never read Emily Dickinson'—"

"—lobbying for a theme issue devoted to Lapp authors—"

"—'You mean Angie?' he says to me—"

"—not a single uppercase letter in the entire—"

"—of the nineteenth-century resistance movement—"

"—I mean, how on earth did he get into Harvard?"

"—manuscript. 'This is *not* poetry,' I told them—"

"—and he starts telling me he knows William Dean Howells personally—"

"—*female* nineteenth-century Lapp authors—"

"Hey, girls." I pound on the door. "You're boring the hell out of me. Get out already."

The voices skid into silence. After a brief interval the door is unlocked and thrown open, and storming out in an eddy of dark skirts and tasseled boots is the big-nosed trio from Dunster House.

One of the girls rams a shoulder at me as she bowls past. "How did you get in, anyway?"

"Ow. What?"

"Into the Advocate, I mean."

One of the other girls taps my arm. "Did you have to bribe Gino, honey?"

I frown at her. "What did you say?"

"I didn't know he liked older women."

"Does she go to Harvard, d'you think? I haven't seen her around before."

"D'you like her haircut?"

"Her mascara's running."

"I wonder how much she paid Gino?"

"Dunster House sluts!" I scream, careening into the bathroom and turning the lock. Breathlessly I slope against the door, watching the mottled, water-stained ceiling throbbing from the tumult of dancers above. Then as I stare open-mouthed into the mirror it takes me a while before I realize that the pale, wild-haired girl I'm eyeing so suspiciously is actually my own reflection.

Somebody knocks on the door. "Just a minute," I say, twisting around trying to get a look at my behind in the mirror. It doesn't work. The most I can see is a painfully hunched shoulder blade. Grumbling, I go into the stall and unzip my jeans. The knocking on the door continues, more forcefully. "Okay, okay," I say irritably, and it's then that I discover that I've started my period.

Biting my lip, I peep out of the stall and nod. No more paper towels. I improvise a flimsy little pad out of toilet paper, maliciously pleased to be using up the last of the roll, zip up my jeans, and emerge from the stall. Meanwhile, the rapping on the door has become still more insistent, and now I can hear someone saying, "Candygram. Special delivery. Candygram."

I unlock the door and open it a crack. Instantly a huge soft bluish thing plunges at me and I'm mashed up against the mirror, face to face with a giant grinning mouth bristling with sharp white teeth. I let out a little bleat of horror.

Next I hear laughter, and slowly my assailant pulls away. Then as I wilt against the basin wheezing softly I see Gerard standing in the doorway with his arms around the plastic shark, both of them rocking with mirth.

"Land shark, Miranda." Gerard giggles. "Land shark."

I straighten up. "You know, Gerard," I say, brushing a strand of hair from my forehead, "sometimes you really get on my nerves." Head held high, I sweep past the two of them and march to the door, which Gino opens wide for me.

"Leaving so soon?" he says affably.

"I'm afraid so." I pause on the steps. "I didn't find the person I was looking for."

"Oh, really? Who is it? If he's in there, I would've seen him come in."

"Yeah?"

"Of course. I'm the doorman. Nobody gets in without my okay first."

"Right."

"So who were you looking for?"

"I was—I was—oh, mind your own beeswax."

"Listen." Gino comes so close that I can't even smell his leather jacket over the scent of hair pomade. "Can I tell you something?"

"What."

"I'm really sorry."

"About what." I'm trying desperately to keep my lips from quivering.

"About not letting you in tonight. I didn't know."

"Know what."

He leans even closer. "About you and Jackson."

I tilt backward. "What about us?"

"I didn't know the whole story. I'm really sorry."

"Great," I snap. "At least one of us does." And then, before I can turn away quickly enough, two large tears slide down my face.

"I'm really sorry, Miranda," Gino calls after me. "Anytime you want in at the Advo, honey, you just come to me. I'll take care of you."

"Bryan? I didn't wake you up, did I?"

He grunts. "Just a minute." There's the sound of a lamp being switched on. "What's wrong?"

"Oh god. You were asleep, weren't you?"

"It's three o'clock in the morning. Why would I be asleep?"

"Oh god. I'm sorry. I'll call you tomorrow."

"If you hang up on me now I'll kill you. What's wrong?"

"I can't sleep."

"Jackson?"

"Yes."

"What happened?"

"We ended up sitting at the same table at dinner tonight."

"And?"

"We talked about the weather."

"Jesus."

"I didn't have much fun."

"I'll bet you didn't."

"And when we started comparing the weather this winter with the weather from last winter I spilled my coffee all over the table."

"Spill any on him?"

"No, he wasn't sitting close enough."

"That's too bad."

"That's what I thought too." My voice trembles.

"Then what happened?"

"I made a joke about crying over spilled milk and got up."

He sighs. "That's my girl."

"And then Anthony comes running over and wants to know why I don't want to go out with him. Like I want to discuss this standing next to the salad bar."

"Right."

"Then Master Ackerman sashays over to congratulate me on winning the Boylston Prize, puts his arm around me, and exhales baked scrod all over my hair while he's telling Anthony how proud he is that Adams House got me."

"Badly put."

"Yeah. And then his wife comes along and starts telling us all about little Jim's latest bout of diarrhea, looking at me like it's my goddam fault the kid's got problems with his lower—"

"I get the picture."

"Exactly. And then Gerard walks by with his little sister, who's visiting for the weekend."

"Great."

"He says something to her and they both wave at me."

"Oh lord."

"Bryan, she's five feet tall and she was wearing pink pants, pink shoes, and a pink blouse."

"What color were her socks?"

"Guess."

"No thanks. So what did you end up doing?"

"After I peeled Master Ackerman off me? And outran Anthony? I went to the Widener stacks till closing time. Then I came back here and I've been doing some reading. And how was your day?"

"Never mind. Look, I want you to get some sleep. Will you try closing your eyes and just not thinking about all this?"

"Got any Valium?"

"Forget it. Get into bed and start thinking about ways we can get into the black-tie party at the Fogg this weekend."

"I could do that."

"I'm counting on you. So brush your teeth and get under the covers, okay?"

"Okay."

"Good. And call me back if you still can't sleep."

"Really?"

"Yes. You want to have dinner tomorrow?"

"Can I come up to North House?"

"Yes."

"Okay. Good night, Bry."

"Night."

"Thanks."

"Don't mention it. See you tomorrow." We hang up.

The streets are cool and still. Slipping along Mount Auburn Street, my sneakers silent on the pavement, I realize I need to blow my nose. By the time I draw near the Lampoon, I'm soppy enough to pull up the neck of my t-shirt and use it to wipe my nose.

"Ooh, disgusting!" somebody yells from the Lampoon turret.

I look up and there's Teddy Anson leaning on the ironwork balustrade, grinning and wiggling his fingers at me. He's wearing a big gray Yale Crew sweatshirt, and a Red Sox cap tilts rakishly low over his brow. "Hi, Miranda," he calls down. "What's wrong with your nose?"

"Hay fever," I reply sourly.

"You poor thing. Hey, I finally got my mother a birthday present."

He's looking at me with such bright-faced expectancy that reluctantly I yield. "Yeah, what?"

"A vacuum cleaner."

"What?"

"Yeah, a mondo deluxe Hoover."

"You're joking, right?"

"No, of course not," he answers, sounding hurt. "Why would I joke about a thing like that?"

"Why would you buy your mother a vacuum cleaner for her birthday?" I wipe my nose again, this time using the back of my hand.

"Ooh, gross me out."

"Doesn't the poor woman already have a vacuum cleaner, for god's sake?"

"Yes, but the Coop had a sale on Hoovers."

"I see."

"So I charged the biggest one I could find and had them gift-wrap it and ship it out to her."

"Why didn't you just use Federal Express?" I say disagreeably.

"My folks don't have a charge account with them."

"Good thinking." I nod up at him. "I'll bet Federal Express doesn't gift-wrap either."

Teddy doubles over with a loud whoop of laughter. "Hay fever!" he cries, slapping the balustrade. "Oh god, Miranda. You slay me."

Tapping my foot, I wait for the chuckling to subside. "Well, Teddy, I'm afraid my nose and I have got to be running along now." I flap my fingers at him and turn away.

"Wait!"

I halt. "What."

"Why don't you buzz on up? We're just starting our Helen Reddy retrospective."

"No thanks." I haven't taken more than two paces when Teddy calls out again.

"Wait!"

"What, for god's sake?"

"You haven't called me Theodore once tonight." He leans over the balustrade to peer down at me. "What's wrong?"

"Mind your own beeswax." I turn away.

"That's okay," he cries. "It happens to the best of us." He says something else too, but I can't make it out over the rising strains of "Ain't No Way to Treat a Lady" pouring out from the second floor.

I cross Plympton Street, and as I'm going down the stone steps to Adams House I spot the pear-shaped junior ahead of me, opening the door. "Hey, wait up," I blurt, rushing to catch the door before he lets it swing shut behind him. I grab it just in time and squirm inside, bearing down on him by the C-entry mailboxes. "Hey," I say, tapping him on the shoulder.

He jerks around with such a look of dread upon his wan doughy face that automatically I recoil too. "Oh, sorry. Did I frighten you?"

He just looks at me, gripping his books to his chest, and in the silence I find myself noticing that the color and texture of his skin reminds me, strangely enough, of a plucked chicken.

"Hey." I try to smile. "My name's Miranda. What's yours?"

His back straining against the mailboxes, he seems to be willing himself to disappear behind his massive armful of books. His pale eyes dart erratically in their sockets.

"I said, my name's Miranda. Who are you?"

At last he garbles something in a thin asthmatic tremor. "Mahnmzlrzn."

"Pardon?" Leaning forward, I cup a hand to my ear. "What did you say?"

He looks ready to crawl into one of the mailboxes. "Ahsd, mahnmzlrzn."

"Oh. *Larson*." I break into a toothy smile of relief, and my nose starts running again. "That's some Southern drawl you have there."

"Ahmntsuthn."

"Oh, really?" I give a loud sniff. "Then why's your face so red all of a sudden? Looks to me like you're blushing."

"Izmallrgeez." His eyes are skittering wildly.

"What? You have hay fever?" I exclaim. "Say, you wouldn't happen to have a Kleenex I could borrow, would you?"

Drawing a long sibilant breath, he hoists his books a little higher on his chest. "No," he says, very distinctly. "Ah don't. Now y'all leave me alone." Then he lunges past me and scuttles across the corridor into the men's room, locking the door behind him.

Leaning against the mailboxes, I use my t-shirt again to wipe my nose. Then I pick at my cuticles for a little while, yawning. "Hey, Larson."

Tomb-like silence from the men's room.

"Aw, come on out. I won't bite you, I promise."

Nothing.

"Come on, don't be such a stick in the mud."

Still nothing.

With a sudden flash of resentment I find myself wishing I had Gerard's shark right now. *Candygram. Special delivery.* "All right then. Be that way."

Nothing.

"It's no skin off my nose, pal." I sniff again, even more loudly. "But how do you ever expect to make any friends if you're going to be such a loner?"

Then I slink off, without so much as a simple *Ciao* to give him fair warning that I'm gone. *When the cat's away . . .*

As I trudge up the C-entry stairs, I'm wondering if poor pear-shaped Larson will end up spending the night in the men's room, staring bleakly into the mirror or perhaps even doing some reading from one or another of his textbooks. Still, there are worse fates, I tell myself philosophically, and then I realize with an abrupt little jolt that UHS was actually right. I'm not pregnant after all.

That's it, I vow. *I'm never having sex again.*

My feeling of cheerful resolve barely lasts the time it takes to ascend a single flight of steps, and in its wake comes the unwelcome yearning to cry. As I bite my lower lip, a dimly remembered voice floats through my head, echoing softly. *It's a party, remember? It's a party, remember?*

I pause on the landing, confused. *God, who said that?* I can't seem to think, and shaking my head I keep plodding upward. When finally I reach the door to C-45, I take a deep breath and straighten my shoulders before letting myself in.

Inside it's that ponderous dead-of-night darkness, shadowing everything with an eerie amorphous underwater dimness. In the living room the furniture seems transmuted into vague, unfamiliar objects, shapeless and threatening. *Oh god, are they moving toward me?* I start to look around for the night-light, then catch myself. *You little dope. Grow up, why doncha.*

I creep back into the hallway. The door to Jessica's room is halfway open, and from her bed comes the low rippling growl of her snoring, rising and falling in a slow, steady glottal cadence.

Quietly I shut the door and go down the hallway into the

bathroom, where I swipe one of her Tampax. After I shower I step onto the cool floor, toss the empty shampoo bottle into the waste-basket, and lackadaisically towel myself dry. I brush my teeth, avoiding my image in the mirror, and just this once I skip the floss. Then, wrapped saronglike in my towel, I pad back down the hall-way, hesitating at Jessica's door to listen for a moment to her snoring.

My room feels cold. Shivering, I drop the towel onto the floor and get into bed, too tired to look for my only pair of pajamas, which in fact, I suddenly recall, I borrowed from Michael for last year's pajama party. Grimacing, I blow my nose, toss the soggy Kleenex in the general direction of the plastic garbage bag in the corner, and pull the covers tightly around my shoulders. I stare up at the ceiling in the blue-black darkness, listening to the tiny electric hum of my clock-radio. Then I curl up onto my side and close my eyes, numbly wondering if this chilly, pinching sensation in my chest will ever relax its hold.

SUNDAY | 5

|||||||||||||||||||||||||||||||||||||||||||||||||||||||

I cross Mass Ave in the brilliant morning sunlight, and as I round the corner onto Quincy Street I see Walt coming toward me on the uneven brick sidewalk. He's dressed in gray sweats and white hightop athletic shoes, and has on a pair of dark sunglasses that look rather like the ones I myself am wearing.

"Well, hi," he says, smiling. "Aren't you the early worm."

"Bird."

Walt ducks. "Where?"

"It's just an expression."

"Oh." Slowly he straightens up. "You English majors."

"What about us?"

"You talk funny."

"Do you mean funny ha-ha or funny strange?"

"And nitpicky too. Do you have a cold?"

"No. Why?"

"Because your nose is red and you sound stuffed up."

"Who asked you?"

"You did." He looks at his watch. "Oh my god. I'm late."

"The White Rabbit. Spoken like a true English major."

"What?"

"A literary reference."

"See? You're talking funny again."

"Then why aren't you laughing?"

"Say, shouldn't you be out doing your pre-brunch jog right about now?"

"I have a cold."

"You poor thing."

"Plus I'm on the rag and I'm bloated to twice my normal size."

"Yes." Walt clears his throat. "Love your shades."

"Thanks."

"Are yours Raybans too?" He leans so close our noses bump. "I can't see a thing in these."

"Maybe you need glasses."

"You think so?" Worriedly he bumps his nose against mine again.

I step back a few inches. "I think you should come to brunch with me at the Union."

"Why aren't you having brunch at Adams House?"

"Because I went around the Spee last night with a lampshade on my head," I say evenly. "I can't show up at the Adams House dining hall until dinner at the earliest."

"A lampshade, really?" Walt marvels. "How could I have missed that?"

"Maybe that's why you need glasses."

"Oh dear."

"Walt. I'm kidding."

"You mean you didn't walk around the Spee with a lampshade on your head?"

"I mean I'm kidding about maybe you need glasses."

"Oh." He looks at me over the rims of his Raybans. "So tell me more about the lampshade."

"I'll tell you over brunch at the Union."

"Can't. Sorry."

"Why not?"

"Why are you scowling at me?"

"I'm not scowling at you." I lift my eyebrows and curl my lips into a smile. "Come on. I'll help you steal Cocoa Puffs."

"Well, it's nice of you to offer, but—"

"But what?"

"And now you're shouting at me."

"I'm not shouting. Why don't you want me to help you steal Cocoa Puffs?"

"Check it out, Miranda." With a crafty look Walt twists around and displays his bulging green backpack to me. "Two Rice Chex, three Corn Chex, four Special Ks, four Cap'n Crunches, and *six* Cocoa Puffs."

"Congratulations."

"Thanks. But I need to hit at least three other houses in order to meet my brunch quota."

"Your brunch quota?"

"Miranda, we've gone over this before."

"Refresh my memory."

"They allot seven dollars for brunch, remember? And my backpack isn't big enough for me to sneak out with enough boxes from a single dining hall. So I have to make drop-off stops at Adams House."

"I'd forgotten it was so complicated."

"Miranda, stealing cereal isn't all fun and games."

"Then why do you do it?"

"Why do I do it?" He frowns, scratching his head. "Nobody's ever asked me that before."

"Just like nobody's ever asked you why you want to be a dentist?"

He's silent for a few moments, peering at his fingernail. Then he looks at me. "I know why."

"Why what?"

"Why I take cereal from the dining hall."

"Well?" My nose has begun to trickle, forebodingly. "Why do you take cereal from the dining hall?"

"Because it's there."

"What?"

"I said, because it's—"

"You're crazy," I interrupt, and am abruptly shaken by a violent sneeze. My sunglasses fly off and I'm still pawing at my nose as Walt, having picked up my glasses from the ground and wiped them on his sweatshirt, holds them out to me. "Thanks." I slide them on top of my bangs, hooking them neatly over the snarl right above the hairline. "That was nice of you."

"No problem." Walt hikes his backpack more firmly over his shoulder. "Well, it's been fun, Miranda."

"Come with me to the Union." I squint at him in the sunlight.

"I'd love to, but—"

"We'll have a blast. I'll stick little gooey bits of raisins between my teeth."

"Sounds appealing, but—"

"Just like old times."

"I'm under a deadline here, Miranda."

"Well, not really old times, but—"

"In fact, I'm sort of behind schedule at this point."

"Are you?" I slide my sunglasses down over my eyes. "So am I. Thanks for reminding me."

He nods. "Going jogging now?"

"No, I'm going to the Union for brunch."

"You're not going to let a little cold stop you from jogging, are you?" He wags a chiding forefinger at me. "Remember, no pain, no gain."

"I don't have a cold."

"Then why aren't you going jogging?"

"Well, it's been fun, Walt." I turn to cross Quincy Street.

"See you later, Miranda," he calls out cheerfully as he strides down the sidewalk. "Hope your hay fever gets better."

I'm trying to figure out just what has happened. Jackson, whom I scarcely know well enough to nod a greeting at, is now gracefully sprawled out on my living-room sofa and chain-smoking unfiltered cigarettes. Didn't he wink at me as we bumped into each other at the coffee machine?

"It's not so bad having parents who are divorced," he's saying. "Especially if one of them lives in France."

"I can imagine."

"Of course I never tell anyone that I went to junior high in New Hampshire." He blows a smoke ring over my head.

"No, why would you?"

"High school was great, though. I got my bac in Paris."

"Wow." I blink at him. His face is so thin and angular, his skin still boyishly smooth and soft-looking. *"That's great."*

He laughs, smiling down at me on the floor, where I sit leaning against the sofa with my knees curled up to my chest, arms clasped around my shins. *"Do you know what a bac is?"*

"Well, no." I feel my face getting warm. *"But I assume you're not talking about musical composers."*

"Clever girl."

"Qui, moi?"

"Oui, toi." Smiling, he blows another effortlessly aimed smoke ring into the air. *"Tu parles français?"*

"No, no. I just did well in French A, that's all."

"You are a clever girl."

"Well, thanks."

There is a pause, during which I notice that my feet are falling asleep. Then Jackson coughs softly. *"You know I broke up with Madeleine Anfang a little while ago, don't you?"*

I stay perfectly still. *"I didn't even know you were going out together."*

"You didn't?" He seems surprised. *"But we all live in Adams House, yes? You must have seen us together."*

"Well, yes, but—" I stop myself from saying But I never really noticed.

"But what?" He stubs out his cigarette with a quizzical air.

"Oh, nothing." I feel myself blushing again, and turn in relief when my roommate Elizabeth suddenly unlocks the door and comes ambling into the room, swinging her Guatemalan bag. She sees Jackson, shoots me an astonished look, says a general hello and without breaking stride goes into her room and shuts the door behind her.

Jackson laughs again. *"Never mind."* Languidly he stands up. *"Let's turn the stereo down a little, shall we?"*

I watch him go over to the stereo and adjust the volume, my eyes sweeping up and down the long-legged span of his body. Then I drop my gaze to my now-numb feet as he turns back around and comes to sit next to me on the carpet, lolling against the sofa.

"Those are nice socks," he says into my ear.

"What?" I meet his eyes for a second and look back down again. *"Oh. Thanks. Ow."*

"What's the matter?"

Gingerly I stretch out my legs. *"These damn shinsplints."* I start flexing my ankles, trying not to grimace at the painful tingling.

"You run, don't you?"

"I jog a little."

"Ma belle, I call that running. I've seen you." Jackson rests his arm on the sofa cushion, almost but not quite touching my shoulders. *"You run at really weird hours too."*

"Do I?" I jiggle my feet.

"Just last week I was coming back from an Advocate party and you nearly ran me down."

"I did? Where?"

"On Mount Auburn Street. Wihout even saying hello."

"Oh, I'm sorry."

"The point is, running at six o'clock in the morning is weird."

"It's the best time to go running on the beach." I feel his hand lightly brush the back of my neck. *"When the tide is out, see?"*

"Yes, I see," he says softly.

I am silent, pretending to listen to the music. Then, when his fingers slide gently along the side of my throat, I take a deep breath. *"I've been meaning to tell you."*

"Yes?"

Oh dear god. *"I've been admiring your blazer all evening."*

"Have you?"

"You wear blazers a lot, don't you?"

"I own a couple of Pierre Cardins." He's smiling at me.

"Ah." Dear, dear god. *"French."*

"Of course." He leans an inch or two closer.

"Ah."

"Yes." Lightly he kisses my temple.

"Jackson?"

"Mmm?"

"This is a stupid question, but—"

"There are no stupid questions." Now he kisses my eyebrow.

"This one is."

"Try me."

"What time is it?"

"Late," he says calmly.

"Oh dear."

"What's the matter?"

"I have to get up early tomorrow."

"Do you?"

"I'm afraid so."

"No problem."

"What?"

"I'll get up with you."

"I mean really early."

"Okay."

"I have a nine o'clock class."

"Fine."

"I like to get there five minutes early."

"We'll set the alarm."

"Really?"

"Crack of dawn."

"Sometimes I even get there ten minutes early."

"I'll set the alarm myself."

"Yes?" With childlike deliberation I graze the tips of my fingers across the warm silky flesh of his cheekbone. *"I'm serious, Jackson. I really do have to get up early."*

"I'm serious too." He stands up, holds out his hands to me, and slowly, prolonging the gesture, slowly he pulls me to my still-tingling feet. And as his arms go around me, somewhere in the back of my mind I find myself wondering if either one of us really will bother to set the alarm tonight.

I look down at the tabletop. *Styrofoam cup*, I say to myself, the syllables rolling unintelligibly through my head. *Plastic utensils. Wheat toast.* I reach for my coffee, but the gesture somehow strikes me as hollow and queer. Have I forgotten to add cream, or do I usually take my coffee black? I push my tray away.

I'm stretched out on my bed, reading by the light of the tensor lamp clamped to the headboard, when my father opens the door, as usual without knocking first, and pokes his head into my room.

"Hey, hey. Anybody home?"

I don't look up from my book. "Hi."

"Mind if I come in?"

"Sure."

He perches on the edge of my bed, his weight shifting the mattress around. I sit up and cross my legs Indian-style, watching him stare around my room as if he's never seen it before.

I clear my throat. "What's up?"

Now he looks around as if surprised to see me. "Hey, what are you doing home on a Saturday night?" *Jovially he taps my knee.* "Why aren't you out bowling with the gang?"

"Bowling." *I feel a tremendous scowl coming on and deliberately I will my face to remain blank. My knee twitches and I look down at the bedspread.*

"What're you reading?" *He takes my book and peers at the cover.* "David Copperfield. What is this, some kind of smut?" *He chuckles and hands it back to me, losing my place as he does so.*

"I'm kind of busy, Dad. What's up?"

His face is suddenly serious. "Your mother," *he begins.*

"What about her?"

"Well, she's mentioned to me that you've been acting a little snappish towards her lately."

"Snappish?"

He's staring around my room again. "She says you jumped all over her when she asked that you wear a little less eye makeup."

"What difference does it make how much eye makeup I wear?"

"A young lady your age—"

"For years she bitched at me for wearing hiking boots and sweatpants." *I close* David Copperfield *and cross my arms, holding it close to my chest.* "Shouldn't she be happy that I'm wearing makeup?"

"I think she feels that—"

"And before that she told me to stop reading Taylor Caldwell books."

"Remember the time she caught you reading Valley of the Dolls?" *He chuckles.* "Now that was a scene, wasn't it? You were what, fourteen?"

"Twelve." I force myself not to glare.

"And the day after that you—" He stops, looking embarrassed.

"Got my period for the first time," I say coolly. "Weird timing, wasn't it?"

"Mmm." He studies the ceiling for a while, his face reddening under the bronze of his skin. Then he clears his throat. "Heard from any colleges yet?"

"Mmm."

"Is that a yes or a no?"

"Yep."

"Well?"

This time I can't stop my lip from curling. "Yale, Harvard, Princeton, Columbia, and Stanford."

"What'd they say?"

"Yep."

"They said yes?"

"Mmm."

"Is that a yes?"

"Yep."

"When did you find this out?" There's a hurt edge to his voice.

"Last week when you were up in Spokane."

"Why didn't your mother tell me?"

"Ask her."

"Mmm." He clears his throat again. "What about financial aid?"

"What about it?"

"They give you any?"

"Yep."

"How much?"

I bend my head, examining my nail polish for chips. "Full scholarships." My breath wheezes a little in my throat.

"That's great, honey."

"Yeah." I peel a ragged pink strip from my thumbnail. "Looks like you'll still be able to build that swimming pool in the backyard."

"Well, the most important thing is that you got in."

"Yep." My chest is starting to feel like there's an enormous claw tightening around it. "Was there anything else you wanted to talk about?"

"No, not really." He stands up. *"I'll tell your mother we got it all straightened out."*

"Yep."

He hitches at the creases in his trousers. "Lighten up on the mascara a little, honey, okay?"

"Yep."

After he leaves I get up and close the door and lean against it, a hand on my sternum. Asthma, *I tell myself.* It's just my asthma acting up again. *Then I start looking around for my inhaler, wondering where the hell I left it after the last time.*

"Earth to Miranda."

"Huh?" I look up from the table.

"Beam me up, Scotty." Teddy Anson pulls out a chair opposite me and sits down, grinning prodigiously. One of his arms is in a sling. "Hey, you little space cadet. What's the weather like out there on Mars?"

"What happened to your arm?"

Teddy's grin actually broadens. "I fell down a flight of stairs."

"What?"

"Right in the middle of 'Delta Dawn,' too."

"Oh, Jesus."

"I know, I know." He shakes his head, his eyes twinkling. "I just can't control myself around Helen Reddy."

"Are you okay?"

"Why are you holding on to the edge of the table like that?"

I relax my grip. "Teddy, are you okay?"

"You bet."

"I'm serious."

"So am I. Luckily it only hurts when I laugh." He flaps his bandaged elbow at my tray. "Is this yours? I'm starving."

"Help yourself."

"Thanks. I'm a sucker for poached eggs on wheat toast." His uninjured hand wields the fork with rapacious glee. "Cold poached eggs on soggy wheat toast."

"Don't forget the undercooked bacon."

"What? Oh, there it is. Thanks." He shovels one of the flaccid little strips into his mouth. "Lucky I didn't fall on my eating hand, huh?"

"Close to miraculous, I'd say."

"Got any butter?" he asks with his mouth full.

"No."

"Margarine?"

"No."

"Jelly?"

"No."

"Jam?"

"No."

"Apple butter?"

"No."

"Oh, and here's coffee." He takes a swallow. "Lukewarm coffee." He takes another gulp. "Got any milk?"

"No."

"Cremora?"

"No."

"Sugar?"

"No."

"Honey?"

"No."

"Sweet 'n Low?"

"No."

"God, you really know how to eat, don't you?" He wipes the plate clean with a last little wedge of toast, which he deftly pops between his teeth. "Lucky for me you weren't hungry." Still chewing, he smiles at me, tiny toast crumbs clinging to the corners of his mouth.

"Teddy, what are you doing here?"

A look of alarm clouds his face. "Oh no, we're not going to talk about religion, are we?"

"I mean how did you know I was here?"

"Oh." The toast crumbs curve upward again. "I ran into Walt Abrams in front of Adams House, and he said you were hiding out in the Union and were desperate for company."

"I didn't know you knew Walt," I say irritably.

"*Know* Walt!" Teddy cries. "Walt and I are like that!" He waves his uninjured hand at me with the forefinger and the middle finger clamped together. "Why, we're practically blood brothers."

"Oh?"

"Sure. Walt's the Lampoon business manager, you know."

"What?"

"Didn't you know that?"

"No."

"Seriously? It was Walt's idea to market those *Helene Does Harvard* videos."

"I see."

"I had a bit part in the *Head of the Charles* trilogy," he discloses boastfully. "I played a dumb jock from Kirkland House."

"Imagine that." I push back my chair and stand up. "Well, I hate to eat and run, but—"

"You're leaving?" Teddy looks up at me in surprise. "But I just got here."

"I've got a lot of work to do."

He nods. "Well, I guess I'll have seconds and then head back to the UHS emergency room."

I pause. "Why?"

"Because I'm still hungry."

"No, why are you going back to UHS?"

"So I can pick up a prescription for Percodan which I'm going to sell to a friend of mine from Dunster House."

"Great." I push in my chair. "See you around."

"A fellow Helen Reddy fan," Teddy says, giggling. "Ouch!"

At six o'clock the reading room closes. As I'm walking underneath the Wigglesworth archway toward Mass Ave, my head swims dizzily and I lean against the wall for a moment until my vision clears. As if on cue, my stomach growls, and then I realize that I seem to have skipped a meal or two today. Still feeling a bit light-headed, I walk back to Adams House, peer into the empty C-45 mailbox, and, unaccountably dashed, plod into the dining hall.

Virginia the checker sits erect at her post, pen poised over her list of names, her face nearly invisible behind her big eyeglasses and cheery expression. "Take one of these, hon," she orders by way of greeting, holding out a sheet of paper as I pass by.

"Thanks." I use it for a placemat on my tray.

Serge tosses me an apple over the glass counter. "Hey, I saved this one for you."

"It's gorgeous. Thanks."

"I sure can pick 'em, huh?"

"You bet." I put the apple on my tray. "How are you, Serge?"

"Great." He's bouncing up and down on his toes. "It's my last night here."

"What?"

"Yeah, I'm moving down to Florida to live with my grand-parents."

"Can I have a banana?" A scrawny sophomore girl stands next to me. "And an orange?"

"Sorry. Apples tonight." Serge holds one out to her.

"No bananas?"

"Ran out at brunch."

"How could you have run out?"

"People were eatin' 'em, I guess."

"Well, never mind then." She turns and walks away.

Serge grins at me and puts the apple back in its bowl. "Yeah, I'll miss this place."

"Why are you going to Florida, Serge?"

"Aw, you look so sad," he says delightedly. Then he shrugs. "I dunno. Better weather, right?"

"It doesn't snow so often in Florida."

"That's right," he says, laughing. "I'm gonna learn how to water-ski."

"It's easy." I try to smile. "Just hang on to the rope."

We are silent for a moment, and then he says: "Well—"

"No, no." I take a step backward. "I'll come say goodbye on my way out."

I'm standing in the dim wood-paneled gloom of the Freshman Union, squashed up against the bread station and gripping my tray as I look around for a place to sit. It's packed and noisy and I curse myself for having come to dinner during rush hour. Three, four, five people stream past, each bumping into me with a cheerful "Sorry." Trying not to scowl, I follow in their wake as if I'm with them, covertly peering around for anybody I might know from these first few weeks. Even one of my room-mates would be a welcome sight right now. Shit, shit, shit. Just as I'm resolving to start coming to dinner at five o'clock, regardless of when I might actually be hungry, I spot an empty seat in the middle of the long wooden table on my left. I squeeze my way in, slip into the chair, and gratefully pick up my spoon.

"Oh, you're probably confusing him with my uncle," says the girl directly across from me, a big-shouldered redhead with about a thousand freckles sprinkling her face. "My uncle's the television producer. It's my father who's the president of—"

Oh shit, I think to myself, staring down at my yogurt. These are the glammies I've already learned to avoid, the ones who all seem to know each other, who wear expensive, handsomely outworn clothing, are in-timately familiar with New York, speak several languages, and are prone to lapsing into composed silences when they don't feel like talking, no matter how expedient it might seem to keep up their end of the conver-sation. I take a long breath, and smell cigarette smoke. Didn't anybody tell them that this is a nonsmoking area? My mouth tight, I suppress a cough. What would they think if I got up right now and left?

"I thought your name sounded familiar." The kid on my left gestures triumphantly, flicking ashes all over his tray and into my yogurt. "My dad's a department head over at NBC. Don't your folks have a summer place in Montauk?"

I accidentally drop my spoon and it clatters onto my tray, more loudly than I would have thought possible. The kid on my left looks over at me and nods casually. "Yo," he says.

Now I recognize him from my English-lit class. "Hi."

"Don't you think the food is worse than usual tonight?"

"Definitely."

"I thought so too. You go to class today?"

"Sure. Didn't you?"

"Nah. Too boring. Hey, what about your dad?"

"No, he didn't go to class either." I pick up my spoon and stir the ashes around in my yogurt.

"No, I mean would I know him."

"Maybe." My throat is constricting.

"Yeah? What's he do?"

Feeling several pairs of eyes upon me, languidly I wave the smoke away from my face. "My dad?" I say, slowly. "Well, I'll tell you one thing." I lean back in my chair. "He's got a fabulous suntan."

There is utter silence for a moment, and then they all laugh. The kid from my lit class pokes me with his elbow. "I think I know your roommate Jeanne. Aren't you the one from California?"

"Fer sure," I say, deadpan, waiting for them to start laughing again. Instead the kid on my left points his cigarette at me and announces to the others: "We're in English 10 together." Then he offers me one of his Gauloises and they start asking me questions about L.A., what classes I'm taking, have I gotten my Coop card yet, and whether I actually plan to attend the freshman picnic on Saturday.

By the time I'm describing to them some of the more sophisticated techniques of bodysurfing, and Ryan, the kid from my lit class, has asked me to help him study for the midterm, and Leona, the redhead sitting across from me, has complimented me on my eye makeup, some strange, subtle, half-familiar circuit has flipped over in my head, leaving me with a sensation uncomfortably close to a headache.

Pulling the piece of paper out from under my bowl of cottage cheese, I dab at the coffee rings with my napkin and peer at the first paragraphs through the damp blurry puckers.

<u>OCS-OCL Senior Survey</u>

Dear Member of the Class of 1982:

We'd like to know more about you and your future plans. Please take a few minutes to answer the following questions. The results of this survey will enable us to better serve the Harvard community, and will be published in a future issue of *Harvard Magazine*. Please be sure to write clearly and legibly.

1. Describe your plans for the upcoming year. Will you be attending graduate school? Beginning a job? Traveling? Include mailing address and telephone number(s) if available.

I take a bite of apple and chew it carefully. Then I pull a pen from my bag and hunch over the table.

I've joined the Navy's Deep-Sea Research Program. No telephones where I'm going! I'll write as soon as I get back.

I give Virginia my survey, hand my tray to the dishwasher, and dump my napkin and half-eaten apple into the garbage. Turning, I see Beatrice and Alicia coming in my direction, their legs in red tights flashing underneath their black leather miniskirts. *Shit.* Trapped on either side by the big garbage bins, I swallow and step forward.

But Beatrice and Alicia sail by, completely ignoring me. I'm staring after them, blinking, when somebody says behind me:

"They heard about the lampshade."

"Huh?" I spin around. It's Carlos, standing there with an empty plate dangling from his fingers. I notice he's wearing the same loud Hawaiian-print shirt he had on the last time I ran into him at dinner. When was that? Wednesday night? It seems like several eternities ago.

"Yeah, the lampshade." He shakes his head. "They heard."

I look into his dark enigmatic face. "Very funny."

"You think so?"

"Not really."

"Man, I wish I'd seen you with that lampshade on your head. That was some party, huh?"

"Yep."

"I haven't had so much fun since the day that kid cracked up in my psych class. Threw his books at the professor and ran out screaming."

I stare at him as he practices his Frisbee wrist action with his plate, until finally he switches over to his other hand and glances at me. "How's your hay fever?"

My teeth grit. "I don't have hay fever."

"Really? You look like you're having a bad allergy attack."

"I'm fine."

"That's good. So what about that lampshade?"

"Nice talking with you." I turn away.

"I'll bet you look good in a lampshade," he calls after me. "You're tall, so you can carry it off."

"Thanks." I walk toward the exit without bothering to wave goodbye.

C-45 is empty and quiet. Taped to my door is a sheet of Harvard Athletic Department stationery on which Jessica has neatly typed a little note.

Telephone messages: Michael (once), Richard (twice), two un-identified creeps who hung up as soon as they heard my voice. I'd like to stick around and take all your phone calls but I do have a thesis to write. I'm staying over at my thesis adviser's place and using her PC in exchange for feeding her icky neurotic cats while she's at Club Med. See you Friday. Meet me at the cocktail party in the History & Lit lounge around 5 if you want.
                                        Jessica Marie Hartsfield

I leave the note on the door and go into the bathroom, where I lean against the basin and pick up my toothbrush. No sooner have I opened my mouth to sneer at the mirror than I see that there are several little white clumps of cottage cheese wedged be-tween my front teeth. Dropping my toothbrush, I clamp my lips together and stare at my reflection.

Through the air shaft I can hear someone singing "Get Happy" in his bathroom. Then there is only silence and suddenly I'm press-ing my forehead against the icelike surface of the mirror, staring down at a basin in need of a good cleaning. *Dear god, this is it. I'm cracking up.* The phone rings and I jerk in surprise, bumping my nose against the mirror. "Ouch. Goddam."

I brush a few wisps of hair off my brow and open the cabinet behind the mirror, rooting through the various bottles and tubes until I find Midol and Sudafed. I swallow two tablets of each and then brush my teeth until my gums hurt.

The phone rings again. I go back into the living room and wait for the rings to stop. Then, after a second's hesitation, I pick up the receiver and start dialing.

After the fourteenth ring I slam down the phone. "Jerks," I whisper. "Let me guess. Bridge with the Taggarts, right?" I look at my watch, which of course says twelve-thirty. After a while I get up and go into my bedroom to check my clock-radio. It's only a little past eight. Maybe I can go running today after all. I bend from the waist, touching the floor with my palms, and in an instant I'm completely congested again.

Straightening up, I blow my nose, drop the tissue on the floor, and punt it under my bed. Frowning, I clamp my hands around my left hamstring. Is it my imagination, or does the muscle already seem a little flabby? My eye lights upon the big garbage bag next to my bureau and I poke my foot at it, trying to remember what I shoved inside last night. *My, aren't you just the cutest couple. Maybe you two'll win the prize for best costumes.* I give the bag a vicious kick and go back into the living room.

Restlessly I do a few arm windmills and then stand by the window, looking down at the brightly lit stretch of sidewalk in front of Harvard Pizza. There's Anthony and Skip sauntering out, each carrying a big flat white cardboard box, and crossing the street without looking for cars. Five or six football players pass through the narrow doorway, jostling one another and nearly trampling the Adams House English tutor, who's got his arm around a blonde girl who looks vaguely familiar. Then I think I catch sight of Henry walking along Plympton Street toward the Charles.

"Dear god," I say aloud, my breath misting the windowpane. The tall dark-headed figure in the dark jacket vanishes past the Lampoon, and frantically I scramble for my shoes.

I bolt down the stairs and out of Adams House and start racing down Plympton Street. When I come to the corner at Mount Auburn Street I plunge across the intersection against the light, and head for the river. My legs are stiff and cold but I force myself to keep lengthening my stride as I lope along scanning the sidewalks and streets.

Crossing Mem Drive, I come to a halt on a gravelly path near the garbage-ridden bank of the Charles. I look around, panting a little. This isn't exactly a terrific place to be alone, I remind myself, particularly at night. Yet I remain until my breath evens out and the abrupt urge to cry has subsided, and then I turn back toward Adams House. Though I'm now feeling less than energetic and I hate running in Keds which have no arch support whatsoever, I launch into a fast jog up Plympton Street. As I'm crossing Mount

Auburn Street my nose starts tickling; I put up a hand to swipe at my nostrils and collide with a strange bouncy resiliency into an Arpege-scented form barreling out of Harvard Pizza.

"Oh, shit!" It's Jeanne, my freshman roommate, reeling with laughter as she points at the slice of pizza lying on the ground between us, its mangled tip pointing at me in a cheesy *Je t'accuse.*

"No, pussycat, it's mozzarella." Her companion, his plump round chest swathed in a HARVARD MODEL U.N. t-shirt, laughs too. "Not shit. Mozzarella."

"You must be Carl," I say sourly.

"That's right." His lips glint in a grease-smeared smile. "And you must be Miranda. I've heard all about you."

"Oh?"

"Same old impetuous Miranda," Jeanne says indulgently. "Still running around like she's got a lampshade on her head."

"What?" I take a step closer, towering over her.

Her eyes twinkle up into mine. "I just wish you'd watch where you're going, sweetie. That slice had extra cheese and mushrooms."

I just wish you'd shove it up your ass. I wipe my nose with the back of my hand and notice that they're goggling at me, their smiles fading. Dear god, did I actually say that aloud? Folding my arms across my chest, I stare right back. "And furthermore—"

"How about another slice, pussycat?" Carl wheels around and hustles back into the pizza shop, the thighs of his blue jeans hissing as they rub together.

"And furthermore—" I hesitate, sniffling. *I wish I had a dollar for every time I've seen you talking on the phone wearing a big white Jolene mustache.* "You know, Jeanne, I really hated the way you'd leave your pubic hairs all over the soap."

"I—what?"

"Frankly, it really grossed me out." I nod and stalk away. As I'm crossing Bow Street I hear Carl sing out behind me: "Here you go, buttercup! Extra cheese and mushrooms."

Buttercup, I say to myself as I'm climbing the C-entry stairs. *How unutterably perfect.* It's not until I'm back in C-45, taking off my jacket, that I recollect what took me whirling outside in the first place. I go back to the window, dragging my jacket on the floor behind me. The sidewalk in front of Harvard Pizza is deserted.

Henry. I'm leaning my shoulder against the window frame, remembering Henry's gleeful predilection for hugely oversized thrift-store blazers, his unfailing interest in whatever shade of lipstick I happened to be wearing, which he would affably compliment and then gently dab off with one of my tissues. *Do you mind?* he'd say. *It looks wonderful, but I don't like the taste.*

There's a tiny cool breeze coming in through the window. I look down at the street one last time, and then I turn and throw my jacket, hard, onto the couch. It lands with a sharp little *plop* and I go into my room and start taking off my clothes.

MONDAY | 6

||||||||||||||||||||||||||||||||||||||||||||||||||||||

I slam the little door to the C-45 mailbox shut, clutching a stiff white envelope in my hand. My head is pounding. I go around the corner into the ladies' lounge, where I lie down on the slippery flowered divan and rip open the envelope. *Seniors graduating with a job that pays over fifteen thousand dollars a year are cordially invited to apply for an American Express card.*

"Right," I mutter aloud. "Don't goddam leave home without it."

"Look, honey," my father is saying, "he's your son."

Hunching lower over the kitchen table, I turn another page in my algebra book. Through the open windows their voices float in from the backyard, where they are sitting in lawn chairs facing into the last of the afternoon sun.

"I just can't believe Andy doesn't want to spend the summer with us."

"Is that what he said?"

"He said he'd rather stay out in Denver."

"Maybe he's going to summer school," my father says tentatively. "Or maybe he's got a girlfriend out there."

"I'm sure he put Andy up to it." I hear ice cubes rattling against glass. "It's just the kind of thing he'd do."

"Now, Annie—"

"If he knows I want something, he's just got to do the opposite."

"I'm sure he's—"

"Divorced fifteen years and he's still trying to make me miserable."

"I don't think—"

"Fifteen years of gloating about what a terrific father he is. Haven't I insisted that Andy spend his summers with us, even if it's screwed up our own vacation plans?"

"Now look—"

"I'll tell you one thing." My mother lowers her voice. "I sure as hell wish I'd gotten my tubes tied before I met you."

There is a long silence, punctuated by the soft whooshing cadence of the sprinkler jerking around and around over by the honeysuckle trellis.

My father sighs. "You want another drink?"

"No, I want you to talk to Andy."

"Why do you want me to talk to your son?"

"I just want you to talk to him. Man to man."

"He's sixteen years old."

"Just talk to him. Is that so much to ask? Tell him how much we're looking forward to seeing him. Tell him he can use your car."

"Hey, hey, let's not get carried away here."

"Tell him we'll pay for his guitar lessons."

I close my algebra book and gather up my papers into a neat little stack and go upstairs to my room, where I put on socks and sneakers. Then I go back downstairs, slipping through the kitchen and into the garage, and get my bicycle where it leans against an old rickety bookcase my mother keeps insisting she's going to give to Goodwill the first chance she gets. I'm not too worried about the algebra test on Monday anyway. I haven't dropped below a 95 yet.

The toilet flushes in the adjacent bathroom. I turn my eyes to the top of the application, where, I note, the NAME OF APPLICANT line has already been filled in with neat computer type: *Mrs. Mirinda Walker.*

There's the sound of water running in the next room and then somebody's nose being blown in soft vigorous puffs. Involuntarily I give a little sniff of my own. *Please describe your employment history, including summer job(s), listing most recent first.* Video games, I muse, does that count as full-time employment?

"Wanda!"

I look up from the section describing the billing agreement in print so minute it makes my head throb even more violently. Angela stands there, a brush in one hand and a large handbag in the other. Her eyes are red, or maybe it's just a reflection from her maroon sweatshirt with RADCLIFFE embroidered over the heart. "Hi, Angela. How's everything?"

"Awful."

"Oh?"

"Guess what I've been doing."

"Smoking pot in the loo?"

"No, I've been crying." She sits on a stool in front of the mirrored vanity. "Philip and I are having an argument."

"What, again?"

"In the dining hall." Her voice is low and excited. "I just stormed out on him in the middle of dessert."

"My." I realize that I need to blow my nose, and start poking around in my bag for a tissue.

"Wanda?"

"Mmm?"

"Do you think I'm wrong to want breast implants?"

"Well—" I blow my nose and stick the Kleenex back into my bag. "I'm not really sure if it's a question of right or wrong."

"That's what I keep telling Philip." Her lower lip starts to tremble. "Will you come help me, Wanda?"

"I don't see how—"

"Come and help me talk to Philip."

"I'm sure you're doing a perfectly good job already."

"I just want you to—"

"After all, isn't that what a liberal-arts education is all about?"

"I really need you to—"

"Improved communication skills, right?"

"Wanda, please. He likes you. He respects your opinion."

"Really?" I say dubiously.

She gives a little sob. "Please."

"Okay, okay. Just don't cry, all right?"

"Thanks, Wanda. I knew you'd come through." Then her look of relief is displaced by an anxious pucker. "Oh my god."

"What's wrong?"

"I hope he hasn't left the dining hall already."

"We'd better hurry then." Slowly I fold up the letter from American Express and put it into my bag.

"If Mariel Hemingway can do it, why can't I?" Angela says for the third time.

Philip sighs and stands up, empty coffee cup in hand.

As soon as he's out of earshot Angela turns to me and whispers, "How do I look?" She gropes in her bag and pulls out a hand mirror.

"Fine, fine," I mumble through a mouthful of split-pea soup and smushed-up cracker.

"My hair looks awful."

"No, no—"

"I look like I've been dead for two days."

"No, no." I swallow laboriously.

"And he doesn't even offer to bring me more coffee, the selfish creep."

"Does he always drink this much coffee?"

"Only when he's upset."

"Calms his nerves, does it?"

"Will you look at these pores? God, I hate my complexion."

"Angela, your skin is beautiful." I crumble another saltine into my bowl.

"You won't *believe* what he said to me the other night."

Oh shit. "Have you had a facial lately?"

"He's lying right on top of me and he looks at me and says—"

"I hear oatmeal soap is marvelous."

"I mean, the bed is *dripping* wet and he has the gall to tell me—"

"Benzoyl peroxide," I say loudly. "Jessica swears by it."

"And then he says, 'I've been meaning to tell you some-thing—'" She breaks off as Philip returns and sets his cup on the table in precisely the same spot it was before. Without looking at us he sits down again, adds sugar to his coffee, and stirs, his spoon making little rhythmic clinks against the inside of the cup. Angela puts the mirror back into her handbag, closing the snap with a sharp twist of her fingers. I'm staring down into my bowl, bent on mashing the cracker around until I've achieved the perfect sodden green consistency.

"You'd have dissolved granite in there by now." I glance up, but she is addressing him.

"I like to stir my coffee." He doesn't stop. "Is that okay with you?"

"Listen," Angela begins.

"If you mention Mariel Hemingway one more time—"

"All I was going to say was—"

"All you've done for the last week is talk about your breasts," he says wearily. "How do you expect me to get any work done when you're running around the room without a shirt on?"

"If you cared about me—"

"Angela." Philip sighs again. "I just don't think getting breast implants is such a good idea."

There is a leaden silence, and then Angela pinches my thigh under the table. "Ow!" I exclaim. "Don't do that."

"Go on," she hisses. "Talk to him."

"Oh." I look across the table to where Philip is still stirring his coffee. "Well, gang, let's just approach this thing rationally, shall we?"

"Good," Angela whispers, nodding.

"Thanks." I nod back, and fall silent.

She pinches me again.

"Ow!"

"Keep going," she hisses.

"Oh." I stifle a sigh. "Well, I mean, look. Maybe somebody should tell me why Angela wants to get breast implants in the first place."

"Some jerk claiming to be from—"

"A senior photographer from *Playboy* has asked me to—"

"Wants her to take all her clothes off—"

" 'Girls of the Ivy League' pictorial—"

"Take her picture standing stark naked in the middle of Harvard Yard—"

"*Tasteful* partial nudity—"

"Right in front of my freshman dorm—"

"And he'll help me get a modeling contract." Angela smiles gloatingly. "He says he knows Eileen Ford personally."

There is another silence. I look down at the green mush in my bowl, wondering if this was such a good idea for my stomach after all. I push my tray away and use one of my napkins to blow my nose.

"He's so self-absorbed, Wanda. He doesn't pay attention to my needs at all."

"Well, if it comes to that, she never—"

"Him and his little hidden agendas—"

"How does she expect me to get my work done?" Philip leans toward me, his round little wire-rimmed glasses glinting in the overhead light. "How am I supposed to study for my finals? My thesis review is on Thursday—"

"I've got emotional requirements too, you know."

"And the final paper for my psych seminar is due in two weeks."

"Hopes and dreams like everybody else."

"And I've got med school to start thinking about—"

"Is it such a terrible thing to want to be on the cover of *Vogue?*"

"And right after my finals are over I've got to register for my psych classes at summer school—"

"They're not *his* breasts."

"And all she can do is worry about her cleavage—"

"Sandy Duncan has breast implants."

"Eye implant," I say absently, rooting around in my shoulder bag to see if maybe I overlooked the aspirin the last time I checked.

"You're missing the point," she wails.

I look up to see if her lips are trembling again, but she's gazing at Philip.

"Barbra Streisand got her nose fixed," she says tremulously. "I'm sure there are dozens of girls who'd feel the same way if a chance like this came along." Angela knits her brows and then gyrates her head toward me. "Wanda, wouldn't *you* get breast implants if a senior photographer from *Playboy* wanted to use you in a 'Girls of the Ivy League' pictorial?"

I shrug. "I avoid major surgery at all costs."

"But if it meant a modeling contract—"

"Well, if we're going to talk about ignoring needs." Philip's eyeglasses are glinting my way again. "Back me up here, Miranda. Put yourself in my shoes."

"I hate Topsiders."

"What would *you* do if you were trying to get your work done, trying to *focus*, trying to *concentrate*, and your girlfriend kept running around without her shirt on, crying and carrying on like it's the end of the world?"

"I'd probably offer her a Kleenex."

"Wouldn't *you* go to the library to study?"

"Sure. Listen, you don't happen to have any aspirin on you, do you?"

"See?" Philip turns to Angela. "She says I'm right."

"She does not. She said she'd go to the library and do you have any aspirin."

"Yes, do you?" I look from one to the other, but they are busy frowning at each other across the table. As if for the first time, I find myself noticing the startling resemblance between them, with their wavy blond hair flowing off handsome broad foreheads, their clear gray eyes, their smooth pale skin ever so slightly freckled from summers on the Cape. My stomach gives another stabbing cramp and I lean my elbows on the table and prop my forehead in my hands. *What next*, I ask myself. *My nose, my stomach. I wouldn't be surprised if my arms were to fall off.*

"She says *I'm* the one who's passive-aggressive. *I'm* the one who's sending out subliminal messages of rejection—"

"Wanda." Angela nudges me. "Philip's talking to you."

"Ouch." I raise my head. "What."

"She keeps telling me how insensitive I am, right? So the last time we had sex, you know what she said to me?"

Oh god no. "Well," I say, shifting in my chair. My nose tickles in a panicky sort of way. "I think I'd better be—"

"She has the gall to—"

"Hate to eat and—"

"—the absolute gall to—"

"—studying to do—"

"—comment about the size of my—"

I sneeze, clapping my hands over my nose, and in the hush that follows I peek over my fingers to see if my arms are still attached to my shoulders. I give a little sigh of relief, and then my stomach cramps again. "Pardon me," I say faintly.

"Bigger this, bigger that," Philip goes on irately. "She'll probably want us to move to Texas after we're married."

"Eh?" I tilt my head in despair. *This is it. My goddam hearing is going.*

"Didn't you know?" Angela says gaily. She waves her left hand in front of my face. A round little diamond twinkles on her fourth finger, glittering yellow, pink, violet, blue. "We're engaged. I thought everybody knew that already."

I feel my jaw drop. As I'm looking back at her, a riptide of fatigue suddenly overwhelms me; it's all I can do to move my lips. "Congratulations."

"Isn't it wonderful?" She is glowing, two spots of pink blooming on each patrician cheekbone. "We're going to Italy for the honeymoon."

"Italy."

"Assuming my first year in med school goes well, of course." Philip finishes the last of his coffee. "Otherwise we'll have to postpone until after my second year."

"That's what *you* think, buster. Mummy's already reserved space for the reception hall."

"We'll see," he says austerely.

"So what do you think, Wanda?" Angela turns to me.

"About what?" I'm still staring at her ring.

"About the breast implants."

"I think—" Blinking, I draw a long breath. "I think you should—"

"Yes?" She's giving Philip a victorious little smile.

"I think you should remember that my name is Miranda." I push my chair back and slowly stand up. "Not Wanda. Miranda."

I turn and start walking toward the exit, so tired I feel as if I'm moving in slow motion against some powerful current. Behind me I hear their voices, floating toward me as if from a vast distance.

"What's wrong with *her?*"

"She just walked out on us."

"She left her tray."

"Wanda!"

Limping a little, as though I've run too hard or ignored burning calf muscles, I keep walking. I make my way out of the dining hall, through the foyer and past the mailboxes and up the C-entry stairs, pausing at each landing to rest for a moment, just as if I were an old, old woman.

"'And as he stood there in the snow looking at her, he found that he had nothing more to say. No words, no sounds, just the snow falling everywhere, covering the ground, falling lovingly on their heads, caressing their faces like little white fingertips. And he knew, as he watched her, that somehow his life had changed in such a way that he would never be the same again. He wanted to reach a hand out to touch her but it seemed unnecessary somehow, so he just stood there and watched her, and felt the snow falling onto his head, white and inviting, soft white fingers somehow cold and warm at the same time.'"

Kerry pauses for a moment and then slowly lowers the last sheet of paper onto the table. She looks around the ring of faces and when nobody says anything she adds in a loud voice: "That's all, folks."

Then come the sounds of rustling papers, yawning, coughing, people stirring in their chairs. Gradually it all subsides into another deadly quiet.

Kerry looks around, frowning. "Hey, it's your turn now, remember?"

There's a sharp crackle of gum, and somebody laughs quietly. I'm sitting chin in hand, gazing across the table at Stephanie Kandel, who keeps her eyes fixed on her lap, when Winky whispers into my left ear: "Miranda?"

"Yeah?" I whisper back.

"I was supposed to hand something in today."

"Yeah?"

"Writer's block," she murmurs. "I had writer's block."

"Again?"

Mr. Tate finally looks away from the window, pushes his glasses higher on the bridge of his nose, and tries to smile at Kerry. "You're done reading?"

"Yes." She frowns at him too. "I thought it was obvious."

"Well, these days it's hard to know for sure." Mr. Tate shakes his head, and his glasses slip down again. "The new fiction and all. Can't tell if you're coming or going."

"It seemed pretty clear to me that the story had ended."

"Well, you're the author. You had some inside information."

At the word *author* Kerry has brightened, but doggedly she pushes on. "I tried to make the ending dramatic. You know, memorable. Memorable and—and compelling." She draws an invisible circle in the air. "Strong sense of closure."

"Oh, really?" Harris says. "I thought you were parodying the ending from 'The Dead.' "

She stiffens. "What's 'The Dead'?"

He gives her a sardonic look. "It's the book they made *Dawn of the Dead* from."

"What?" She glares at him. "Are you implying that my story is about a bunch of zombies?"

"Oh, for god's sake, Kerry, relax." One arm thrown over the back of her chair, Erin blows a shimmering pink bubble and pops it between her teeth. "He's pulling your leg."

"Well, he'd better stop."

Harris runs a hand through his curly red hair. "Say, are you threatening me?" He looks like he's about to laugh.

"Hey now." Mr. Tate rotates his head in a dilatory semicircle. "Let's just confine our remarks to the text, okay?"

"I refuse to sit here and be attacked." Kerry's earrings swing chaotically against her cheeks.

"You're the one who's getting all hot under the collar," Harris points out. "I simply made a teeny-weeny literary comparison and you jumped all over me."

"I wouldn't jump all over you if you were the last man on earth."

He simpers. "Fresh."

Mr. Tate lifts his hand about six inches off the table and lets it drop again. "Let's talk about the story, okay?"

"Great idea." Erin's jaws are working rhythmically, reminding me of an oil derrick pumping at full speed.

"Miranda?" Winky whispers.

"Yeah?"

"How come you keep staring at Stephanie?"

I look over at Winky. "Because," I say, very, very softly, "she's got a huge hickey on her neck."

"Really?" Winky puts her glasses on and gapes across the table. "Oh my goodness."

"Since it seems to be something of a point of contention," Mr. Tate is saying in his soft, enervated voice, "maybe we should start with the ending."

"Or maybe we should end with the start." Harris snickers.

Mr. Tate goes on as if he hasn't heard him. "Let's talk about the very last scene."

"I tried to make it dramatic and compelling—"

"No, no. It's their turn, remember?"

"Oh. Right." Kerry subsides unhappily.

Winky is still gawking over at Stephanie and finally, turning away from her myopically bulging eyes, I crane my head to get a look at Mr. Tate's watch. My neck crackles and he catches me peering at his wrist.

"Miranda, why don't you begin the discussion?"

"Discussion? Me?" Studying his drawn, not unattractive face, I find myself speculating if it's really true that he's on antide-pressants.

"Miranda?"

"Do I have to?" I wonder if anybody has bothered to tell him that he's got a short story in this month's issue of *Esquire.*

"No," he replies with that sad sweet smile of his. "But I wish you would."

I sigh. "Oh, all right."

"Big of you," Harris says.

Something goes off inside my head, like a tiny internal fire-cracker, and for one confused moment I think Erin has popped another bubble. But when I glance at her I see that she is in fact doodling quietly on the back of Kerry's story, her mouth for once perfectly still. I lean back in my chair. "Frankly, I thought the ending was derivative and contrived."

"And just what do you mean by that?" Kerry is bristling again.

"Oh, come on." I cross my arms over my chest. "Snow falling like little fingers? I'm sure."

"It's a simile," she says hotly. "Personification."

"It's a cliché. Boring."

"What do *you* know about snow? You're from California."

"Well, I'm no meteorologist," I drawl, "but I know what I like."

Harris snickers again. Mr. Tate's back to gazing blurrily at the window, and Erin pops another bubble. Stephanie Kandel is still staring down at her lap, her lank brown hair straggling over her shoulders. There is a small dreamy smile on her face.

Kerry's earrings are batting about. "I was talking about inno-cence and—and knowledge."

"I thought you were taking about snow."

"It's a simile!"

"It's a cliché!" I mimic her querulous intonation.

"Ooo-ee," Harris says. "What's with you today, Walker?"

"What do you mean, *Frick?*"

He quails a little, but presses on. "Get up on the wrong side of the bed? Or are you just on the rag?"

"Interesting question, Frick. Which reminds me. What kind of name is Frick anyway?" I give him an insolent little show of teeth. "It's kind of unusual, wouldn't you agree?"

"None of your business," he mutters, flushing.

"It's lucky your parents didn't name you Richard, isn't it? Can you imagine people calling you Rick? Or Dick?"

"Listen, Walker—"

"And what if you married a girl named Frack? And she wanted to hyphenate your last names? You could go into the sewing-notions business."

"Shut up!" His face is as red as his hair.

"Ooo-ee. Aren't we touchy today?"

"You don't know what you're talking about. So why don't you just keep your mouth shut for once?"

"Frick," I say pensively. "Frick. Now where have I heard that name before? You *are* a fine-arts major, aren't you?"

"I said *Shut up*."

I look at him across the table. If he lunges for me I'll have to swat him away with my notebook. In the silence I can practically hear the eyeballs bouncing back and forth between Harris and me. At the far end of the table, Erin works peacefully away on her gum. Then Kerry says in an urgent little bleat: "Mr. Tate?"

His head jerks up. "Eh?"

"Isn't it time for our break?"

"Break?" He tries to focus on his watch. "Oh. Sure. Take ten, everybody."

The room clears out except for Mr. Tate, Harris, and me. I yawn protractedly, without bothering to cover my mouth, and Mr. Tate looks over at me with his soft melancholy eyes.

"You're usually a bit more tolerant, aren't you?"

"There's only so much that flesh and blood can bear."

"That's true." Mr. Tate nods, slowly. "I often tell myself that." He heaves himself up from his chair and makes a desultory attempt to tuck his shirt back into his trousers. "Well, if you'll excuse me. It's time. . . ." He drifts out into the hallway, leaving me alone with Harris, and I start staring at the window. There is a short silence.

"Look, *Miranda*." Harris speaks with ostentatious calm. "I didn't want to pick a fight with you, you know. It's just that you're being such a bitch today."

"Am I?"

"My god, yes. Even more than usual." Smiling, he leans forward in his chair. "Why *are* you being such a bitch, anyway? Nothing's wrong, I hope?"

I gaze at him across the tabletop. Even his eyelashes are that same bright, sickly red color. "Wrong?"

"You can tell me."

"Tell you what?"

"What's bothering you."

I lift my eyebrows. "Why would anything be bothering me? Aside from your stupid questions, that is."

"Oh, come on, Miranda." After a few seconds he gives a sharp little laugh. "Oh, I get it. You're being snotty because you've already had *your* stories critiqued. You feel safe now, don't you? You can be all high and mighty about it, right?"

"Frick, try not to be more of a dope than you already are."

"You think your stories are so great. So that means you can rip on everybody else."

"Dear, dear Frick."

"You think you're better than everybody else." His voice rises screechily. "You're nothing but a snob. A snob, do you hear?"

"Frick, Frick," I say gently. "Why don't you take your little old trust fund and go jump off a pier?"

"You think you're so great," he whispers. "Cunt."

Raising my eyebrows again, I look straight at him. "Frick." Then, whistling a little, I pluck a Kleenex out of my bag and leisurely proceed to blow my nose. We maintain a torpid silence as the rest of the class straggles back in, taking their seats and eyeing us curiously. Mr. Tate, the last one to return, slides into his chair and looks dreamily around the table. His glasses tilt crookedly across his eyes.

"Well, then." He sighs and pokes at the papers in front of him. "I guess it's time to move on to the next story."

There's another anticipatory rustling of papers and shifting of chairs. Erin blows three quick little bubbles, *pop pop pop*. I feel an irrepressible smile curving my lips.

"Okay," Mr. Tate says. "Who's next?"

Pop pop pop. My smile widens. Folding my arms across my chest, I glance across the table. "It's Frick's turn," I say, pleasantly.

———

Trying to keep myself from sobbing aloud, I'm hunkering on the steps leading down to the huge paved courtyard that separates the towering Catholic church on Bow Street from the equally massive parochial school across the way. School has let out and there are what seem like dozens of Catholic schoolboys playing ball in and around the neatly painted basketball courts below. Some of the boys just lean idly against the fence that parallels Mount Auburn Street, their black caps tilted back on their heads. Is it my imagination, or are they staring at me as I sit here jackknifed on the steps weeping into my knees?

Frick's words loop relentlessly through my mind. *You feel safe now, don't you? You think you're better than everybody else. Cunt. Cunt. Cunt.*

I grip my head more tightly between my hands, wanting to squeeze my brain into utter silence. But now I hear my mother's voice, high-pitched and thinned out over telephone wires. *You'd better get off that high horse of yours, young lady. I don't know what they're teaching you at that fancy school of yours over there, but I can tell you one thing: you're no better than the rest of us. You and those kooky clothes of yours, that makeup, walking around with your nose in the air like you're some kind of princess.* A huge silent sob grips me.

"Whatcha doin'?" says a little voice.

I look up from my knees. "Huh?" Standing below me on the steps is one of the young schoolboys. He gazes up at me, swinging his satchel in a gentle arc.

"I said, whatcha doin'?"

"I'm—I'm—well, I'm—" The late-afternoon sun is turning his light-brown crewcut into gold. *Like a halo. Dear god.* I force myself to remove my hands from my hair and to take a deep breath. "I'm—I'm suntanning."

"Oh, yeah? Then why's your face all wet?"

"Uh, because it's raining?"

"No, it's not," he replies, his face serious. "It's sunny out."

I tilt my head up toward the sky. "Are you sure?"

"Sure I'm sure."

"You're right, it's not raining. So I'm suntanning, okay?"

"Naw, you're crying. How come?"

"How come?" I stare at him. *Jesus, he looks so frail,* I think wonderingly, *he's all spindly arms and legs*. His face is uncannily handsome, his fine, strong features almost too keenly formed, without any softening baby fat to obscure the angles of pointy little chin, sharp cheekbones, slanting long-lashed eyes. His skin is clear and soft-looking, almost luminescent in the golden afternoon light. I shudder with another noiseless sob.

"Yeah, how come?"

"I—I—somebody's been calling me names."

"Is *that* all?"

"They were—bad names."

"So what? People call me names all the time."

"What? Why on earth would anybody call you names?"

"People are jerks."

"Oh." I blink. "Hey."

"Hey what."

"What's your name?"

"Timmy." He's busy scuffing the cement step with the toe of his shoe.

"Are you a Tim or a Timothy?"

"Huh?" He pauses briefly and then resumes his scuffing, this time with the other foot. "Oh. Either. My mom calls me Timmy. Timothy when she's mad at me."

I watch him scuff, gazing at his serious little downturned face as he systematically scrapes away the polish on his formerly shiny black shoes. "Hey."

"Hey what."

"Don't you want to know what my name is?"

He scuffs a few more times, then stops and looks up at me. "Well?" he says impatiently in his clear thin voice. "What's your name?"

"It's—" My breath catches in my throat and I stare back at him. "It's Miranda," I say at last.

"What? Tarantula?" His face lights up delightedly. "Your name is Tarantula?"

"Well, actually—" I feel myself starting to smile too.

"Neat! I've never met anybody named after a spider before."

"Well, I—"

"Can you crawl up walls too?" He laughs, a flat, ironic little bark.

"Well, it's not exactly my name," I hedge.

"What? Why not?" His face darkens suspiciously. "You mean you made it up?"

"No, no. It's—it's a nickname. Like your name is Timothy but your mom calls you Timmy. See?"

"Oh." He scrutinizes me unblinkingly. "Okay," he says, noncommittally.

"You can call me Tarantula if you want."

He is silent.

"I don't let many people do that, you know."

"Okay." He starts swinging his schoolbag again.

"Timmy."

"What."

"Uh—" I wipe my nose with the back of my hand. "So do you play with your friends after school?"

"Sometimes."

"Is it fun?"

"Sometimes."

"It's not always fun?"

"Sometimes it's a drag."

"Why is it a drag?"

"Because sometimes my friends are jerks."

"Shouldn't your friends be nice to you?"

"Some of them are."

"Only some of them are nice?"

"Yep."

"What about the other ones?"

"They're mean."

"You have mean friends?"

He shrugs.

"They call you names," I venture.

"Yep."

"What do you do when they call you names?"

He shrugs again.

"Doesn't it bother you?"

He looks up at me for a moment, then drops his eyes back down to his schoolbag. "Who cares?" he says, with another humorless laugh.

"Why do you have them for friends if they're mean to you?"

"They're not always mean."

"But still."

He lets out an impatient puff of air. "Sometimes they're nice, and sometimes they're mean," he says as if talking to a complete dullard.

"Your friends should always be nice to you," I persist. "Don't you think so?"

He lifts his shoulders in another shrug, and then starts scuffing his shoe again. Clutching my knees to my chest, I watch him in silence for a little while.

"Timmy?"

He doesn't look up. "What."

"Do you live around here?"

"Nope."

"Are you waiting for the schoolbus?"

"Nope." He switches to his other shoe. "I'm waiting for my mom."

"Oh. She picks you up after school?"

"Sometimes."

"What about the other times?"

"My stepdad picks me up."

"They take turns then."

"Yep."

"You're doing a nice job on your shoes," I say admiringly.

"Thanks."

"Is your mom late today?" I look around the schoolyard. "Most everybody else is gone."

"Sometimes they won't let her out of work early." He stops scuffing and sits down two steps below me, holding his satchel between his knees.

"What about your stepdad?"

"What about him?"

"Does he come on time?"

"Sometimes." He looks down at the courtyard, narrowing his eyes against the sun.

"Do you like your stepdad?"

"Sometimes."

"Do you like your mom?"

"Sometimes." He shrugs. "Most of the time."

"That's good." I gaze at his small, finely molded profile. "Isn't it?"

"I guess so," he says indifferently.

Having cried most of the way home, I've silently let myself in and have crept into the den, where I climb up into the big leather desk-chair and pick up the telephone receiver. On my third try I get the numbers right and my grandmother answers the phone in her soft crackly voice.

"Hello?"

"Gram," I say quaveringly.

"What's wrong, Mirabelle?"

"I gave him my pencil box."

"You gave who your pencil box, honey?"

"Tommy." A sob shakes me.

"And what happened? Tell Gramma."

"He told me he liked it and then he walked home with Laura."

"No," she breathes. "The dirty rat."

"My new pencil box."

"Not your new orange one? The one with the picture of Twiggy on the front?"

I sob again. "It had four pencils inside."

"Oh, honey."

"And my favorite eraser."

"The pink horse that you got at the dentist's?"

"Yes." My tears fall onto the desktop.

"And the rat didn't even walk home with you?"

"No," I say forlornly.

"After you gave him your brand-new pencil box." She sounds angry.

"Gram, why did he—" I break off as the door to the den opens and I see my mother standing in the doorway, her body a dark figure-eight outline against the sunlight in the hall.

"Mirabelle? Miranda?" my grandmother is saying. *"Are you there, honey?"*

My mother comes into the room, a cigarette in one hand. *"Who are you talking to?"* Her eyebrows are squeezed together into a single thin line.

"Gram," I whisper, looking up into her face.

She takes the receiver from me. *"Mom?"* she says, and listens for a second. *"I've told you a million times, you've got to stop spoiling her."* She is quiet, exhaling a long silvery-blue breath of smoke, and then she says sharply, *"I don't have time for this. I'll talk to you later."* She hangs up the phone and looks down at me. *"Haven't I told you not to come into your father's study?"*

"He doesn't care." I wipe my nose with the back of my hand. *"He's never here."*

"Don't argue with me, young lady." She puffs once, twice on her cigarette, the tip glowing red like a wicked little eye. *"And stop wiping your nose with your hand."*

"I need a Kleenex."

She's looking down at the desk. *"You've gotten Daddy's papers all wet."* She takes me by the shoulder and pulls me from the chair. *"From now on you stay out of Daddy's study. You hear me?"*

"It's the den," I say feebly, feeling the tears starting to slip down my cheeks again. *"It's not the study, it's the den."*

"Will you ever learn? It's not the den." She gives my shoulder a little shake. *"We're calling it the study now. And just stay out."* Holding me by my wrist, she marches me into the hallway, slamming the door shut behind her. *"Now go upstairs and blow your nose."*

"Hey. Hey." Timmy pokes my knee with his forefinger, once, and pulls his hand back. "Hey, spider woman."

My eyebrows wrinkling, I look down at him on the step below. "Hey what."

"Do you go to school too?"

"Yep. Just like you."

"Are you waiting for someone to come pick you up?"

"Nope. Just hanging out."

We sit silently for a while, and then I wipe my nose with the collar of my t-shirt. "Timmy."

"What."

"Do you have a pencil box?"

"A what?"

"A pencil box. You know, a box to keep your pencils in."

"Nope."

"Well, what do you keep your pencils in?"

"I don't have any pencils."

"You don't? Then what do you use to write with?"

"They make us use pens." He laughs mirthlessly. "And get mad at us when we make mistakes."

"Are you serious?"

"No, I'm making it up," he says darkly. "Like it's raining today too."

"You're right." I poke him gently on the arm, once. "People are jerks."

"Yep." He looks at his arm. Then he shrugs. "But who cares?"

"You're right." This time I'm the one giving the bitter little chuckle. "Who cares?"

We're quiet again for a while. I'm clasping my knees to my chest, watching the sun tint his hair a tawny gold. Suddenly he jumps up, swinging his schoolbag.

"It's my mom."

"Where?" I look around in confusion.

He points across the schoolyard. "There. In the green car."

A small green Toyota has pulled up to the curb on Mount Auburn Street. Through the fence I can see a blur of face and hair, a hand waving from the driver's side.

"Well—" He looks at me for a second. "So long." Without waiting for a reply he turns and hops down the steps. When he reaches the bottom he stops, stands stock-still for a moment, and digs into his satchel. Then he runs back up the steps and thrusts something at me. "Here."

I hold my hand out and he drops something onto my palm: a green plastic ring. "What's this?" I look at the ring and then over at him.

"My Spiderman ring."

"No, no. I can't. Not your Spiderman ring."

"Take it," he says impatiently.

"No, I can't. It's too much." I hold it out to him. "Really."

"Don't you want it?"

"Of course I want it."

"Then take it, stupid."

I look at him and then my fingers curl around the ring. "Okay." From across the schoolyard a car horn honks. "Thanks."

"You girls are so dumb." He turns and runs down the steps and across the yard. He gets into the Toyota, which after a few seconds pulls out onto Mount Auburn Street and drives away, merging swiftly into the traffic.

The courtyard is deserted now except for two priests walking toward the church, heads bent and hands clasped behind their backs. Alone on the steps, I look down at my hand, observing how the sunlight lends my skin a faint golden sheen, and slowly, smiling a little, I uncurl my fingers.

"Ow," I say aloud. I'm slumped on the sofa with Jessica's hot-water bottle resting on my stomach. "Ow!" I frown at the ceiling. How long can it take for three Midol to kick in?

I pick up the *Lampoon* again and turn to the next article. It's called "How I Made a Killing in the Stock Market" and above the title is a full-color picture of a hatchet dripping with bright-red blood.

"Oh Christ." I flip the *Lampoon* into the fireplace. From the street below I hear a car radio blaring some thumping disco song by Queen, a voice wailing high over the bass: *"Another one bites the dust, another one bites the dust."* The sound rises and then falls, slowly dying away as the car drives off down Plympton Street. I readjust the hot-water bottle a little lower between my hipbones, and then I close my eyes and try to drift off into sleep. Twisting my head on the sofa cushion, I recall that Midol has caffeine in it. "Oh Christ." I force myself to count backward from a hundred in French. But even as I'm finally starting to go limp, without warning I find myself remembering Richard's voice, strong and plaintive through a bright misty blaze of turquoise.

> *Your crown don't it weigh too much*
> *See it glitter, see it shine*

Yeah shimmering it reflects the light
But it weighs too much, it keeps you down
Do you remember, do you know
Can you take it off at night

For a moment I'm tempted to get up and turn on the radio, and then the phone rings. Lacing my fingers over the hot-water bottle, I look at the ceiling and silently count. On the fifteenth ring I jump up and pounce on the receiver. "What?" I snarl.

"Hi, Miranda."

"Who's this?"

"It's me."

"Look, I don't have time for this. Who's calling?"

"It's Tim."

"What?" *Little Timmy?*

"Tim Lazare. Remember me?"

"Oh. Hi."

"Listen, can I come up? I'm downstairs."

I sit down on the couch, sagging against the cushion. "Yeah, sure," I say slowly.

When I open the door to him I think for a brief moment that he's going to hug me, and I start backing into the living room. "Come on in. Have a seat."

"Thanks." He sits on the sofa, one arm stretched along the back. He looks up at me, smiling.

"Well," I say.

"Yep."

"Well, well, well." I'm standing in the middle of the room, my hands gripped together. "Would you like something to drink?"

"Sure. What have you got?"

"Water."

"That's okay. Thanks."

"Sorry."

"Are you going to sit down?"

"What? Oh. Okay." I sink into the armchair.

"So."

"Yep."

"It's nice to see your room again. I haven't been here in a while."

I find that I'm holding on to the arms of the chair with fingers that have gone white. "So," I say evenly, "what brings you around these parts?"

"I just thought I'd drop by."

"Drop by?"

He's crossed one leg over the other and is jauntily swinging his foot back and forth. "Yeah, I was just in the neighborhood."

"I see." I make myself let go of the chair arms. "Tim?"

"Yeah?"

"Can I—" I hesitate, startled all over again by the complete symmetry of his features, even to the cleft in the exact middle of his chin. I feel a fiery blush start to flood my face. "Can I ask you something?"

"Sure."

"It's about that night we spent together."

"Yeah?"

I'm gripping the chair again. "Why the fuck did you have to go and tell Bryan and Jessie?"

"Huh?" The foot stops swinging.

"You had to go and blab." My voice trembles. "Why couldn't you just keep your goddam mouth shut?"

"Well, I—"

"I mean, it wasn't like it was the goddam eighth wonder of the world or anything."

"But I—"

"Don't you realize I almost threw up on your bedspread?"

"I know, but—"

"Tim, nothing happened."

"Well, I just—"

"Why the hell did you have to tell them?"

"I told everybody."

"What?"

"Yeah." He smiles at me. "I just thought it was so neat."

"Neat?"

"Yeah, you're so cool, and so pretty, and I—well, I just thought it was neat."

"Well." I can feel another rush of heat cascading down my face. "My own impressions were somewhat different."

As Tim opens his mouth to reply, I hear the door to C-45 being unlocked. "Hello?" Jessica calls out. "Anybody home?" She comes whirling into the living room and abruptly halts, her skirt flouncing around her calves.

"Hi, Jessie." I sense my face irrationally collapsing into lines of guilty distress. "Welcome home."

"Hi, Jessica," Tim says from the couch.

She's looking straight at me. "I'd like to speak with you."

"Yes." I glance at Tim. "Well, thanks for dropping by."

"Oh. Sure." He stands up, and I follow him to the door, avoiding Jessica's eyes. At the threshold his arms go out as if to embrace me and I recoil, whispering sharply, "Stop it. Jesus."

"Oh. Yeah. Sorry."

"Jesus."

"Well, bye, Miranda." He smiles at me. "It was nice seeing you again."

"So long." I close the door in his face, and turn the deadbolt. I lean against the door just for a moment, listening to him whistle as he goes down the stairs.

"I'm fucking tired of your taking everything I own."

"You've used *fucking* fourteen times in the last twelve sentences."

"I'm fucking tired of your fucking taking everything I own." Jessica is pacing around the living room. "My clothing, my sheets, my shampoo. Nothing of mine is safe from you."

"Sixteen."

She glares at me. "You're the reason my socks don't match."

"Jessie," I say gently, "you know that's not true. You do it on purpose, remember? Your antibourgeois fashion statement." I'm sitting in the armchair watching her stump back and forth.

"Okay, forget the socks. But everything else. Don't you know the meaning of property? Of trampling other people's boundaries? Of invading interpersonal territories?"

"Sure. I took Soc Sci 15 too."

"A vulture, that's what you are. Just waiting to descend." She flaps her arms in the air.

"Now just a minute."

"A vampire," she screams. "Sucking me dry!"

"Jessica." I uncross my legs. "Listen to me."

"You take fucking everything." She points a pale accusing finger at me. "You even took Tim from me."

"Don't be ridiculous."

"You knew I liked him, and so you couldn't keep your hands off him."

"I thought we'd gone over this," I say wearily. "And would you kindly get your finger away from my nose?"

"It's all the same to you, isn't it? Shampoo, clothing, men."

"Jessie—"

"The grass is always greener, right?"

"Jessica—"

"And then you bring him up here and flaunt it in my face." She pivots violently. "Were you planning to fuck on the sofa? Or on my bed?"

"Christ, Jessica."

"D'you have to rub it in my face?"

"Jessie, he called and asked to come up, and—"

"That's right," she sneers. "You're just the girl who cain't say no."

I swallow. "That's uncalled for."

"Don't tell *me* what's fucking uncalled for." Her chin juts rancorously. "How could you do that to me?"

"Look. I made a mistake. It should never have happened. I'm sorry, okay?" My heart is battering against my chest. "I'm sorrier than I can ever tell you."

"You're sorry. Big fucking deal."

"Jessica—"

"Where's my goddam Christian Dior twelve-dollar lipstick?" she screams.

"Do you think I'm having *fun?*" I say in a low voice. "That I'm doing this for laughs?"

She stares at me, her hands hidden in the folds of her skirt.

"Do you really believe that this is my idea of fun? Is that what you think?"

"Well, what I really think," she says coolly, "is that I'd like you to let go of the chair before you break the arms off. It's mine, if you recall."

"I asked you a question."

"I know you did." She snorts, tossing her head. "I know you. It's just your way of twisting things around, trying to put me on the defensive."

"That's not true." Suddenly a half-remembered voice corkscrews through my brain. *That Miranda. She could sell shoes to a snake.*

"Oh yeah? If I don't watch you like a goddam hawk, in five minutes you'll have me on my knees begging for forgiveness."

Who said that? "Listen. Will you listen?" Now I feel a headache coming on. "I'd just like an honest answer, that's all." *Jackson? Teddy? Master Ackerman?* My mind churns uselessly.

"Oh, Jesus. An honest answer. Now I'm rooming with goddam Demosthenes. How fabulous." Shaking her head, Jessica plunks herself onto the sofa. "Jesus," she screams, jumping up. "Christ!" She digs into the cushions and pulls out the hot-water bottle. "What the fuck is *this*?"

"A hot-water bottle."

"*Whose* fucking hot-water bottle?"

"Your fucking hot-water bottle," I say politely.

"That's right, *my* fucking hot-water bottle. Why don't you use your own fucking hot-water bottle, for Christ's sake?"

"I don't own a hot-water bottle. Or a fucking hot-water bottle, for that matter."

"Oh, you're funny."

"Not really."

"Why don't you buy your own?" She drops the bag as if it's contaminated by something unspeakably foul. It lands on the floor with a soft gurgle. "They're found in any drugstore. Any idiot can buy one."

"I'm not sure I like what you're implying."

"Jesus, you're such a goddam hypochondriac." She lowers herself onto the couch with conspicuous gingerness. "For such a healthy person, you're pretty goddam sick."

"That's a compliment, right?" My stomach cramps, and secretively I slide a hand over my abdomen.

"No, it's not a fucking compliment."

"Oh."

"I'm sick of hearing about your goddam lymph nodes. All you do is worry about your body, do you know that? Jesus, you act like any minute it's going to goddam fall apart."

"How do you know it won't?"

"You're twenty-one years old! You're a kid!" she screams. "Stop worrying about every single twinge, for Christ's sake." She waves her arms in exasperation. "I swear, you're worse than my crazy old grandmother. Every time she loses a fucking *eyelash* she runs crying to her doctor, begging him to surgically glue it back on again."

"I see." My head droops, and I prop it up by cupping my chin in my hand.

"These are the best goddam years of our lives, and all you do is complain," Jessica rages on. "You're always feeling so goddam sorry for yourself."

I look at her through my eyelashes. "Somebody has to."

After a moment she laughs disagreeably. "I haven't slept in three days, I'm living on Spaghetti Os and granola bars, I'm surrounded by three balding cats who keep trying to hump my leg, and *you're* feeling sorry for yourself?"

"Why are you living on Spaghetti Os and granola bars?"

"That's all there is in my thesis adviser's goddam apartment. That's what the goddam cats eat too."

"Why don't you buy some groceries?"

"Because, in case you haven't noticed," she replies icily, "I've got a thesis to write."

"Then why are you wasting time fighting with me?"

"I came back for some clean towels. I suppose you've used them already too?"

"You're in luck." *Goddam.* I can't take aspirin, now that I've already taken the Midol. "I haven't had a chance to sink my fangs into your washcloths yet."

"Aren't you flip." She gives that scathing laugh again. "Her royal highness, the queen of the fast comeback."

There is a silence. Involuntarily I sniffle, softly.

"Don't just sit there sniffing down your nose at me, you shit."

"I need to blow my nose." I glance at her. "But I'm afraid you'll start calling me names again."

"Go ahead," she screams. "Use my Kleenex, why don't you?"

I wipe my nose with the back of my hand. "Are you through hollering? For the moment?"

"Why?" She eyes me suspiciously.

"Just asking."

"Why? What do you want to take now?"

I stand up. "Well, if you'll excuse me, I'm going to my room."

"That's right," she calls after me. "Go feel sorry for yourself."

My hand on the doorknob, I pause. "Jessica?"

"What? What the fuck is it now?"

"You probably won't take this in the right spirit, but—" I look at her for a long moment. "Good luck with your thesis." Quietly I shut the door.

WEDNESDAY | 8

||||||||||||||||||||||||||||||||||||||||||||||||||||||||||||||||||||||||

*E*yes closed, I lie in bed with my hands on my thighs, trying to detect the presence of new fat. Have my muscles gone slack? Have they begun to atrophy yet? I squeeze my quadriceps, recalling a magazine article I read somewhere about how inactivity reduces fitness at a geometric rate more or less approximating the speed of light.

Wincing, I pull the covers closer around my shoulders. I hear my next-door neighbor in C-41 laughing shrilly. *How long have I been in bed?*

I open my eyes and look over at the clock. It's four-thirty. I've been lying here for almost fifteen hours. Folding my arms behind my head, I gaze up at the light fixture. Taking twice the recommended dosage of Nyquil, it seems, results in a proportionate amount of sleep.

A quavering scream comes skewering through the wall, and I pinch at my waist for excess flesh. Then, sighing, I slope upward against the pillows and blow my nose. The Nyquil doesn't seem to have helped much with my congestion, I think crossly, flicking the

Kleenex onto the floor, and suddenly I sit up straight. It's Wednesday. Late Wednesday afternoon, to be precise. Another Soc Sci 33 class missed. I start to yawn, and then into my mind comes the image of Jessica pacing a distraught little figure-eight in front of me. *That's right. You're just the girl who cain't say no.*

There's the sound of something smashing next door, and I look away from the wall, gazing at the gray attenuated shadows slanting in under the half-drawn blind. They look like trees, I tell myself, mutant trees. Or like those weird deep-sea creatures that never see the sun. *No, dope, they look like lettuce leaves.*

My stomach gives a long, hollow-sounding gurgle. I look over at the clock again. It's been nearly twenty-four hours since I've last eaten. Slouching down against the pillows, dreamily I contemplate what I'll have for breakfast. A big plate of waffles swimming in maple syrup? A mushroom-and-cheese omelette with heaps of toast and freshly squeezed orange juice? Or maybe I'll skip straight to dinner and have a hamburger and french fries, with lots of ketchup. And Tab. And maybe some frozen yogurt from Baby Watson's for dessert.

Humming, I throw off the covers and stand up. But when I lean forward to do a few toe touches, I find myself staring at my knees. When was the last time I went running? *No pain, no gain,* I hear Walt's voice echoing thinly in my ears. *You're not going to let a little cold stop you from jogging, are you?* Exhaling deeply, I touch my palms flat to the floor, ignoring another despairing gurgle from my stomach. Then I straighten up, trying to shake the tinny little voice snaking through my head. *No run, no fun. Go ahead and feel sorry for yourself, why doncha.*

"Sister," I say aloud, bouncing on my toes, "you can kiss that mushroom-and-cheese omelette goodbye."

I do a few dilatory waist twists. The way the day is going, I reflect bitterly, I may as well drag myself downstairs to the Adams House library and check out some Soc Sci 33 readings. I sigh again and then start scrounging around for some clean clothes.

Dressed in sweatpants, sneakers, and my ancient Minnie Mouse sweatshirt with the ripped sleeve, I pass the mailboxes, forbidding myself even a fast peep, and stalk along the entryway. From the

Gold Room come sounds of raised voices, laughter, and off-key piano tinkling. As I'm passing by, eyes fixed upon the curving staircase that leads up to the library, through the massive gold-leafed double doors I hear someone squeaking out:

"Look who's here!"

"*Meer*iam!"

The Bicknell twins dart out, each of them taking one of my wrists in a surprisingly strong grip.

"Come on in!"

"Join the party!"

I look left and right at them, both wearing identical pale-blue dresses with dainty lace collars, and finally I concede that I'll never be able to tell the two of them apart. "What's up, girls?"

"First Boston's throwing a cocktail party."

"For prospective job applicants."

"Why don't you come in?"

"We're having lots of fun."

"Well, I've really got a lot of studying to do—"

"They're giving away the cutest little miniature briefcases."

"There's going to be a slide show later on."

"Some of the guys are really cute."

"And the buffet is fantastic."

"Buffet?" I look over at Stacey or Beth, whichever. "I don't suppose they have cheese balls, do they? Those mushy little orange things all studded with nuts?"

"Sure they do!"

"Trays and trays!"

"Well, I don't know. It's just that I'm way behind in my Soc Sci 33—"

"They're giving away door prizes."

"A gift certificate to the Coop."

"Tickets to a Red Sox game."

"Plus there's an open bar."

"A Red Sox game? No kidding?"

"Cross my heart!"

"Hope to die!"

"Well, maybe I'll pop in for a minute or two."

"Yay!"

"Hurrah!"

"But there's just one thing."

"What?" they say in unison.

"Maybe you could let go of my wrists before we go in."

"Oh, bad luck!"

"Your turn, Marlene."

"My turn already?" I lean against the piano, blinking. *What am I doing here? Who are these guys? And why am I wearing a tie over my Minnie Mouse sweatshirt?* I hear another soft *ptui* on my right and then I remember I'm in the middle of an orange-seed spitting contest with two young associates from First Boston, using orange slices we've stolen from the bar and martini glasses for targets. They've taken off their jackets and have rolled up their sleeves to the elbow. It's Ned's tie I'm wearing, a handsome silk paisley, loosely knotted around my neck. "Wait a minute. I thought it was Peter's turn."

"No, no. He just spit on somebody's back."

"Forgot the seed." Peter grins.

I look over to where Ned is pointing. "Hey, that's our house master."

"Well, that's Peter for you," Ned says proudly. "Always aiming for the top."

Peter slings his arm around my shoulder. "That's the way we do things at First Boston, Marlene." His breath smells of gin and oranges.

"Spitting on people's clothing?"

"No, no. Aiming for the top."

"And succeeding," Ned adds. "You can bet your bottom dollar on that." They both laugh.

"That's right, little lady." Peter's arm tightens around me. "We don't know the meaning of the word failure."

"Is that so?" I look over at him, noticing dimly that I'm slurring my words. "Then how come I'm the one winning the contest?"

Ned laughs loudly. "You Radcliffe girls. Cute *and* smart." He throws his arm around my shoulder, getting tangled up with Peter's arm in the process.

"Oh, Ned!" Peter coos. "I didn't know you *cared*."

"You pussy-faced dick." Ned pulls his arm away, nodding at me. "None of that stuff at First Boston, Marlene. You can rest easy on that score."

"We don't go in for that kind of shit," Peter agrees. "No way. Nothing but real men at First Boston, Marlene."

"That's good to know."

"Say, Marlene." Ned leans close again.

"What." I take a big swallow of my drink.

"You're a Radcliffe girl, right?"

"Woman." Peter squeezes my shoulder.

"I guess so." I take another swig. "Who cares?"

Ned looks around, then whispers, "Is it true what they say about intelligence being an aphrodisiac?"

I blink at him. "I don't know. What do you mean?"

"Well, I hear—" He lowers his voice even more. "I hear there's a correlation between your IQ and how good you are in bed."

"Oh, I see. Well, I sleep pretty soundly, I guess. But maybe that's because I always leave my window open."

"No, what I think they mean is—"

"Maybe it's the fresh air."

"No, I—"

"Just a tiny bit, even in winter." I blow my nose in a cocktail napkin.

"Yuck," Peter says, wrinkling his nose. "That's what you get for sleeping with the windows open."

I crumple up the napkin and pitch it into one of the martini glasses. "Two points," I say lightly, fighting down an oncoming sensation of *déjà vu*.

"Just a minute here." Ned clears his throat. "Who says it's two points?"

"A napkin is lots bigger than an orange seed. It should be worth twice as much."

"But you blew your nose in it."

"Then make it four points."

Ned starts to think it over, and I grin at him, showing all my teeth. No one speaks for a moment.

"Heard a great joke today," Peter says brightly. "An investment banker meets a commodities trader in a bar, see—"

I look across the room, where Stacey and Beth are gleefully waving their Red Sox tickets in front of the slide projector. Standing by the bar Master Ackerman watches them without expression, paying only nominal attention to the two enthusiastically gesticulating juniors in sports coats who flank him, their mouths moving almost as rapidly as their arms. Then I see the pear-shaped Larson in earnest conversation with a First Boston representative, who wears an expensive-looking navy-blue suit with an equally expensive-looking paisley tie. I can't help noticing that both he and Larson are eating cheese balls. Behind me at the piano somebody is playing "Moon River" badly.

"—and so the trader says to him, 'Pork bellies? Well, pal, I guess that means you're overdrawn!' "

Ned and Peter erupt with laughter, jostling me merrily with what seems like a disproportionate number of elbows. I laugh too, jabbing them back, although in the middle of a particularly high-pitched peal it occurs to me that I have no idea what I'm laughing about. Mid-giggle I look out into the foyer and see Michael going toward the dining hall.

"Michael. Yoo hoo."

He turns. "Y'all just yoo-hoo me?" Hands in pockets, he gazes at me through the doorway.

"Yes. Hi."

"I'm goin' to dinner. Y'all wanna come?"

"We'd love to." Ned gives another spurt of laughter, jabbing me again.

"Ow. He means me."

"Oh, darn." Peter's fingers creep in through the rip in my sweatshirt to tickle my armpit.

"Stop it. Michael—" I realize I'm still grinning and foggily I try to stop it, but I'm afraid my face will crack if I do. "Yoo hoo."

Slowly he comes toward me, long-legged in jeans and boots. "What's doin', gal?"

"Michael—"

"Ned Billings. As in Montana." Ned sticks out his hand. "And this good-looking guy over here is Peter Ainsley."

Peter waits for Ned to relinquish Michael's hand before sticking out his own. "Call me Pete."

"Howdy-do." Michael puts his hand back into his pocket. "Some shindig y'all got goin' here. Somebody's birthday?"

"No, it's—"

"First Boston, Mike."

"That's right, Mike. We're looking for a few good people."

"We're aiming for the top."

"In fact, we've already offered Marlene here a summer internship."

"Marlene?" Michael's eyebrows go up.

"She'll be working in arbitrage, Mike."

"Five hundred clams a week."

"Starts first week of June."

"Subsidized housing."

"Company pays for lunches and cab fare."

"Possibility of staying on full-time."

"Twenty-eight thousand a year to start."

"Plus a bonus in January."

"Profit sharing."

"Free checking and automatic deposit."

"Discount membership at the New York Health and Racquet Club."

"Neat, huh?" I say weakly.

"If y'all say so."

Ned puts his arm around me again. "Yep, we think Marlene will be an important member of the First Boston team."

"Very important." Peter slaps me jovially on the back.

"Ow. Michael." The Gold Room has begun to slowly sway back and forth. "I think I forgot to feed Edgar."

"Edgar?" Ned asks, breathing gin and oranges into my face. "Who's Edgar?"

"My asparagus fern." I struggle to straighten up under the dead weight of his arm. "If I don't water him on time, he starts dropping his needles."

"Dropping his what?"

"Needles. Hypodermics." I feel an abrupt urge to laugh. "You've got to be careful not to step on 'em, you know. They go right through your shoes."

"Yeah, yeah, sure." His big genial face looks perplexed.

"Didn't I tell you that I'm pre-med?" A tiny risible bubble is expanding inside my chest. "You know. Cutting open frogs and dead people, that kind of stuff."

"Neat!" Peter exclaims. "Frogs, really?"

"Edgar, Edgar." Finally I succeed in freeing myself. The floor feels rubbery under my feet. "Michael?"

"Gal?"

"We'd better hurry, don't you think?"

"Sure."

I step forward and take hold of his arm. "Bye guys." I try to focus on their faces. "Nice meeting you."

"Bye, Marlene."

"See you in June."

"Bright-eyed and bushy-tailed." Ned winks at me.

"Don't forget your briefcase." They both laugh.

"Your dinner," I say, face-down on Michael's bed, feeling it tilt languorously from side to side. "Yoo hoo."

He sits next to me, leaning against the wall. "I'm right here. You don't need to yell."

"I'm sorry. Your dinner. I'm sorry."

"It's okay."

"I'm sorry."

"Don't worry 'bout it."

"Michael?"

"Yeah?"

"Did you take my shoes off?"

"Yes'm. Why?"

"I was just wondering." The bubble in my chest has tightened into a dense little ball that's making it hard for me to breathe. And my left arm is tingling painfully. "Michael."

"What?"

"I think I'm having a heart attack."

"What makes you think that?"

"My left arm hurts. They say that's the first sign."

"Maybe that's 'cause you're lyin' on top of it."

"Oh." He helps me pull my arm from underneath me. "I guess maybe it just fell asleep, huh?"

"Guess so."

The bed lists precariously, and I give a little moan.

"Kitten?"

"Huh?"

"You okay?"

"Can't complain," I say into the pillow.

"Good girl."

"Michael?"

"Yes'm?"

"I only had three drinks."

"They sure do go a long way, don't they?"

"Empty stomach."

"That helps too." He laughs softly. "How's your arm?"

"Much better."

"Good."

"Michael?"

"Gal?"

"I think I'd like to sit up now."

"Okay."

I twist over on my side and he helps me slide up against the pillows. Everything reels for a moment and then settles into a gentle oscillation.

"Michael?"

"Yeah?"

"My chest still hurts."

"Your chest hurts?"

"Yes. Here." I take his hand and place it on my breastbone.

"How come your chest hurts?" he says quietly. His hand rests warm and motionless right over Minnie Mouse's face.

"Heart attack?"

"Are you okay? Tell me the truth." I feel his breath against my face, and then I smell peppermint and Paco Rabonne.

"I'm fine."

"Then how come your chest hurts?"

"Michael." I curl my hand around his neck and tilt toward him. For the merest second we are kissing and then he leans away and takes his hand off Minnie Mouse.

"Honey."

I am very still. The tightness inside me seems to have frozen into a hard cold ball.

"Honey. Look at me."

"What?"

"Look at me."

With an effort I raise my eyes. "What."

"It's not that—" He runs a hand through his hair. "It's not that—I mean, it's not that I—"

"Don't you think it would be nice?" I say in a small voice.

"Very nice."

"Then why don't you want to?"

"I believe we've had this talk before." His smile is half-wry, half-sad. "I've noticed you have a tendency to not be friends with folks afterwards."

"It wouldn't be that way with you."

He touches my cheek for a moment. "I don't think I wanna take that chance."

"Big of you."

"Honey—"

"Don't honey *me*, buster." I'm wheezing as I speak. "When did you become the king of discipline?"

His smile twists. "Now you're makin' it tougher than it already is."

"Tougher for who?" I lean over the side of the bed and start fumbling for my shoes. "Where the fuck *are* they, goddam it?"

"What're you doin'?"

"Looking for my goddam shoes. Do you goddam mind?" I locate one sneaker and shove my foot into it.

"Miranda." He touches my shoulder, and I shake him off. I find the other shoe and jam it on. Without bothering with the laces, I take as deep a breath as I can and stand up.

"Well, thanks for everything."

He stands up too. "Look, kitten—"

"I've got a lot of work to do." I'm swaying only slightly on my feet. "If you'll just excuse me."

"Why don't you just stay till you're feelin' better?"

"I feel fabulous," I hiss.

"Let me walk you to your room."

I avoid his eyes. "I'm fine, thanks." I walk into the living room and toward the front door, carefully planting my feet as I go. At the threshold I turn my head and look just past his right ear. "Have a nice day." Then I turn and start down the stairs, one hand gripping the rail, the other trailing against the wall for balance.

"Be careful," he says, in a voice so sad that it's all I can do not to turn around again. But I force myself to keep my gaze fastened on the steps, as one by one I painstakingly descend.

Shit. Shit. Shit. I'm at the house phone outside of B-entry, waiting for my eyes to refocus. I've already dialed two wrong numbers, and now I'm standing here blinking at the receiver like I've never seen one before. *Shit.*

"Well, hi."

"Huh?" I jerk around, clutching the phone to my ear. It's Clark, the A-entry junior, standing there holding a Heineken in each hand. My heart bobbles uncomfortably. "Waiting to use the phone?"

"No, I was just watching you."

"Why, for god's sake?"

"You were standing so still, I thought maybe you were asleep."

"Asleep on my feet?"

"Horses do it."

"Birds do it, bees do it." I glare at him.

"Really?"

"No, I was just practicing." I take my hand off my chest. "I got a job in a wax museum."

"Really?" He blows into one of his Heineken bottles, making a tuneless whistling noise. "I heard First Boston made you an offer."

"My, doesn't good news travel fast." I suppress a belch. "But the pay sucks."

"That's funny. I heard they offered you thirty-five thousand to start."

"Forty."

"Wow, neat."

"Well, if you'll excuse me, I have a terribly important phone call to make."

He doesn't move. "Want to come to a party?"

"No thanks."

"You should check it out. It's a great party."

"I've had my quota for the day."

"Okay." He takes a swallow from the other bottle. "See you around."

"Yep." I turn back to the phone.

"You look great tonight, by the way."

"Thanks."

When I hear the B-entry door shut, I depress the hook and then I dial, listening intently to the rings. One, two, three, four—

"Yeah?"

"Hi, Jackson. It's Miranda."

There is a tiny pause. "I know. How are you?"

"Are you busy? I'd like to see you."

Another little pause. "No, I'm not busy. You want to come over?"

"I'm outside B-entry."

"I won't bother to clean up then."

"Want a drink?"

"What have you got?"

"Vodka straight up."

"Okay."

I sit in a corner of the sofa and watch him pour two drinks into heavy-bottomed rocks glasses. He's got the Rolling Stones on the stereo, and holding both glasses in one hand he turns down the volume with the other.

"Stoli okay?"

"Sure. Got any lime?"

"No." He sits in a low-backed leather director's chair across from me.

"Lousy bar you run here."

He shrugs and picks up a pack of Camels from the coffee table. Tapping out a cigarette, he offers it to me. "You smoking or non-smoking these days?"

"Non. Why?" I take two, three, four small quick sips at my drink, trying not to make a face at the taste.

"It's good, isn't it?" Jackson laughs as he lights his cigarette.

"No." I keep sipping.

He exhales and crosses his legs, eyeing me through the pale gauzy smoke. "You look pretty."

"Thanks. So do you."

"Flattery."

"No, no. I always thought you were prettier than me."

"Are you thirsty? You want a glass of water?"

"No. Why?"

He's smiling as he flicks ashes into a blue ceramic ashtray that is balanced on the arm of his chair. "Lousy bar, but we do have water."

"I'm fine."

"Good."

I sit watching him smoke, remembering the first time I'd been here. It was late: the lights were off, and Gerard was lying on the couch watching "The Honeymooners" and smoking pot. He made room for us on the sofa and we watched TV for a while, laughing at all the wrong places. When "Get Smart" came on, Jackson stood up and turned off the TV while I covered the quietly snoring Gerard with an afghan; and then he'd taken my hand and we'd gone into his room.

"Wild Horses" winds to a close, and Jackson coughs. "Depressing song, no?"

"You think so?" I smile, feeling the warmth, heavy and soporific, spreading down my shoulders and through my arms.

"I didn't know this was going to be a formal occasion."

"Huh?"

"Should I have put on a jacket?"

"What?"

"Your tie, sweetie."

"Oh." I undo the knot and slip it off my neck. "It's not my tie."

"Ah."

"It's sort of ugly, isn't it?" I toss Ned's tie on the coffee table. It slithers off the corner and onto the floor. "Whoops."

There's another pause, and then he stubs out his cigarette in the ashtray. "Well, sweetie," he says briskly. "What can I do for you?"

"Do for me?" Again I feel that strange discomfiting urge to

laugh. "Well, actually," I say, trying to keep my voice steady, "I thought we could talk about the weather."

"You came over so we could talk about the weather."

"That's right." I'm noticing the chill tightness in my lungs again, dissipating the lulling warmth of the vodka. "It's been fabulous, hasn't it? Spring is finally here, don't you think?"

"So it seems."

"Sunny and mild, no? Balmy almost."

He picks up his drink. "Look, sweetie, why don't you just tell me why you're here?"

"I was just in the neighborhood." I pick up my glass too.

"And you thought you'd drop by."

"Right."

"A friendly thing to do."

"Exactly."

He sighs. "I think I'm getting bored."

"Bored." I put my glass down, hard, so hard that for a dizzy moment I'm afraid I've broken it on the tabletop. "That's a goddam friendly thing to say, isn't it?"

"Easy on the glass, darling. It's Gerard's."

"I don't give a fuck whose glass it is."

He's smiling. "After what happened at the Spee, one would think you'd have a bit more respect for Gerard's things."

I give a little strangled gasp. "What did that worm say to you?"

Jackson shrugs. "Oh, he didn't have to say anything. There were plenty of other people around to fill me in."

"Worms. Creeps. Scumbags."

"Sticks and stones, darling."

"*Fuck* sticks and stones."

"Look, didn't you come to the Advocate to find him? Or was it Dean you came to see?"

Something wrenches inside me. "Mind your own beeswax."

"Excuse me?"

"And just what the fuck were *you* doing with Stephanie Kandel?"

"An unfortunate construction, darling."

"What?"

"I'd rephrase that if I were you." He shakes his head. "And you an English major."

Speechless, I fold my arms around myself, gripping my biceps with fingers that feel unreasonably cold.

Gently he puts his glass back on the coffee table and takes out another cigarette from the pack. "Now, are you still a nonsmoker, darling? I feel like I've got to keep asking you. I really don't know you anymore."

"Coward, coward," I whisper, so low that he bends politely forward.

"Pardon me?"

I look at him and then I hear myself saying clearly: "Tell me again why we broke up."

He lights his cigarette, inhales, and lazily exhales. "I believe the lawyers would call it irreconcilable differences, don't you think?"

I'm sitting at a table with Benny and Val and Toby and Ross when I catch sight of Jackson walking past, carelessly holding his tray with one hand. Our eyes meet and he nods at me, once, and continues to saunter along toward the north end of the dining hall. I lower my hand and watch him sit down at a table near the windows. In his room later that night, he pulls me onto his lap and whispers, "What were you doing with those people?"

"What people?"

He's kissing the side of my neck. "You wouldn't believe the shit I got at dinner."

"I told you never to eat the chili surprise."

"I mean I got hell from people."

"Why?"

"Trying to explain why you were hanging out with that scraggly crew of wonks."

"I like them." Now one of his hands is at my waist, pulling my shirt out of my trousers.

"Sweetheart, why don't you try sitting with us regular folk?"

"We were talking about seventeenth-century metaphysical poetry."

"Try not to do it in the dining hall where everybody can see."

"Toby has some interesting theories about Donne."

"Have you ever noticed how unattractive they are?"

"The metaphysical poets?"

"No, your friends the drones."

I don't have a chance to reply, for Jackson has gently tipped up my chin and is kissing me, while his other hand continues to unbutton my shirt.

"Darling, your posture is awful."

"Fuck you."

"Aren't we just a teeny bit hostile tonight?"

"Hostile?" I'm gazing at the big bay windows overlooking Bow Street. For a moment I see myself slamming up against the window, glass shattering, splintering into a million crystalline shards, each one a tiny glittering knife. "God, god," I whisper, turning my head away and squeezing my eyes shut.

"Randa?" Jackson says. "Are you okay?"

I swallow once, twice. "Yes. No."

"Miranda." He's sitting on the couch, his arms encircling me. "Sweetie. It's okay."

Dazed, I notice that I don't seem to recognize the cologne he's got on. I give a gummy sniff. "You seemed a little upset about it too," I whisper into his shoulder.

"Well, that's because I was."

"Was? What happened?" My voice is shaking. "I don't understand."

"It was a long time ago, Randa."

"Not so long."

"Look." I feel his chest rise and fall with a sigh. "Those feelings—" He hesitates. "They hurt."

"So?" I open my eyes and stare at the monogram on his breast pocket.

"So they hurt too much." His voice is low, and tight. "So I—stopped having them."

"Stopped having them? How can you just stop?"

"You just do."

"Oh, I get it. There's an on-off switch somewhere, right?" I lift my head. "Huh? Or do you send them out with your shirts to be laundered?"

"Very funny."

"Nice and clean, starched and completely dead."

He lets go of me, his eyes flashing something that looks oddly like hatred. "I'd appreciate it, sweetheart, if you'd stop claiming ownership of my feelings."

"I'm not claiming ownership of anything." I make myself return his gaze. "But just how the fuck do you stop having feelings?"

"Watch your language."

"I'm an English major, remember? I can say anything I want."

"But do you have to talk like a drunken sailor?"

I swallow. "I believe I asked you a question."

"Can we change the subject? It's getting boring."

"No, no, I really want to know. How do you—I mean, how does one stop having feelings?"

"You just do, Miranda." He gives a long sigh that ends in a cough. "You just stop. Simple."

"Just like that?"

"Just like that."

"You make it sound so easy."

"Haven't you ever heard of mind over matter?"

"What about Friday night?"

"Friday night?" He looks blank for a moment. "Oh."

"Memorable, eh?"

"Look, it was nice, Randa. It was very nice."

"And that's all."

He sighs again and leans his head on the back of the sofa. "It was always nice."

"At least we were compatible about something."

"Look. Nothing can change what we felt for each other and all that." He stares over at the fireplace, his eyes shadowed by long curling lashes. "But we broke up, remember?"

"Oh. Right. It must have slipped my mind."

"By mutual consent, if you'll recall."

"Maybe I was lying."

A nerve jumps near his eye, just underneath the smooth skin of his cheekbone. "And now you're the expert on feelings."

"Well, I guess that's my problem, isn't it?" I let go of my arms and look at the marks on my skin. "Well." I clear my throat. "Thanks for being so straightforward with me."

The nerve jumps again. After a moment he says in that tight quiet voice, "I wonder how long the record's been done."

"Not long." Unsteadily I get to my feet. "Thanks for the drink."

"No problem." He doesn't look at me.

For a second I feel sick and I almost sit down again. But I remain standing, looking down at his pale, handsome face, his half-closed eyes and unsmiling mouth, still and exquisite as if carved in alabaster. "See you around."

When I am at the door I hear his voice. "Miranda."

"Yes?"

"Don't forget your tie."

I turn. He's still staring at the fireplace. "I don't want it." I swallow again. "It's not mine, remember?" He does not reply, and carefully I close the door behind me.

I blink in the morning sun. Pulling a Kleenex from the pocket of my pajama top, I blow my nose and bat the tissue into the fireplace. Then I pick up the phone and start dialing.

"UHS, Mental Health."

"Ha."

"Hello?"

"Yes, I'd like to cancel an appointment."

"Yes, with who?"

"Whom."

"Sorry."

"With Mary Froelich, tomorrow morning at nine."

"Let me see here. Miranda Walter?"

"Walker. With a K. As in karate."

"Yes, right. I've canceled the appointment for you, Miranda. When did you want to reschedule for?"

"Reschedule?" I look at the Matisse print over the fireplace. Has somebody actually bothered to straighten it? "I don't want to reschedule."

"Um. You're a regular patient of Mary's, aren't you?"

"I guess so."

"Why don't I just ask Mary to call you about arranging another time?"

"No, that's okay. Thanks." I hang up. I rebutton my pajama top so the buttons align, listening to the Bicknell twins scampering out of their room and down the stairs, reminding each other to get toilet paper. Out on the street by the Lampoon somebody calls out: "It wasn't my idea!" A police siren wails and then dies away. "It's not my fault," the voice shouts. "It's not my fault."

"Sit up straight, Mirabelle. Don't slouch. It's not good for your lungs."

"I know." I draw myself up, trying to keep my shoulders from curving in toward my chest. "It's hard, Gram."

"I know it is. But keep trying."

"I remember and then I forget. And then I remember and I forget."

"And then you remember and then you forget."

"Right. So why bother?"

"One day at a time, Mirabelle."

"Like the TV show, huh?"

"Whatever."

We look at each other across the table, resting between games of double solitaire. She peers more closely at me through her jeweled cat's-eye reading glasses, the ones I like to tease her about.

"Is that a new brow pencil you've got on?"

"Yeah." I raise my fingers to my face. "Is it too heavy? Did I put too much on?"

"No, no, it looks lovely."

"Really?"

"It looks beautiful. Makes your eyes even bluer."

"She said it looked—" I stop, and am silent for a few moments. "Hey, Gram."

"What, sweetie?"

"Can you keep a secret?"

"I don't see why not."

"It's kind of a big secret."

"Try me."

"Okay. I got my PSAT scores back."

"Did you?" She reaches over to take one of my hands. "Tell me."

I stretch out my arm so she doesn't have to lean. "I did okay."

"Good for you!" She squeezes my hand. "I knew you would."

"Thanks."

"I didn't doubt it for a second."

"Thanks." I look down at the small pale hand grasping mine, at the delicate veins crisscrossing her flesh like little blue rivers. "Hey, Gram."

"Sweetie?"

"There's more to the secret."

"Tell me."

I lean forward. "Gram, I did really well."

She squeezes my hand again. "I figured."

"Did you?"

"Of course."

I look up at her and then down at her hand again. Suddenly I am blinking rapidly, engulfed by a black dizzy conviction that the ceiling is about to give way, collapse, certain to crush me under its weight. The dizziness passes, but the oppressive sensation, dark and relentless, remains lingering in my chest, flooding my lungs, almost as if somehow I knew that three weeks later Gram would fall as she was going down the stairs to the basement to put her wash into the dryer, injuring her hip and impairing her mobility to the point where my parents would decide to place her in the Seaview Retirement Villas in Santa Barbara, a sunny, exquisitely landscaped compound of charming bungalows from which, as it was to happen, Gram would not return.

"Mirabelle?"

I catch my breath. "Gram?"

"Sit up straight." She looks at me through her funny glasses, smiling. "One day at a time, remember?"

"Like the TV show, right?"

"Whatever."

"Okay."

"Good girl. Now pick up your deck and let's play."

I slouch lower in the armchair. "Goddam it, Gram," I say aloud. "Why the hell couldn't you watch where you were going?"

But there is only silence in C-45. I tilt my head, frowning. *I should have a hangover. Why isn't my head aching? Why isn't my stomach doing a flamenco on my small intestine? Why at least don't my shinsplints hurt?*

"Dear god," I say softly. "What's wrong?"

I open up the C-45 mailbox and flip through the mail. Two flyers from Crimson Travel, a postcard inviting me to an opening at the Fogg, another bill for Jessica from the Coop, and a letter for me from Columbia. I go around the corner into the ladies' lounge and sit on the edge of the flowered divan.

Dear Miss Walker:
    We are delighted to inform you . . .

I've finished the reserve readings for Soc Sci 33 and am staring down at the small stack of manila folders, one hand curled around the nape of my neck, when I hear soft footsteps, rhythmically sounding upon the corridor on the other side of the stacks. They turn along the eastern edge and come up behind me, muffled on the hard gray floor. Idly I run a finger over the cool beige surface of the top folder.

"Miriam."

I swing my head around. "Richard."

"Hey." He leans down and kisses me lightly, his mouth just barely touching that tender curve of flesh right above the lipline.

"Hi."

"Hi." Perching on the edge of the wooden desktop, he takes his sunglasses off and puts them on top of my reserve readings. He's wearing the tie Ric Ocasek gave him, a narrow strip of black leather negligently knotted under the collar of his white shirt. "How are you, baby?"

"I'm okay. How are you?"

"Okay."

"Good."

"Your neck hurt?"

"What? No, it's fine."

"Good."

"Richard?"

"Yeah?"

"How did you know I was here?"

"Lucky guess."

"Yeah?"

"I've been trying to track you down, baby." One of his feet in its pointy black demiboot is jiggling back and forth, the zippers clicking softly against leather. "I get a little worried when you don't return phone calls. And stop answering the phone."

"I know. I'm sorry."

"Well, stop doing it."

"I'll try. It's nice to see you, Richie."

"It's nice to see you too."

I look at his foot, and then up into his face again. A long spiral of hair, dark and glossy, curls down over his forehead. "Richard," I say, "are you okay?"

"Sure."

"Good."

"Yeah." He's staring out the window. "Listen, I came to say goodbye."

"What?"

"You know, aloha. Bye-bye birdie and all that shit."

"Oh, no. You're not going to Hawaii, are you?"

"No, I'm going to New York."

"What? Now?"

"Yeah."

"What about graduation?"

"No time, baby."

"You're not going to graduation? That's against the law, isn't it?"

He laughs. "Maybe. But I ain't going."

"What's in New York?"

"You really want to know?"

"Of course I want to know. What's in New York?"

He hesitates, leaning back against the carrel wall. "A recording contract."

For a moment I am completely still. Then I reach over and take his hand, squeezing it hard. "Congratulations."

"Thanks."

"I'm really happy for you, Richie."

"Thanks. Babe, you're hurting me."

"Oh god." I loosen my grip. "Your guitar hand. I'm sorry."

"That's okay."

"Richie?"

"Yeah?"

"You don't seem excited."

"No?"

"You're bummed about missing graduation, right?"

He smiles. "That's right." His eyes, fixed on something beyond the window, are shadowed with bluish bruised-looking arcs of fatigue.

"What about your diploma?"

"I guess they'll mail it to me."

"Don't you have any finals?"

"Two."

"So you're coming back to take them?"

"No, they're setting up proxy exams for me." His fingers tap soundlessly on the desktop. "Right in the goddam studio, probably."

"That should make your producer happy."

"Yeah."

"Don't let the other musicians copy from your bluebook."

"Okay."

I touch his arm. "Hey."

"What?"

"How does it feel, now that you're about to be a rock 'n' roll star?"

His fingers stop tapping. "I don't know."

"Keep me posted, okay?"

"I will. So what are you doing after graduation?"

"Me?" I blink. "I don't know. I got accepted into Columbia."

"Yeah?" He takes my hand and holds it lightly in his own. "That's great."

"I guess so."

"You don't seem—shit, how did you put it?"

"Excited."

"Right. Thanks. So why aren't you?"

"I don't know. I just found out about it a little while ago."

We look at each other for a few moments. Then Richard lets go of my hand and stands up. "I'm staying at my brother's for a while, just till I get my own place." He gazes down at me, heavy-lidded. "Got a pen I could borrow?"

"Sure." I reach into my bag.

"And some paper."

I hand him my notebook and a pen. He opens the notebook and scribbles something on the last page.

"Here."

"Thanks." I twist the notebook around and look at his writing.

"That's my brother's number."

"Okay. Thanks." I close the notebook.

"Don't lose his number."

"I won't. Where I go, my notebook goes."

"Sort of like an American Express card."

"Sort of." I smile. "Richie?"

"Yeah?"

"How soon do you have to leave?"

"Yesterday."

"You can't stick around for just a little while?"

"No."

"I was going to ask you to the Radcliffe Senior Soirée."

"Yeah?"

"Yeah." I sigh. "I was going to buy you a corsage and everything."

"Miriam." He leans forward and kisses me hard. I've barely had time to breathe in the familiar smell of him, the leather, the smoke, the faint musky scent of his skin, when he's straightened up and stands there looking at me. "I'll take you out to CBGB's, okay?"

"Okay."

"Look, I gotta run." He flicks the unruly curl off his brow. "Hang on to that number, okay?"

"I will."

"Good." He turns and starts walking away between two ceiling-high tiers of stacks.

"Richard?" I call.

"Yeah?"

"Can I be on the album cover?"

He pauses, poised on the balls of his feet. "I'll work on it."

"Thanks."

He starts walking again. "Sure." He reaches the corridor and makes a left toward the elevator.

When his quiet footsteps have receded into silence, I lean back in my chair and gaze out through the window, trying to gauge the time by the slope of the afternoon light. I'm due at Robbins by six. Sighing, I look down at the desktop, and see that he's left his sunglasses on top of the manila folders. I hear his voice from that first night at Dunster House, soft and calm under the thumping of "My Sharona" on the stereo: *Yeah, I just started this new band. We're hot. You wanna be my first fan?* Smiling a little, I skim my fingers through my hair, ruffling my bangs, untangling a snarl or two in the back, and then, carefully, I slip my notebook and the pen, his sunglasses and the reserve readings, into my bag.

As I close and lock the door to Robbins, it occurs to me that I've only snapped twice at people tonight, and have even politely suggested to Raphael that he first let me stamp the date cards in the last two copies of *Fear and Trembling* before he carried them out in his Bergdorf Goodman bag. In fact, he consented with such alacrity that I didn't even get a chance to tell him about my being an astrophysics major. *I must be slipping.* But at least, I console myself as I'm walking down the stairs, I didn't go so far as to actually start reshelving books.

Outside, standing on the steps to Emerson, I breathe in the mild spring air and look out at Mem Yard, gazing at the newly-leafed trees silhouetted against the darkness by soft opalescent floodlights from Widener and Mem Church, and beyond, at the freshman dorms and University Hall, rising tall and regal, illuminated from within by cozy-looking yellow lights.

"Jesus," I hear myself saying aloud. "Thank god I'm graduating." And then my stomach gives a loud protracted gurgle. I blink, looking over toward Widener, where somebody in a track suit is running methodically up and down the broad white stairs. I watch him for a little while, and then all at once a synapse flickers keenly somewhere in the back of my mind, and I start walking down the steps.

"You want butter with that muffin?"

Tommy slops a cup of coffee down next to my plate. Leaning an elbow on the dingy Formica-topped counter, I reach for the little metal pitcher of cream. "No thanks." I'd smile at him but I know he hates that, so instead I grin at the back of his stained white jacket as he lurches off to the grill to attend to the steaming basket of french fries, cigarette stub lolling acrobatically on his lower lip.

I take another bite from the huge lopsided corn muffin in front of me. A couple of pinball games are going on over in the corner, and behind me the jukebox blares continuously. As I'm chewing, I'm wondering if Tommy still has "Singing in the Rain" sharing the "R" button with Rick James' "Superfreak."

"You want more coffee?"

"No, that's okay." I brush some corn specks from my shirt. "You did a good job on the muffins today."

Tommy doesn't reply, and if anything his thick black eyebrows draw together even more, but when he takes a toothpick from his jacket pocket and drops it next to my plate, I can tell he's pleased.

Humming under my breath, I take the cellophane wrapper off my toothpick. *She's a very funky girl* . . .

"Well, hi. Long time no see."

You don't take home to Mother. I crumple the cellophane and drop it in an ashtray next to the creamer.

"Hey, Miranda. You deaf or something?"

I put the toothpick between my lips and then turn my head to look at Pablo Esperanto. "What?"

"I haven't seen you in ages." He sits on the stool next to me. "Since our little rendezvous at the Ha'Penny, in fact. What have you been doing with yourself?"

"Studying." Gently I probe the space between my upper left incisors. "School and all that."

"Listen, there's a whole bunch of us over there." He jerks his thumb at the row of booths against the wall. "With some folks I know'd love to see you."

"They've got eyes, haven't they?"

"Oh, come on, Miranda. Have some fun for once."

"Fun?" I look over at the booths. "Let me guess. You're sitting with Dean, Anthony, and Roald."

"You're such a bright girl. I love that." He puts his arm around my shoulder. "How come we never went out together, you and me?"

"Darn." I stand up, dislodging his arm. "I *knew* there was something I forgot to do." I walk over and slide into the booth next to Roald. "Hi, guys. How's everything?"

"Hi, Miranda." Roald smiles at me. "I heard about your job with First Boston."

"Did you?"

"Yeah, that's great. Fifty thousand a year to start."

"Sixty."

"Wow, great."

"Free business suits."

"Wow."

"Six weeks' vacation a year."

"Neat."

"Doesn't Miranda look great?" Pablo squeezes in next to me. "Don't you think so, Deano?"

"Sure." Dean looks at me obliquely across the table.

"Yeah, gorgeous," Anthony chimes in wistfully.

I watch Dean take a long drag on his cigarette, his hair gleaming in shimmering brown waves under the fluorescent light. Shifting my toothpick to the other side of my mouth, I ponder if he hasn't perhaps let it go too long between shampoos.

"Want some Coke?" Pablo thrusts a cup at me.

"No thanks."

"I'll have some," Roald says, reaching across me.

"Get your own." Pablo pulls the cup away.

"You look really great, Miranda," Anthony says. "Did you do something different with your hair?"

"No."

"Oh."

I lean back against the booth, watching Dean. He studies the overflowing ashtray and exhales smoke right in Roald's face, who doesn't seem to notice as he picks away at a scab on his cheek.

Anthony sighs, poking at the soggy remains of a plate of french fries. "You really look great, Miranda."

"Thanks."

Pablo nudges me. "Hey, Miranda. You're coming to Roald's big party tomorrow night, aren't you?"

"What big party?"

"We're throwing another big party in our room tomorrow night," Roald explains. "John and Clark and me."

"John and Clark and I," Dean says quietly.

"Oh, are you helping throw the party?" Roald looks confused.

Pablo grins at Roald and then at me. "It's a reincarnation party, Miranda."

"What's a reincarnation party?"

"It's a come-as-you-were party." He laughs. "Get it? Get it?"

I slide a little closer to Roald to avoid Pablo's elbow. "No."

"You smell nice, Miranda." Roald sniffs at my neck and I veer an inch or two back toward Pablo, who's flexing his fingers in my face.

"I'm coming as Chopin. The child prodigy, natch."

"Ringo Starr," Roald says, beaming. "Yeah, yeah, yeah."

Pablo frowns at him. "He's not dead, chump."

"He will be someday."

"Who are you coming as, Miranda?" asks Anthony.

When the cat's away . . . I take the toothpick from my mouth and flip it into the ashtray. "Good question. Maybe I'll wear a mouse outfit."

Roald peers at me. "A mouse outfit?"

"Ask Dean."

He's lighting another cigarette, eyes downcast.

"What about you, old boy?" Pablo is smiling again. "I was thinking Ashley Wilkes would be a good choice for you."

Dean blows out his match and with a graceful arch of his wrist he drops it in the ashtray, but the tiny wooden stick tumbles off the pile of butts and napkins and french fries, landing on the tabletop, still smoking a little.

"You'd look sharp in a cravat," Pablo goes on. "Don't you think so, Miranda?"

"I don't think I'm qualified to say." I pick up Dean's match, puff on it lightly, and toss it on top of the little pile. "But I know he looks good in gray."

Dean lifts his head, his mouth tight. "Funny."

Anthony looks back and forth between Dean and me. "Why should Dean come in a mouse outfit?" he says suspiciously. "I don't understand."

"Don't let it bother you."

"That's right." Sniggering, Pablo rattles the ice in his cup. "Ignorance is bliss, huh, Miranda?"

"Oh, I don't know." I look over at the pinball machines and see the three big-nosed Dunster House girls from Saturday night standing in front of Jungle Lord. "You're such a bright boy," I say to Pablo. "Help him figure it out. Would you excuse me, please?"

As I'm sliding out of the booth, Roald says, "You're coming to the party, aren't you?" He looks up at me, a tiny trickle of blood running down his cheek. "Huh, Miranda?"

"I've got a lot of work to do."

"Please? It won't be a party if you're not there."

"You might have to struggle along without me."

Pablo slides back in next to Roald. "How about if Dean brings the cheese?" he says with a malicious smile.

I look at him. "Such a bright boy." I turn and walk over to the pinball machines and tap one of the girls on the arm. "Excuse me."

She turns. "Oh, hi." The other two swing around also. "Hi," they chorus.

"Hi. Listen, I just wanted to apologize for calling you guys Dunster House sluts the other night."

They look at each other, then at me. "That's okay."

"We'd forgotten all about it."

"Besides, we're not from Dunster House."

"Ah."

We all nod pleasantly, and I turn away. When I'm at the door, Roald calls out:

"Miranda!"

I pull the door open and gaze over at him.

"Help me figure what out?"

So that's why it's called higher education. "Never mind, sweetheart," I say loudly, holding the door open to let some people in. Then I release the handle and step outside.

FRIDAY | 10

IIIIIIIIIIIIIIIIIIIIIIIIIIIIIIIIIIIIIIIIIIIIIIIIIIIIIIIIII

*E*ven with a quick detour into Lamont to flip through the latest issue of *Rolling Stone*, I'm still ten minutes early when I get to Soc Sci 33. Taking a seat in the center of the lecture hall, I open up my notebook and uncap a pen, then sit quietly as the room fills up.

At five after eleven Professor Nimitz arrives, teaching fellows in tow, and strides up to the podium, where he takes his notes from his briefcase and removes his pipe from his mouth. Then he nods at us and begins to speak, his voice deep and measured.

"As I walk along the familiar streets of Cambridge, with their stately homes, their historic buildings, yes, with their busy restaurants, their bustling shops, the crowded movie houses, well, ladies and gentlemen, the issues of social responsibility are never far from my mind. This morning at breakfast I said to my wife Sheila, 'How in good conscience can we justify these blueberry pancakes, no matter how delicious they might be, when *everybody* doesn't have blueberry pancakes for breakfast?' Now as you can imagine, Sheila, who makes what are quite possibly the best blueberry pancakes in New England—"

I must have fallen asleep, for when I jerk my chin upright I realize that I'm just about to start drooling all over my notebook. Swallowing hastily, I shift my head and find myself being scrutinized by my section leader, Stu, a dead ringer for Chagall. He's sitting across the aisle and a few rows up, so close that he doesn't even bother to put on his glasses. I give him a little wave and turn my attention back to Professor Nimitz, who is, as I surmise from a peep at my neighbor's wristwatch, wrapping up today's lecture. I wait for him to tie it all together with a remark about breakfast foods, or about lunch perhaps, since it's now twelve o'clock, but instead he closes by reciting a passage from this week's reading assignment. I listen appreciatively, and join in with the applause that follows his final dramatic pause, clapping till my palms hurt. Looking gratified, Professor Nimitz sticks his pipe back into his mouth and his papers back into his briefcase, and hustles down off the proscenium and out the fire exit before anyone can catch up to him.

When the crowds have thinned out I make my way over to Stu, who stands in the aisle listening to a reedy-looking kid I remember seeing sitting in the front row directly in line with the podium.

"I've got it all on floppy disk, right? Chapters one through five. Bibliography, title page, table of contents, the works. So I run out to the Coop to get a new ribbon so the print will look nice, right? I come running back to my room, I've been gone ten minutes tops, okay, and I'm ready to stick the disk back into my PC and start printing it out, right? And then I look underneath my desk and there's Edgar, chowing down on my floppy. I couldn't *believe* it. I almost started crying all over my disk drive."

"Edgar? Who's Edgar?"

"My dog."

"Let me get this straight. Your dog ate your computer disk."

The kid nods. "Appendix, photo captions, suggestions for further reading, everything."

"So what do you want from me?"

"An extension."

"Well," Stu says slowly, "the final paper, as you know, is due a week from today. Can I make a suggestion?"

"Yes, absolutely."

"Get your dog's stomach pumped." Stu looks over at me and sighs. "Hello, Miss Walker. Did you have a good nap?"

The computer whiz swings around, snickering balefully. "Refreshing, huh?"

"Just remember one thing," I say to him. "Garbage in, garbage out."

He stops snickering. "What's that supposed to mean?"

"Think about it the next time Edgar wants to go outside."

"What?"

"Stu, can I speak with you privately?"

"Certainly, Miss Walker. I assume it's a matter of some delicacy?"

"Rather."

We're moving toward the exit when the computer kid says: "Now wait a minute."

I look at Stu. "Now he'll be forced out of pride to tell you he doesn't have a dog."

"Stu, can I see you afterwards? About that extension?"

When Stu and I are outside in Mem Yard standing in the leafy green shade of a tree, I lean against the tree trunk and clear my throat. "I guess you know why I wanted to talk to you."

"It's about your final paper, perhaps?"

"Yes, exactly."

"And you want an extension."

"Oh, no, no, no."

"You don't want an extension?"

"No, why should I?"

"You tell me."

"I just wanted to let you know that it'll be in on time. In case you were worrying about it."

"Well, that's thoughtful of you." He runs a stubby-fingered hand down his beard. "Perhaps I was jumping to conclusions based upon your attendance record."

"If I'm not mistaken, my running average in the class is an A."

"That's correct."

"I think it's safe to say my grasp of the material is strong."

"Undoubtedly."

I'm shaking my head. "It's just that this damn combat training has absolutely shot my schedule to hell."

"Combat training?"

"Sure. Didn't you know?" I widen my eyes a little. "Didn't I tell you at the beginning of the semester?"

"Tell me what?"

"I'm ROTC."

"I beg your pardon?"

"You know, be all you can be and all that."

Stu looks at me blandly. "If I might say so, Miss Walker, you don't quite seem the type."

"Army intelligence." I nod, once. "Undercover work."

"Ah."

"Yep. What with karate classes, pharmacology research, and my work in miniaturization technology, I'm lucky if I can grab a few minutes to read my mail."

"Miniaturization technology?"

"You know, little briefcases with video cameras in the handle."

"I see."

"And then of course there's my fieldwork, which takes up about twenty hours a week."

"Fieldwork?"

"Pistol practice, skydiving, high-speed chase simulations. You know."

"It sounds a little dangerous."

"Not really. You just need a steady eye and a firm hand."

"Ah."

"Either that or a firm eye and a steady hand. Either one will do."

"Of course." Stu's stroking his beard again.

"Anyway, that's why I've been a little erratic in my class attendance."

"Are you sure you don't want an extension? I wouldn't want to interfere with pistol practice."

"Oh, no, no, no. I just wanted to let you know that you'll definitely get the paper in on time."

"Well, I certainly appreciate your letting me know."

"You'll understand if there are a few bullet holes in it."

"Of course."

"Thanks, Stu." I square my shoulders. "And thanks from Uncle Sam too."

"You're both very welcome." Stu lets go of his beard. "Very good, Miss Walker. If I don't see you in class next week, you can just drop your paper off at my office."

"Thanks again, Stu."

"Certainly."

"Stu?"

"Yes, Miss Walker?"

"Can I interest you in a good used parachute?"

"No, thank you."

"Are you sure? A little old lady from Framingham only used it to go skydiving on Sundays."

"I'm afraid I'll have to decline. But I appreciate the offer." Nodding, Stu walks briskly off along the path toward the Science Center. But not briskly enough, for just as he's about to pass the azalea bushes by Mem Church, a wiry little form trots up behind him.

"Stu! Can I see you for a minute? It's about my dog."

Legs crossed, I'm sitting on the steps of Sever Hall putting on nail polish. I've just finished the second coat and am holding out my hands to admire them when the bells in Mem Church ring two o'clock. Standing up, I blow on each of my nails in succession. When Bryan finally comes through the massive double doors, I push my sunglasses to the top of my head and wait for him at the foot of the stairs.

When we are level with each other I give him a little poke. "Hi."

"What's that all over your nails? Bubble gum?"

"Cutex. A Rose Is a Rose Pink. Whose stupid idea was it to stop talking, anyway?"

"I thought it was yours."

"I thought it was yours."

"Do my eyes deceive me," he says, "or have you gotten

taller? Or is it just that you're standing up straight for once?"

"When are you going to throw out those awful jeans? They don't flatter you at all."

"When you finally get a decent haircut."

"I'll think about it."

"About time. Listen, I'm starving. Coming to lunch?"

"Sure. Then I've got a few errands to run."

"Like trying to bamboozle the Coop into giving you a free cap and gown?"

"I already got my yearbook pictures free."

"No shit. How?"

"I told them Eileen Ford was paying for the prints."

"That's my girl."

We start walking through Mem Yard, and then I pause and tuck my arm through his.

"I just have one thing to add."

"Yeah?"

"Love," I say, batting my eyelashes at him, "means never having to—"

"Keep moving, girlie," he says, and tugs me forward.

On my way out of the Coop I take a last look at the class-ring display, my mind spinning busily, and bump into somebody by the postcard display. "Oh, sorry."

Gerard picks up a couple of postcards from the floor and puts them back in the rack. "Hi, Miranda."

"Hi. Is your shoulder okay? You really slammed into that rack."

"It's fine. Are you leaving?"

"The Coop, you mean?"

"Yes, are you leaving the Coop?"

"Yes, I was just stopping to glance at those class rings."

"Aren't they hideous? My father insisted that I let him buy me one."

"You mean he actually paid for it?"

"Of course he paid for it. How else would he be able to get it for me?" Gerard holds the door open and lets me pass. "Can I help you with that bag? It looks a little heavy."

"No, that's okay. You seem a little burdened down yourself."

"This?" He waves a small white Coop bag. "It's just a book."

"What'd you buy?"

"Kafka. I'm trying to cheer myself up."

We dart across the Harvard Square intersection onto Mass Ave and start walking toward Adams House.

"Why do you need cheering up?"

"I just accepted a job."

"Congratulations."

"Try condolences."

"Let me guess. You got a job at Burger King."

"I wish."

"Gerard." I shift my Coop bag to the other arm so that I can lightly tap his shoulder. "What kind of job is it?"

"Editorial assistant."

"That doesn't sound so bad."

"At *Cosmopolitan*."

"Oh my."

"Helping their fiction editor," he says gloomily.

"Well, the Advocate got you somewhere after all."

"No, my father got me the job. He's a VP at Hearst."

"Oh."

"The only good thing about it is that I'll be subletting my aunt's apartment in Morningside Heights."

"That's up by Columbia, isn't it?"

"Yep. It's one of those huge university apartments with high ceilings and bathtubs with claws on 'em. It's been in the family for generations."

"I see."

"Guess how much rent I'll be paying."

"Tell me and I'll hit you with my shopping bag."

"What's in there, anyway?"

"Presents for Jessica."

He peers over the edge. "Shampoo? Hair conditioner?"

"You think she'll like 'em?"

"I don't know. But I love the wrapping paper."

"You don't think the typewriter motif is too loud?"

"Oh, no. Very handsome. Say, that's a new ring you're wearing, isn't it?"

"Yes, it is."

"It's nice.'"

"Thanks."

"What is it?"

I switch the bag back to my other arm. "It's a spider quartz."

"Spider quartz?"

"You've heard of spider quartz before, haven't you?"

"Of course I have. It's a semiprecious stone, isn't it?"

"Oh, no. It's quite precious."

"Well, it's certainly unusual-looking."

"Thanks."

"Can I look at it again?"

"Maybe later."

There is a short silence.

"Miranda?"

"Yes, Gerard?"

"Listen. About Saturday night."

I pause in front of Schoenhof's bookstore. "What about it?"

"Well, it's just that—" Gerard leans against the window, running a hand through his unruly reddish-brown hair. "I just wanted to apologize."

"Apologize?"

"Yeah, I was sort of fucked up that night. I'd been off coke for two weeks, you know, and then I thought, well, I'll just get a little bit for the party, and not drink anything. But I went kind of overboard, I guess. I don't think I behaved very well toward you."

I stare at him, holding my Coop bag in the crook of my arm. "At least we finally got to dance together."

"Yeah, it was fun. You'd be a pretty good dancer if you'd just relax a little. But the other stuff—well, I just wanted to let you know that I'm sorry."

"Gerard." I blink at him. "Love means—" I stop, and laugh. "It's okay. No hard feelings."

"Good." He looks relieved. "And Edgar felt pretty badly about it too."

"Edgar?"

"The shark." Gerard grins at me.

"I see." I start walking again.

"Hey, Miranda," he says, catching up with me at the corner. "What are you doing after graduation?"

"I don't know. First Boston offered me a job."

"First Boston? Yuck."

I look at him curiously. "I also got accepted into Columbia."

"Great," he exclaims. "We'll be neighbors. You can come over and borrow a cup of yogurt."

"We'll go through your aunt's closets and try on hats."

"You can sneak me into the gym."

"You can get me free copies of *Cosmo*."

"We'll go to the top of the Empire State Building and drop gum on people."

As we're approaching the entrance to Adams House I spot the mysterious Larson coming up Plympton Street, his thick squarish glasses glinting like beacons in the sunlight. I clutch Gerard's arm with my free hand.

"Gerard, who's that?"

He follows my gaze. "Oh, you mean the pear-shaped kid?"

"Yes. Who is he?"

Larson turns and disappears down the steps.

"You mean you don't know who he is?"

"No, why should I?"

"Miranda, he's practically the most famous kid at Harvard, next to the Kennedys and Jodie Foster."

"Jodie Foster goes to Yale."

"Oh."

"Tell me who he is already."

Gerard leans close and whispers something in my ear. "What?" I say indignantly. "He lied to me. He told me he wasn't from the South."

"Haven't you ever noticed how he smells of chicken fat?"

"Oh my god. No wonder he's so—"

"How would *you* like to go through life as the grandson of—"

"I'm picturing him with a goatee."

"The spitting image."

"Oh my god."

As we're walking down the stone stairs into the entryway, Gerard abruptly halts. "Oh, shit."

"What?"

"I've got to run over to Dunster Street."

"What's on Dunster Street?"

"The cleaners. I forgot to pick up Jackson's shirts."

"Really?" My smile is an odd mixture of amusement and melancholy. "Why can't he pick up his own shirts?"

"He's a lazy bastard."

"You think so?"

"Yeah." Gerard turns away and then turns back again. "He said you broke one of my glasses."

"He's full of shit."

"Yeah, I thought he was lying. He kept staring at the fireplace with a stupid look on his face."

I call information in New York, scrawl the number in my notebook, and dial. After three rings, there's a click and a recorded voice begins, clipped and impatient. I wait for the beep, holding the receiver tightly against my ear.

"Henry, it's Miranda. I know you must be incredibly busy with school and all, but I was wondering if you were—if maybe—well, the thing is, I need a date for the Radcliffe Senior Soirée. Call me, okay?"

I hang up and then dial another number.

"Michael?"

"Gal?"

"I have a serious question for you."

"Yeah?"

"Want to go to a movie with me tonight?"

"That's a pretty serious question, all right."

"I promise I won't try to put my arm around you during the scary parts."

"You payin'?"

"Are you kidding? Dutch, baby, dutch."

"I shoulda known."

"I'll buy the popcorn."

"One condition."

My fingers tighten on the receiver. "What?"

"I get to pick the movie."

"Oh, all right. Listen, are you going to the tea this afternoon?"

"They havin' brownies?"

"Is Master Ackerman losing his hair?"

"Maybe I'll mosey on by."

"I'll see you there, then."

"Thanks for callin'."

"Sure. *Au revoir.*"

"*A bientôt.*" He pronounces it *ah-bean-tote.*

We hang up, and I look out the window for a little while. Then I stand up, do some waist twists, and go into my room and start digging my running clothes out from the tangled jumble on the floor.

Standing in the doorway of the history-and-lit lounge, I'm a little surprised to see Jessica over by the buffet eating cream cheese on Melba toast. But then again, I tell myself as I'm weaving my way through the crowd, tastes change.

"Hi, Jessie."

Her head swings around. "Hi."

"You get it in okay?"

She pauses, a piece of Melba toast at her mouth. "Get what in?"

"Your thesis."

"I finished my feces," someone says loudly, giggling. "I turned in my feces."

"Sure I did. Why do you ask?"

"Just checking." I hold out the Coop shopping bag. "Here."

Jessica looks at the bag, then at me. "What is it?"

"Thesis presents. A tradition from the old country."

"Everybody! Let's sing!" Over by the bar someone starts crooning: "I'm dreaming of a white feces, just like—"

"I wish Professor Jenks would shut up already." Jessica takes the bag and puts it on the floor. "He just can't carry a tune." She pulls out a package. "Great wrapping paper."

"Really? You like it?"

"Everybody. Sing!"

"Sure. I love the little accordions."

"They're typewriters."

"All together now!"

"Oh." She starts unwrapping. "Have a cheese ball."

"No thanks."

"Socks." She holds them up. "With little accordions on them. Neat."

"They're typewriters."

"Oh. Well, thanks."

"Do you like them?"

"I love them. They'll look great with my argyles." She's unwrapping another package. "Combs."

"Cheez-its!" somebody cries. "Mouses! Meeces!"

"No!" screams a voice by the bar. "Where?"

"Jessica, is this a theme party?"

"Huh?" She's busy with another package. "What's this? A box of Ivory Snow?"

"Family size," I say proudly.

"I usually get Tide."

"I know. But I like Ivory Snow better."

"Oh, really?"

"I thought I might borrow some."

"Ah."

"Jessie, you've got a little piece of olive in the corner of your mouth."

"Oh. Thanks." She dislodges it with the knuckle of her forefinger. "You sure you don't want a cheese ball?"

"No thanks."

"Some champagne? You should see what they're using for glasses."

"Maybe later."

"Okay."

"Jessie?"

"Yeah?"

"Who's that over there with the lampshade on her head?"

Jessica looks up from the Coop bag. "Oh, that's just my thesis adviser."

"It looks good on her."

"Yeah?" She squints. "It clashes with her dress."

"Yes, but she's tall, so she can carry it off."

"I guess so." Jessica tears the paper off a bottle of nail polish remover. "You've met her already, haven't you?"

"No, but I guess it's kind of hard to meet people when you've got a lampshade on your head."

"Yeah. Oh, Jesus, Herbal Essence." She unscrews the cap and sniffs. "It smells like air freshener."

"Oh." I feel my face fall. "I thought you liked Herbal Essence."

"I do. I said it smells like hair freshener."

"You mean that?"

"I mean everything I say."

"I can take it back if you want. I still have the receipt."

"No, I love it, really. Listen."

"Yeah?" I'm eyeing the cheese balls.

"Speaking of mean."

"Mmm?"

"Are you listening to me?"

"Sure." I pull my hand away from the table. "Speaking of mean."

"I may have been a little touchy lately."

"You?"

"A bit short-tempered."

"You think so?"

"Those dandruffy cats were driving me crazy."

"I can imagine."

"I can hardly wait to go home and shampoo my legs."

"Well, it's nice of you to say so. But you can use soap if you want."

"Did you buy any?"

"No."

"Then I'll use shampoo."

"Oh."

"Anyway, I just wanted to say—"

"Jessica."

"What?"

"Love means—"

"I'm vomiting."

"Which reminds me. Since when do you like cream cheese on Melba toast?"

"If you'd been living on granola bars and Spaghetti Os for a week, don't you think it'd look pretty good to you too?"

"I see your point."

"Have a cheese ball."

"No thanks."

"Anyway, it's an acquired taste."

"Ah."

She holds out a piece of Melba toast. "Bite?"

"I'll pass."

"Okay."

"Well, anyway, I just stopped by to—"

"Miranda?" she says, chewing.

"Yeah?"

"I've got it figured out."

"You've got what figured out?"

"It came to me in a blinding flash of light."

"What did?"

She swallows. "The meaning of life."

"Really?"

"What do you mean, really?"

"It's just an expression."

"Oh. Well, don't you want to know what it is?"

"The meaning of life?"

"Yes," she says impatiently.

"I'm not sure."

"Oh, come on. Humor me, okay? It's my party, after all."

"Oh, all right. What's the meaning of life?"

"Guess."

I roll my eyes. "Ninety-three."

"Close."

"Really?"

"Yes. It's like this." She wipes a little dab of cream cheese off her chin. "If you have a pimple, be grateful it's only one."

"I'm not sure I follow you."

"Wait, there's more."

"Oh, good."

"And if you have two pimples, be grateful it's only two."

"Can I try?"

"If you feel up to it."

"Okay. If you have three pimples, be grateful it's only three."

She nods excitedly. "And if you have four—"

"And so on—"

"And so forth—"

"Until it's time to go to the dermatologist."

"Eureka," she exclaims, hugging me.

"You make it sound so easy." I sniff covertly at her hair.

"Well, it is. Stop smelling my hair."

"Sorry."

"Miranda?" Her voice is muffled by my sweatshirt.

"Yeah?"

"Speaking of smelling."

"Yes?"

"You smell awful."

"I beg your pardon." I lean away. "I believe you mean to say that my running clothes smell awful."

She lets go of me. "Anyway, the whole point is to be grateful for having only one pimple, see? Or two, or three—"

"Whatever. I get your drift."

"And I'm not even drunk."

"Imagine that."

"Just a little champagne. I had mine in a Dixie cup."

"That's my girl."

"Are you sure you don't want a cheese ball? They're going fast."

"That's the way it is with cheese balls."

She's chewing again. "Well, thanks again for the presents. I can't wait to wear one of those socks with the little accordions on it."

I laugh. "They'll look great with your Elvis Presley bobby socks, don't you think?"

"Yeah." She grins at me through a mouthful of Melba toast.

By the time I reach the Weld Boathouse, the tightness in my muscles has finally dissolved into an easy lope. Breathing hard and rhythmically, I spin around and start on the way back, swinging my arms in a loose-wristed cadence. As I dodge a pair of bicyclists barreling along taking up most of the path, I find myself pondering Jessica's new theory. Maybe there is something to it after all. I try to remember when was the last time I had a pimple.

Ah, I think, *this is a sign.*

One, two, three, four. One, two, three, four. I'm picturing Michael and me at the master's tea, whispering and sniggering over our mugs of apple cider. Maybe I'll even try one of those little cucumber sandwiches.

Yes, and maybe I'll start taking aerobics classes at the IAB.

One, two, three, four. One, two, three, four. I'm still grinning as I brush my bangs off my face, swiping a hand across my sweaty forehead. My sweatshirt is damp and clings stickily to my back. Without breaking stride I raise the collar to my nose and sniff.

"Yuck," I say aloud. Jessica was right.

I need to do the laundry, and soon. Particularly before Jessica discovers that I've borrowed another pair of her underwear.

What else?

Shaking out a swift little spasm in my shoulder, I begin drawing up a mental list of things to do.

Laundry
Clean up room
Get watch fixed
Call M & D (collect)
Get cap and gown free
Soc Sci 33 paper
Soap, toilet paper (?)
Haircut (?)

It seems like rather a lot to think about all at once. Loping closer to Weeks Bridge, carefully I inscribe the list on an imaginary blackboard somewhere in the back of my mind, and then, with a quick glance down at my Spiderman ring, I turn my attention back to my stride. Left, right, left, right.

One step at a time, as Gram might say.